Sara Whym's enigmatic poems open onto a shifting, oneiric world in which characters drift in & out and fade away and reappear, leaving in their wake hazy and shimmering traces like the hide-and-seek of dreams. The stories they tell — in fragments, allusions, feints, anamneses — are both heartbreakingly personal and a screen onto which our own stories unfold. *Dreamscapes* asks a lot of its reader and gives a lot in return.

—Mark Polizzotti, author of *Why Surrealism Matters* & *Revolution of the Mind: The Life of André Breton*

Sara Whym's *Dreamscapes* bring to mind authors whose worlds are unforgettable (Beckett, Shakespeare, Kafka, or the playwright Kantor) because each element (sentence, sequence, episode, poem) appears just as suddenly, with the same sort of stupefying, as well as poignant, intensity. To be sure, there is nothing here that is not absolutely unique, starting with the — outright spectral! — density of the maternal experience. Yet naming such worlds helps me name, in turn, the mix of *disquiet* and *happiness* that I feel upon reading these *dreamscapes*. Their own world is one where *everything happens*, the dead return, the living behave like the dead, like gods, like animals — and human beings! A world of extreme concentration & extreme distraction, of bedazzlement, of scattering, and, within all that, of *magnetizing love*. Silhouettes (voices, bodies, figures, clothes: characters almost) gradually settle in my memory, as though at home there: at times as if in a salon, at times as in a train car, a stagecoach, a wagon, a rocket, and so many other unlikely vehicles, lodging their unreason in each while being introduced by a voice that crosses paths with them, welcomes them, runs from and searches for them, protects them or protects itself from them; a voice that is not mine, but wanders freely in my head. And so these poems are like little theaters, each oneiric landscape staging a scene that is always unstable, flexible, elastic and metamorphic — like dreams themselves do; but staging it further, and better, than they do, thanks to the infinitely *graceful* effect of powerful writing.

—Hélène Merlin-Kajman, author of *Rachel* & *Lire dans la geule du loup*

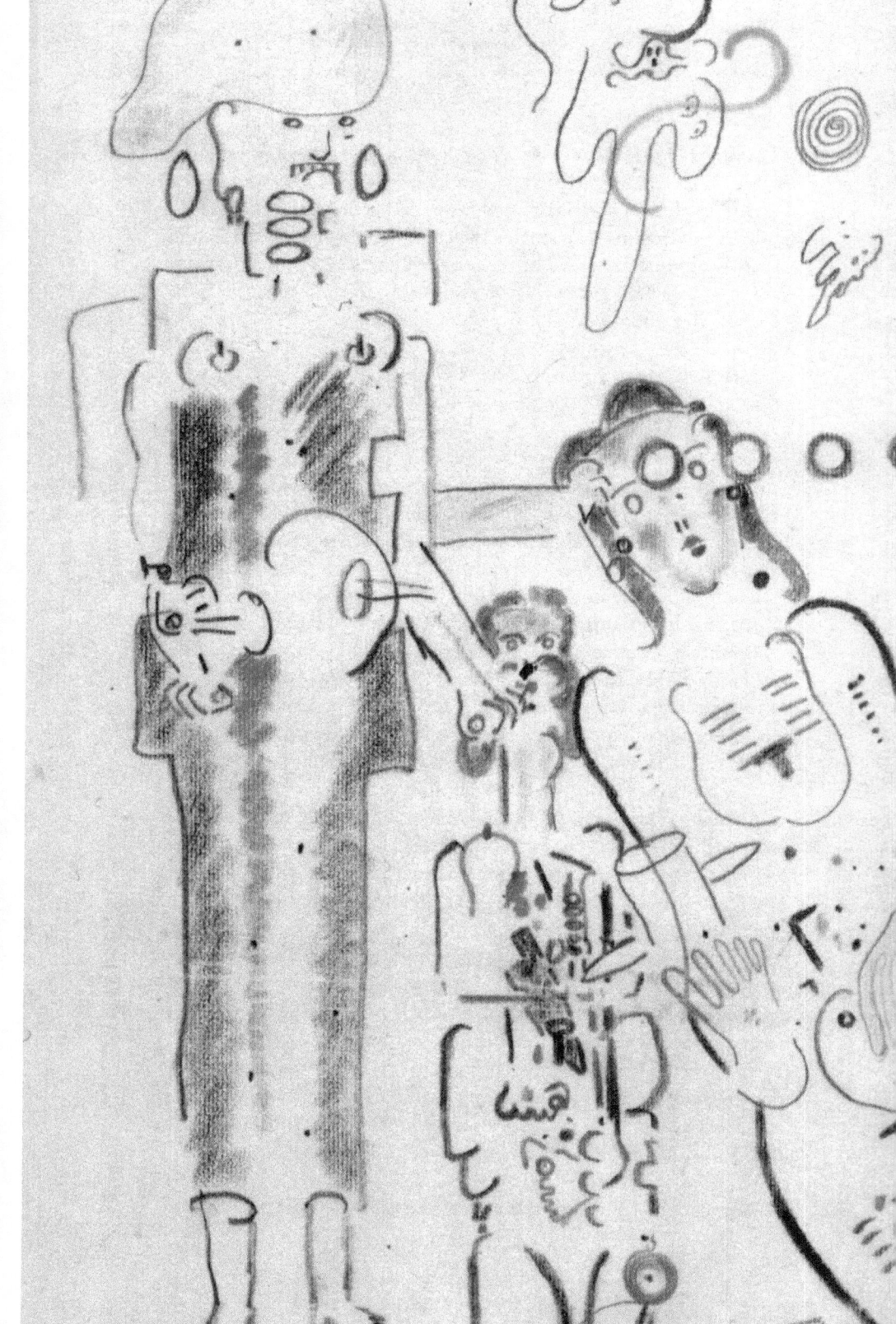

Dreamscapes I

~

Betrayals

(101 & 202 Nights)

Dreamscapes I

~

Betrayals

(101 & 202 Nights)

Sara Whym

Contra Mundum Press   New York · London · Melbourne

Dreamscapes I — Betrayals
(101 & 202 Nights)
© 2025 Sara Whym

First Contra Mundum Press
Edition 2025.

Library of Congress
Cataloguing-in-Publication
Data

Whym, Sara
Dreamscapes I — Betrayals
(101 & 202 Nights) / Sara
Whym

—1ˢᵗ Contra Mundum Press
Edition

466 pp., 6 × 9 in.

ISBN 9781940625737

   I. Whym, Sara.
   II. Title.

2025931910

101 Nights

NE LE RACONTE PAS!

—Beckett

just like that i begin. i call — knowing what is, absolutely. asking you to draw me: a practice, a discipline, a resolution. hands & feet crawling through an opening, fingers tapping. i who never could do the mark-up, will seize hold of every type of punctuation, try to learn what goes together. find out how it's possible to keep going — trim and smooth and clip.

suspended in the air, it's unlikely we'll grab hold of many characters. but i might be able to tweak out the tail of some exchanges. i anticipate these and remember. that's how i know where i've been. swings and slides to baked realities will be saved — outside.

here i'll just try to remain lucid, not capitulate, not cave in.

it's not certain that our story can be ongoing, but it's certain that it's going on. that's why i've come — to keep track of it. i'm hoping you'll become... something. not exactly emerge, jump out, and grab anybody, but just take on some definite contours. your voice, already faltering, has found — its way in. i can feel it. sustain it. i want to live here with you as much as possible and know all things can't be carried over the threshold. wary people, places, and accounts. but reminiscences must be allowed. like threads and fantasies to propel me.

> time throttle that suspends
> the hummingbird
> — shivering
> perfectly still

for instance, the live horizon of the trees yesterday opening and suddenly shut. a feathered patch around the square white mail truck. that is something i need to remember. and there is always (and always) that face, the third one, yesterday, that's been keeping me attached through hours, years even, making the whole (or)deal worthwhile: the dispersion, the death, the birth. i saw that triple face yesterday, the first one, andrew's — light and quivering, the second, angelina's — warm and penetrating, but in the manner of cherished imprints, the third one, matthew's — more material, round and smooth, still enough to hold on to. these faces are with me everywhere.

and there is also that unstable presence of another — olivier — who always meets me on the threshold — welcoming. no wonder i'm not desperate, despite my tendency to be missing, despite the fact that i am hardly ever "in."

2

by night and day i lose my way. can't remember a blooming thing. this morning, the wee one asked me to tell him a story — backwards — but i couldn't, i was blank. my project? just slightly different from the usual, trying to create some space in time. can't accept anymore the dispersion — scattered thoughts, splattered spots, tattered dreams.

need… to string some parts into an ample pattern, that's why i made the decision. bound to make a place down here. the world made by words is different. neither heaven nor hell, not purgatory. it is, but comes definitely from in-side. under the rest and not beyond.

caves indeed, these worlds of words, little habitats. sleepy hollows within the natural wood. it took me *long* to come to a commitment, because i kept on looking to escape. but i'm willing now to settle for the winter, not wander at the return of spring. from inside this place my-opic eyes see a store house of beauty, no longer something that i have to touch. enough to contemplate what might have been. perhaps that's why i had to grow old first? add some farsighted beams.

a wrinkling writer that's what i'll be
and i'll rock wounded hearts on my wobbling

the first concerned turns out to be angie. she said "tears" in the middle of the night. then remarked about the weirdness of the morning. something in between darkness and light, she said. never had a fear (she) about dispersion. daredevil heart. always pulls herself in from the outside, then throws out a perfect line. the second has to do with poetry. perfectly fine in that world to dart in and out, offer only signs, no resting place (if you do your words sell out). but here, in prose, where all reflections are inhabited, introductions must be made and promises (at least) to continue. no disappearing once the words get going. no vanishing into thin air. i need to learn something from my daughter about how to survive down here.

3

it's the third day or perhaps number four. the temptation to bring in markers is overwhelming. what i seem to be discovering is that i'm stuck, always beginning in the moment. that's why i need to shy away from poems. she who treads this path doesn't have a clue about the future, nor does she have a sense of history. how could she? just waking up from being born.

my fits of verse haven't done me any damage, i see much better than before. but nothing so close-snipped can master demons, especially the compulsion to capitulate. the moment the other scratches or pulls me, i'll try not to stop or just cave in. i'll continue, toe the line, like my daughter, or just stay huddled with the shadows down here, until somehow i can pick up, find a pathway and go on.

4

it's dark and messy and there's little light. i've not the frame of mind to strike a match and i don't yet know how to put order within. perhaps i need to pull upon the string that holds my daughter. she's been split down here from the beginning. the one (i let be killed)'s behind the other. the one who has no substance is robbing the other's transparency. i need to repair my "girl"?

no. it's rather that down here, within this world of shadows, i've bumped into my unborn firstborn. she, who never made it to the real world, is taking on this life as her own. she appears coming out of the darkness on the left (somehow it seems i did light a candle). and all i can do is look at her. here she is in the (image of) the flesh. strange combination of nadim — the lebanese banker — and me all balled up with... lise, my mother... looking like a small princess. five years old, jumper suit and exaggerated hair-bow, button-down boots from the twenties. olive skin, fluffy, dirty-blond hair. crinkling mediterranean eyes.

5

i'm afraid to return today, but glad to know there's someone waiting. i didn't know you were lurking in the shadows. i didn't even know you were missing. just like me. yesterday, after i left, i was filled, mixed you up with everything, outside. that's where i thought you'd need a name. i saw you also take on more distinct features, planes in your face resembling some of mine, but still more the effect of your father. i thought that it was up to me to name you, and all i could come up with was — *ondine.*

and i began to have some big, long fantasies, "here come and forgive me if you can," "let me raise you up — a queen." i even thought you'd need a nickname. nina? something sounding death that feels italian, but easy to be bandied about.

it's more likely that you'll never speak to me and it's hardly up to me to plot your life. for now, i can do nothing but observe — five years old. a synthesis of me and another with traces of your sister and brothers. all older, yet to come. your face is round and smooth, warm and clever, translucent, jumpy and high-strung.

you're looking at me as with a question, like happy but uncertain that i've finally made my mind up. no wonder that you're worried, ondine. i'm thinking that i'd better start over, that this attempt is really going nowhere. your eyes are folding up, and i can't tell you even one more thing. nothing's happening but that little gesture — one small hand, circling, tugging at the wrist of the other, palm side up. standing at attention in the corner.

will i ever get to hold you, ondine?

6

it's bothering me to realize that i'm ent-like. i want to be rooted, of course, and there's no question i'm in love with trees, but i'd like to be light and beautiful, bow shooting arrows through the breeze. i'm trying to extract some meaning, but it's slipping through my fingers like dirt. how can you build a house when the bricks all shift there crumbling? no sooner i'm collected than i'm strewn about. i learned from dreams i have imagination.

last night, a crazy, like garage-house party, celebrations of an automatic sort. i was sitting in an unmade bed, right in the midst of the commotion. there was struggle with my mother over a story. petty, but at the same time painful. i was the one who had plotted and planned, got everything assembled for the story, but while I was pondering my options, dealing with the fact that i was bound to flunk — something very basic (like math) — she went off and commissioned, on the model of a scene i'd just shown her, another version of *the little engine that could.* i wanted credit for the whole scenario, but then i realized it was funky and fake.

if i never do get out of here, if i never ever do settle in, this will still be a record of my efforts. i refuse to follow up on more false avenues. and i'd love to take a leap, but i can't. if i give myself over to rhyme, i'll end up for sure right back here. and i'm tired of the other kinds of writing. don't see the point now in telling only secrets, even less of stringing other people's thoughts. what i'm wanting is another existence, the creation of another place in time.

no wonder things aren't starting out smoothly. i'd like to think i'm scared of lying, incapable of making things up. and there's something gaining substance in ondine, but i don't have a clue what to do with her. she's just sitting alongside me in this shadow world, measuring my incapacities. maybe that is why she came here, to oversee the limits of my project, make sure i stay committed to what's real.

> can't i dream for just a moment
> that i'm empty?
> nothing but a faint coloration
> merging with the feather-headed trees

heaven knows the days are long that i am ent-like, gnarled shut with yellow eyes and knobby fingers, stomping through the dense and stillborn forest, looking out for orkish spies.

7

are you sure that lady's not your grandmother? true words blurted from a second-grade class. "i hear you," said the kindly teacher (in response to), "my mom had an operation... she's got a bright red nose."

the analogy with rudolph has been charming. i remember pitching it one day, driving along the curved dark road, smiling at the booster seat. thought i'd put the ball in little matt's court, show us both how to spin the situation, bounce off the glow so glaring in the glass. but that was

christmas in july

after the first or second operation. now through the cycles and the seasons, i'm tired of this conglomerate of reasons, always the same old syndrome. having trouble whipping up the good cheer, and luke is in the down and out.

here's the situation with my brother. a life-time of worshiping YOU-GOD while tending mostly to himself. now, hardly a penny to his name. another wife and child on the way. something contradictory in this story, something to think more about...

> i have to wonder
> who the heck our father is
> he who leaves us wandering
> always empty overfull or crying out
>
> some so shaky in their minds
> that they don't know
> how to start the sorting
>
> others so shackled in their flesh
> they need to be attached to metal
> or tear their very insides out

so, i'll have to put sure contours on this project, see which limitations are the right ones. if i don't commit to sound decisions, nothing i can keep will come. that's where the trouble may be lurking. how to forge some integrity here. certain things will have to be thrown over, or, as if packing for a journey — what to take, what to leave out? i know some things cannot stay in here — like, how i spend my feckless days. like, finally, the holidays... are over. the space that i was in was so full. then suddenly i saw

an opening.

and yet these struggles with time are worth recording. it's the rest that breeds distractions and diversions. take place in a world that's cleared of everything but meaning and allow in too... you. how should i really call you? the one in charge of me and all i want to be here. something has changed in my devotions, i know the ONE who gave me sighs is still here,

if not your lips would fill with ash and dust.

but, i can't just use familiar catch words — God, Father, Help, Please — they've grown all hollow on my fingertips, so i'll find some new forms of address. and if it's true that i'm to settle down here, i'll also need to simplify my trials, no more searching out there, when it's here i want to scrape a life.

8

should i even bother and why? yesterday it seemed so clear, all i needed was to sit. yet this morning, i am moving all about. this shift is maybe due to dreams?
i was lonely in a place and had not been noticed for a time. then someone started to call me. and i was glad to know that finally

the lover was coming.

he was following me, and calling me back. but the last calls weren't getting through. they were garbled and strange. cas-sandra, my sister-in-law, was answering the phone, and even relaying messages, *but the wanderer got cut off.*

he was forced to take three trains, for a stomach cure of
sorts. but it was obvious at the end he'd be returning. at least
he wanted to come back, and that was lifting me, making
my senses most pleased.

and then there was a kind of sequel. i had a clean white
dress, and i was getting ready for an academic show. it surely
was a circus with a surly mc, who was also pacing there, icy
cold and snooty in his dull black suit, and as worried about
his look as my own timing. so i saw as i was dressing that my
pretty, white gown had indeed become bedraggled, if not dirty.
i'd have to wear something less fine.

what happened to the present?

your children weren't there,

my love, nowhere about. how could i forget about them and
strive for kicks from hapless strangers? perhaps i was just feeling trapped... what i need is just an open ending. the problem
that i'm facing:

death.

i've been thinking that i need to nail things shut. see what
in my own eyes is worth keeping, dare to throw away the rest.
but how to go about this day by day?

first don't throw the baby with the bathwater.

if i want to survive down here, have a final go, i'll have to stop
squandering the riches that i have.

lest your dreams become of drowning.

i'll need to get my levels straight.

9

the one that i sloughed off has been waiting here 10 days. she hasn't made a move since i left. she needs *me* to make a move and give her life. i'm her puppet master in a way. in an- other, she's controlling my own gait. for instance, if i wanted to erase her now i couldn't. i mean i'd have to start all over again. and even then,

she'd find her way back through.

the proof is that she's tried before. starting in my first apartment — manhattan corner window on the upper west side — in the summer of the year she was not born. a strange kind of prematurity, aborted child trying to break through at six months. and then she almost came to life three years ago, and then i'm sure there were attempts before. always squashed or squandered from the outset, by me or by one of my impedi- ments — enemies i set before me, all and sundry — except my lucky friend.

ondine, she is my long dead daughter (23 years), aborted in the ides of march. i found her in this cave where i have come to live with memories long and short, gone and living members of my family. and i really don't know what to do with her. she's just sitting in the corner, looking hard at me, wanting me to keep her company. hoping that i'll learn to settle in. she surely is the road not taken. will she keep me coming back?

what can you give to one who never came to be?

thanks for coming back to me,

ondine.

10

i said i would keep track of the details, but ended up counting down my lovers. it wasn't that there was nothing to the incident, there was, though i couldn't really see it. a cold january morning, powdered sugar sprinkled all about, and the feeling of venturing i always get along the canal.

there's something so cocoon-like in the taurus, just the opposite i feared — sensation — i was in for from the ct-scan (before they told me it was nothing but a doughnut): shut cold with no recourse to anything but darkness. in the taurus, through the metal, there is lots of muted light. you're wrapped, but very warm and gently with plenty of elbow room and air.

once arrived at the lab, my destination, i encountered no particular hassle, still more noes to most diseases than yesses. only tricky issue — the nose, which inaugurates the rubric of cancer, with the seeming proviso that it's skin. still, no arguing insurance up front. very chummy, the machine assistants, billboards posted everywhere (even in the ladies' room) shouting out the patients' rights. kind enough to ask (as i'm reclining) if i'm pregnant, but marveling at childbirths at 60. no protesting that i might be a grandmother, according to a second-grade class. what i thought would be a doughnut is like a carwash. three-minute sterile stillness, whizzing, spinning sounds while i lay fixed.

firm in the knowledge of your body,

making peace with a calm, green patience,

certain that you're bound to get out.

on my way, i met a kindly mexican, we remarked on the niceties and cookies. mine, shortbread (have somehow disappeared or are still lying, packaged in the car, attached to the

glossy pamphlet). his, chocolate chip, must be eaten. i doubt
he did the questionnaire. he told me that he'd had a chest x-
ray, to which i muttered lamely good luck. i said that because
i'm scared of chest x-rays, anything that shows "i'm doomed."

george is forty-five and a grandfather — some little child's
papa too. but no one speaks to him of modern medicine. he
just had a kid when he was young, and then another, later,
as he was starting to get old. both are daughters, the elder,
matilda, is almost 22, ceci, the younger, is now 6. matilda's got
a three-year old named oscar, george is taking care of all of
them, with his second wife, inès. they came together here from
puebla, more than thirteen years ago. george is a mechanic in
somerville, inès works part time at a dry cleaner's, and sews
on her machine at home. george has had

a cough for three weeks,

it wouldn't quit with rounds of penicillin. so, the doctor said
he'd better have a look. now it seems his body's in big trouble.

but in the end,

he's going to be o.k., because george is a very good man. two
weeks from now, he'll find out he has cancer in his lungs, and
by forty-eight, he'll be dead. but he's going to have a good life
in between, because he isn't scared of living, nor is he

hiding from the darkness of thoughts.

11

it's a glorious spring day. or rather, one that's soft and bright
to close the winter. the kind of day that comes with promises
in the early months, before the summer's on us and it finally

is, turns out to be, too late. that's how my life has gone along, ondine. that's why i couldn't focus on you earlier. you are all about what might have been the spring.

well, mother, can you tell me that story?

(ondine can play the part like other first-borns, take on a wry and grown-up voice). perhaps that could work to move us forward. i'll tell you what i can about five springs.
the first i can remember was in the third grade. in the world, children have to learn with other children, get knocked and prodded, passed through tin cans. something that we call school. i never clicked so well with all that early knocking, for i was

sleepy and in touch with earth.

i could barely see the writing on the chalkboard or notice cars whose wheels were rolling down the road. but i think i saw

another kind of writing.

the one that's always etched into the wall.
thus i remember being (little) on a certain march third. i liked the moment when we scattered from the school bus. they always let us go by the fake and dusty church, which pretended that we're all good protestants, living somewhere normal in america, not as we were in the scorched & thorny desert where tv land has no real matches outside, only drama or vacant lots. the vacant lot between the church and our house held plenty of adventures for the short. you could easily get lost in those bare bushes, might as well have been a jungle. relieve yourself while fearing indians, join or not in all the naked games.

here's another spring. my fourteenth march. i'm sliding
down a mountain, cactus spurs in my left butt. i've grown
despite my laziness and gravity, too often more toward out
than up. but something has been pumping me with air of late,
perhaps my own sequential pounding down the street, accep-
tance of the need for exercise, if only to enjoy the rush of air
and light. i'm wearing red, a striped t-shirt, and cut-offs hold
my padded thighs in. this picnic marks my parents climbing
to the top. they've turned the slope with pride — called fifty.
when i'm alone at home, within the cool dark, there's a bible
that can manage to console me, echo voices come from europe,
remind me of the prayers i heard in spanish. maybe ma and
pa don't know what's up.

the next spring i remember, i am seventeen. in the green
and liquid park of rambouillet. there's a picture of me there,
too pretty (to be short), holding a first blank book. in there
i should have put — my future... there would have been a
place for you, ondine. if i had found this underworld earlier,
instead of sneezing at the outcome of my research... maybe
then... or maybe, what i'm looking for simply can't be found.
but still there is a chance we will make something, if i can
just shake off my laziness, accept my lot and live within this
hole, eliminating rather than producing, clinging to the junk
that's all around.

the next spring i remember i am twenty-three, that's the
spring before you weren't, ondine. i'm lonely and in pain, but
somehow lithe again. i feel the ground i'm pounding daily, up
and down the city bank, the hudson. in the afternoons i'm
reading, three timed hours, or writing, for this task or that.
suspension takes me to the next place. i haven't yet begun to
write — poetry. that will start to happen in the summer or the
fall, but i've begun to tune in to something like conviction, someone should and might be in there. when winter comes i'll waver
and get hit — hard. completely lose my bearings in the wind.

here's the final spring, now i'm thirty-four. have myself
a husband and two children. i'm living next to here, in this
middle state, which really isn't anywhere at all. there's pain
surrounding every side. the spring before, i couldn't see where
i was heading. i was just dreaming and walking in the garden
with my little ones, visiting the secret spots with ichabod and
flopsy. now the toll of lies has gotten serious, now the world's
collected pools of trials. i've inflicted blows of truth upon my
father, and ruined all the wishes of my husband. in the space
beyond the sorrow, i've a friend.

12

i've been missing you for ages, ondine. been afraid for many
days to settle in. you must be lonely in this frozen winter
with no one here at all to keep you, or even start to build you
shelter. perhaps this morning we could make a fire or think at
least about the gathering — the gathering we'll need of time
and wood.
     outside the cold, harsh days are steel-like, promising...
rough road ahead. not sure if it's for me or generations, but
there's bound to be things terrible ahead. i hope this will not
frighten you, ondine.

there isn't any risk to me,

only to our solid bodies. can you show me how to be insub-
stantial? can you teach me how to breathe among the dead? i
don't suppose you are at ease among the others

or i wouldn't have come here

seeking me instead.

come, ondine, let's build a fire. the wood that i will gather comes from all around the place. covered logs, lying rotted, on the outskirts of the lawn, where tangled brush has buried all but trees, random sticks left over by the ever-hungry dog, who takes in as much bark as he puts out. why not even bring a bag of kindling from the store and a wrapped and coated log with fake blue fire? who cares as long as something's crackling. i took your little brother to a movie last night, so easy just to swaddle him and give him to the world. for you, i'll have to

make it all from scratch.

13

what is there today? i see no fire, nothing but your shadow on the wall.

the problem is, this temple is a pit stop. i have to set my life in reverse. another week gone by and what have i retained? last night as i was hearing andrew's touch, answers to my prayers through his piano, i thought that i could take you for an outing. now, i'm wondering if i can even walk or talk. i'll be silent while i'm speaking, ondine. won't try to guide or crush you with a rock, still i know that you must wait on what i'm thinking, not like other children, now set free — free because well-bonded to my body. you must sit and wait on what i am thinking. so here's

...five springs?

let's have you first slide a bit into the sunlight. just outside this cave, an immense shining star, heartbeat all in flames, is covering the earth with light and colors. it's the sun that brings us up and gives us bodies, then drives us shriveled back to earth and dust. if i can stay here for a moment, and help you step outside, you'll draw a breath of fire, but you won't turn to dust. because the sun can only hit you in my dreams.

i can never get outside, mother, did you forget you'll have to keep me "in"?

no, no i've not forgotten, and i'm sorry. let's begin by trying something called "touching." let me have your hand, ondine.

the one hand circling the other, the tugging hand stretched out — ondine.

lord, have you ever seen such five-year-old hands? of course YOU've seen this miracle, you make them, bring them to the light. or hide them where they can't be seen. ondine's hand, it's pink, that i'm now holding, not like it was mine, strong and stable post, but just enough to keep it steady, certain it won't startle at more contact, or shrink away when shined on by a beam. her hand on mine weighs less than any feather, pale and slightly curved, tender palm-side down, fingertips: a rim that's tense and tight.

let's stay like this, for years, together.

just get used to being here in stillness,

then to dreams of moving, light.

14

now i know i'm frightened, ondine. ballerina left perching, balanced by my hand, while i went running wild round the block. at least a hundred times, i had to make sure not to make unfair advances, preserve my stuck-as-usual attitude. but, thanks to you, my unborn, things are different. you have the same power to lead as the others.

utterly so — i am not a reflection.

you are not square one. and though i'd thought of taking you for a splendid walk when the air was filled with ground-hog day and spring, now too much snow has slid between. no chance i'll let you out. blasted by the cold. it's a blizzard out there, not the storybook kind. so let's abandon, for the mo-ment, thoughts of things to come, and sink within this dull, suspended moment.

what, ma, if the next one never comes?

can't say. i've been away so long for those who're growing up (the bacon i've been bringing's passed mostly through my lips), though they too claim that i'm always off & wandering, not remaining hooked to their concerns. andrew underscores my "short attention span," sees the problem as a lack of seated memories. angie rather seizes on my emptiness, the blank that comes and covers up my eyes. matt talks most of loss of hearing. but to them, through these — eyes and ears (and heart) — i can always find my way back... home.

come closer, let's establish something like a rhythm: heart-beat that can hold us here, ondine.

draw from me some life,

before mine slips away. and let me start by reclaiming you full circle. you are mine. i've come to own you, ondine.

15

ondine's agreed to sit upon my lap today. her knees drawn up, her arms around my waist. she's searching for a hook-up to my heartbeat, pressing cheeks and forehead all around my chest. settling now and quiet, her ear is pinned between my breasts. we're happy in this cave together, it's lit now like a warm cocoon. i'm adjusting to the newfound weight of her, happy she can hold some substance, studying each hair upon her head, wavy, blond and dark in variation, guess that's why they call it "ash." then all at once i'm wondering... who tied this velvet bow? pulled up this ponytail? who's kept her from the dank earth?

suddenly, a line around hetna — grandmother, who living tied me to the cave of ancestors and taught me all i knew about death:

> the moment i saw your shadow
> i heard the bird take flight
> and felt again a pulling
> toward the darkness
>
> that bird was my whole future
> and you were certain dust
> but here we are suspended

we don't speak, but i know her too as grandmother, she scooped me from the bottom of the well.

16

ondine, out there, i had my forty-seventh birthday where everything goes rushing forward. but now, inside, the world for me is barren and stunted. remember? i threw you out with stained *&* dirty bathwater... now there is no longer any water. nothing left to do except wither and fade, and at appointed seasons: dread. the littlest child reminds me daily: old skin, old skin. mommy, i don't want you to be dead.

i've always been a fanatical planner. that's why, i guess, i have been ready to begin. and the clean reality of the break explains all this sputtering. it's like father quitting smoking last september. saying it was actually for "her." something he could offer someone else — lise. devoted on her eighty-third birthday? no. i'm sure it wasn't quite so simple. he too was preparing the beginning of the way, clearing his throat, making room for all the coming blood. i'm losing all my water, but still have all my blood. nonetheless, this is the beginning of the final — draining.

and i'm horrified that, here, where i've been building room to live at peace, i've spotted the shadow of hetna. huge figure with problems all her own. upset to find this too must be a family affair. couldn't we just push her back a bit inside the wall? at least a little time? so i can hold you here, ondine, once more in silence, mourn the passing of the bathwater, search for something i can carry on?

ondine laughs for the very first time. and those green-grey eyes that never will shine are glittering at the prospect of a prank: grandma-pushing back into the wall. lucky for me, grandma smiles too, clever twinkle hid behind big sunglasses. she's standing white and tall, beautiful, here. just like in my vision at the barbecue. maybe there's hope for me too.

wait for me, ondine, i'm coming.

forgive that i've been gone so long. the rain's been falling, falling for so many days. and i've been far removed. why should the child accept such excuses? absent mothers, horrible, who just don't care. trembling anxiety, with alibis, for things meaning absolutely nothing, things that are far emptier than air.

squeeze my hand a good bit tighter, and liquefy my all that-does-not-matter. let me grasp here only for the linings, the glow that might survive the instant, the ray that makes your golden hair. sink back within our bright foundation, search for all that's hidden in the dense world, finery that crumples up and vanishes, soon as sore eyes become distracted, into the thin day air.

but how can i be with you anyway, before i've come to grips with my (own) self? i've been gone so long that only crisis brings me back. and i am altogether clueless what to do with you. for this is not the place for poetry. accounts have somehow to be kept, things can't just begin anew.

i've been here with my question-mark eyes. i've been here with my arms around your waist, my ear pinned to your breast. and where, oh where, my mother, were you?

will i always have to reach for memories? fine, then let's begin right where we left off... there was snow all around, and i was dreaming intermittently of sun, of letting rays of light fall on your hair: let it turn to gold, i thought, and substance.

i wanted to bring you closer to my body, and drew you near the real — and dangerous. then as i closed you in, and touched each strand of hair, i noticed that you too have a body, which someone else i know must have been keeping. that's when i spotted hetna. grandmother: the dead one, the keeper of the gate.

and so i ran in terror from you, my girl, scared to feel the downward pull of family, afraid to cross ancestral gates.

17

my dream was just a hiding place, alone, and far from view, from which i could think up a kind of paradise. i tried to settle in, then you appeared — a future

love that all your madness squandered.

now you bring along the whole family?

multitudes and hordes!

i've got to have some time to come to grips with this. i know that i need first to find myself alone. if i am ever going to tell the story, those people can't come in and live here, vie to shut and drown me out. not the living, nor the dead. if i'm ever going to bring you out across the line, i must find a way to make those voices silent — snap my fingers, make them disappear.

but, i'm wanting to progress, and, with your help, i think i can

begin anew

what? something like "raising" you. the words will be the outgrowth of my learning, the fruit of just my loving, you.

18

today i feel quite staticky and nervous. don't know how to sink back in (within) this space. on the surface, there's a clearcut bug on the wall, or perhaps it's just a roachy spider. in any case, a symbol of my feelings. the day is fine today, it's even got some sheer magnificence, and all my things appear to be in order. but still, there is this nasty creature on the wall. or i should say there was, because he's taken off behind the curtain.

i ought to breathe out slowly from my nose, today. that would rest my tired ribs and chest. and take my heavy chore box to the office. assembly of tasks that take me far from you. then i'll bring some finer things tomorrow. we'll build some splendid things together. i'll gather sticks and stones, things for you to wear, and maybe even spin a plot line, spilling now and then little poems. we'll spend a string of time together, here, while i can still breathe air.

19

"papa" is the one who made you? "mom" the one who gave you birth?

today he's had an operation. small cancer spot — one lobe from one (left) lung.

smoked?

at least a billion cigarettes. but still just two small cancer spots of trouble: throat and lung. cancer's always been in our story. i think it might just be the end of mine, hold me back from telling any tales here,

take away my story time.

like when they sent me off to get the ct-scan, after slightest density on x-ray, after all my own fits of coughing lasting for weeks and weeks.

remember what you said of george last winter?

how fast he came and went. in between two snowstorms in the taurus. how did i know then

what turn the tide would take come spring?

i didn't. that's why i've come to track the story.

you never know just what will happen.

and when there is a lag — no action?

then we'll have some time for fire,

time again to stop and build the fire. summers, we'll make do without fire. instead we'll venture out, see what we can see, protecting you from killer rays of sun.

20

i thought as i was whizzing by the water, yesterday, biking down the path with little matt, that you might well be hid-ing in the underbrush, waiting for me there to come out by your side.

so perhaps i ought to do just that this morning, and think about some formal questions. such as, where's the point and place of poems?

do we really ever need a resting place?

a moment of suspense or tenderness, before contending

      what should i do
      with all this
      time

      time
      i should do
      what with all this

21

i've freed myself of complications, can settle fully down to write. right here with you, ondine, my witness, and one who really gives me: life.

why does so much emptiness seep inside my mind, as soon as i begin to clear...

why must you always reach to plug it?

supposing i just let the free air in and try to let this thing
develop? can't stand the heat, the cold, the draft. want to call
my "pa" this morning, balm the wound on cut-off lung, can't
stand to hear the suffering, lingering in his voice, developing
some feeling for his bravery, don't mind declaring love — feel
the pull of love — even though it dictates that i don't.

   grandpa?

yes, i'm going on about your grandfather, son-in-law of hetna,
who's kept you safe down here in bits and pieces — blood
bonds really do come out.

   it's funny that you used to be at home, alone.

no need, or even tolerance for characters, just ONE back there,
an opening that drew up air. now my world is anchored in a
setting, time, and place. it's everything i wished for, a foundation, but now i can't begin afresh.

   get free?

no, no, ondine, don't worry, i don't want to.

   *i think i might be growing, mother. look at how my leg now has
a pale line, just below the edge of my blue sock. grandma says that
might mean sun.*

how ever did you get that color, child?
   (ondine's eyes smile, grab me by the chin, whisper in my
ear a lot of talk)

   *i did go for a walk, and when you spoke of woods, whizzing
by your bike, i latched upon your words and waited.*

then, 5 o'clock this morning, while you were still asleep, i climbed aboard the letters, rode them through our hole. right into the blue-gray morning, where skipping down the street, light and breezy — air — i somehow managed even to take flight.

then, gliding very low, i hunted down the trail, found the way that you and little brother took, "whizzed" by houses drenched in rain and dark. i followed your bike trail, cycled very well, keeping to the good side of the street.

now, mother, you must come and find me.

winter is for hovering (you told me), temple-sweeping, and retreats. summer is for hide and seek.

22

sorry, i've been waylaid, but i did go searching, yesterday.

two deer led you down the path.

i was moving slowly, but the waters raced beside: thick coffee-waters, just like angie said. she's got the touch for metaphors,

splendid daughters all her own.

at the end of the long trail, a fawn jumped out, then darted on and off again the path. he danced across the road (most taken) as if to say the underbrush is livable. follow me, there's magic in these woods.

for sure, it crossed my mind,

that little deer was me

mottled oldest girl, who've just begun to grow, whose legs have barely brushed the ground.

led?

you were by careless, wayward parents, not exactly watched, nor even planted. just left as loot for future treasure hunts, marker of a secret hiding place, from which, it seems, i'm always…

23

the rain falls equally on the just and the unjust, the faithful and the unbelievers, those who do or don't consult the good book. my newfound freedom's really — quite oppressive, i don't know what to do, or not to do with it. i've lost my basic urge to write.

spending time with me, shouldn't need an urge.

you're right, my little deer, but you have no idea what utter trash is on my mind. mortgages and writings terrible to read, nothing i can talk about with you.

no matter, you should stay beside me. i'll just curl up here and go to sleep. speak your empty thoughts. no crime to be distracted, mother. just stay enough to warm my waxing body, and leave me words for future flights.

24

ondine is peaceful, sleeping, lying on the floor. in and out her child's breath, just like albertine's, carries all the world of trees inside it, doesn't leave a residue of thought. pristine — she's counting on my sense of duty, to get us up and out the door. where light is always waiting, i'll make myself some… heartfelt prayers. prayers that i won't fail today in courage, sink inside the mire of my turpitude, waste myself in stickiness of boredom, squander time i owe to generations, squash all of my treasure under thoughts. today though i'm not happy, nor even up to snuff, i'll pretend myself divided in this moment, recognize the fearsome battle, wage it from a distance: above.

god did not create a meaningless world: the plane crash (that i buy with every ticket), cancer (with a big fat c), paranoia over each presentation, strife over the outcome of every this or that. these do not weigh in as miracles. so when a book that's good advises, i should just repeat: god did not create this — and believe it.

but i'm not sure i do.

do you believe in death?

yes, i do. but not as final, absolute reality. there is a perfect peace that lies beyond this place. death is not the end for mine nor me. we are not all decadence and death, our kind, though for sure our bodies move in that direction.

ondine's body's growing slowly out of death, just as mine is moving into it. she's already been to nothingness and back.

ready now to live.

forever, or maybe just a moment with me.

25

angie told me that i shouldn't be that voice that draws the line, say: "by this alone you will succeed." she's right. that's not at all the voice i want to be. let me exorcise my mind control on just myself today, and let you precious children be.

maybe you can keep me by your side while you go out?

maybe teapots
whistle less for being
short and stout
than for wheezes
under pressure standing

ondine is really crying, because i'm bound to go to france. she knows: she'll hear no hide nor hair from me for months. that's maybe why it's rained all spring. the splitting of the family makes a "full house," but there always is a pinch, a pain.

andrew, angie — siblings — why can't they watch over me? who will ever come to fetch me, down inside this cave? now i'm sure i'll never...

perhaps, i could get back to you in letters? i'll see what i can do. if it's the thought that counts, i'll take with me to france

reminders,

thirty days, this time.

you'll take a part of me to france.

26

little one, i'm sorry, scared and frightened. i'm going to be sent down with you in death. no longer in the light with angie,

the daughter of your flesh, the one you brought the world to shine on.

no. now it's down in the narrow straights where grandma lives, down inside the underworld of death. very threatened by this thought, eventuality, realest thing most sure to come. there's the place i'm bound to write from,

just below the deepest shelf.

we have settled, barely settled in this temporary cave,

nothing but a slight depression,

which i'm supposed to turn into a house.

days and weeks and months gone by since you first came to me and i keep flying out in agitation, can't sit still to see what loving you might bring. is it that i'm addicted to every-day thoughts? or am i always running frightened? how odd and terrible to ask for help from you, a child i myself would not let live.

i don't mind that, mommy, i'll be glad to help. just keep coming down to see,

ondine.

come here with your windy, wobbly words. stretch out to me your chubby, wrinkling arms. hold me here, a moment, give me just some thought. teach me how to live and grow a body, and i will teach you how to be — reconcile you with crossing — death — just as andrew, angie, matt have helped you live.

27

a bad thing that... maybe i should shed. you know that i am struggling with running here in place, believing in this truth or folly. waiting just to feel better.

i can't tell you much about that.

but you're... o.k., even though... you've crossed the finish line. not here (because i threw you down the well). and yet...

i am. look at the line above my sock. it's just that my particles work differently from yours. they fly and carry on. not suspended here, not at all attached by gravity.

you're quite a bit made more like my dream body.

tell me, mother, all about your dreams.

i was, for certain, me, absolutely me, yet i was living in another kind of body, inhabiting a dark hotel. all gussied up in black, younger, all alone. there were people who loved me in the distance, maybe even a husband-father figure. but i was lonely and i wanted to get separated. go somewhere, where i would be apart.

so i let myself get loaded like some baggage in a truck. wooden, something like the painted blue truck father had, open but closed, above, in back. something between the willies and a van, where i could only see the outside through the slats. i was sort of *fine*, as i was rolling, traveling along, thinking that i knew what i was doing. then suddenly i remembered: it's a dangerous world, i really don't know where i'm heading, maybe i have walked into a trap. i might be beaten, raped, and turned into a prostitute.

in a moment of lucidity, i decided to jump out — head back for the dark hotel. and then i see the driver, for the first time, in the mirror. the corner of my eye stays pinned to his, and i see that he is really menacing, which gives me courage to jump out of the truck. i hit the ground running and i keep crouched as i advance low along the dark green hedges, running till i catch the bus.

28

then i emerge (in reality) in france, and turn my face toward thinking, from a distance.

you promised you would write

but i couldn't. i was lost, somewhere amidst the ocean. whenever i go forth,

the wind outside blows out my little flame,

drowns my inner world in mud. and i, a hollow shell,

yes, you, the essence of a turtle,

go looking for my soft and working parts. yet, the light that shines on "here" cradles the whole earth. the surface is the same with accidents. water stretches over this, washes over that: rocks, sands, and trees, all our heavenly parts. and just under & above, and all around the cracks, water even washes over words: words to

call for help from me or others.

words to prove you surely don't exist. words to say who cares where we all go, or knows exactly where we come from. articulated first between the heart and throat, then later traced out by the mind and hand.

i guess i'm logocentric, ondine. anyway, it's thanks to just these words that i can say hello. hello to dead and living children. make the small one laugh, cradle teens in prayers, formulated here like this, or that or

left in back of mind, still hanging.

today, when i am far away from those who are grown up, i'm asking you to please plant a seed. remind them that i'm here, i love them, remind me that they love me too.

the talking words of telephones don't always hold. the distance often makes them crack. this month, for him & her, it's like: i've troubles of my own, and me, the same, apart.

you disconnected from your own mother.

because she let me go at just 16...

help me always be there where my children are in need, help me also be a person when they're not.

who needs you completely, living only through your words?

destroyed, ripped out, your tiny growing body.

today, my little deer, the pickings are less than lean. but at least i've come to reach toward you this morning, am trying not to shrink from you in fright.

but how can you grasp me from so far away?

so far from you and further from myself. when we make ourselves bodies, we simplify ourselves. one body brushes up another: there you are.

then it's true outside there's nothing?

i don't believe in nothingness, ondine.

you, i sent you packing to the other side of here, and you're back and all the richer in your being. help me now to reach into that pool i fear and draw out proof of all your shining. no guilt, no fear.

the children of your flesh will not be angry,

they'd want their "older" sister to be saved? if i can bring you back to some sheer substance

you'll be saving them a bit too.

29

i'm not o.k. down here without some paradise. where mind and body go, this writing's turning out to be difficult.

maybe due to paused commitment?

i can't just take two seconds off and jump into a world with no true consequence.

now you have to face the music,

bring a world into being, something that weighs and measures, or resign myself to kicking up dust. you're of course the one who's come to help me, but i feel i simply can't dig in.

how about a little walk then, mother? we tried before and almost made it.

she's talking to me now. i see her, just as clearly as day one. though from then to now she's really changed. she's taller somehow. less nervous, not so prim. it's like she knows she's going to get a shot at growing, have a chance to ease into a body.
and she's learning to rely on reason. she balances to keep us going forward, tries to rein the blow-outs in. but i'm still worried about her living sister.

what's angie going to think when she discovers you? she's my only girl and she's a writer (i don't think my boys will feel concerned).

she's not going to hate me, mother. when she finds out i'm 23 years dead. she won't be upset or frightened. she'll know that i belong to fiction, that you can hold me only with your words.

fine then, i will stay with you, until we have to part. you'll sit right here with me, or play around my desk. come on in the house, ondine.

30

how can she who's never ridden in a car look so much at ease and swing her feet? blond ashen hair, more disheveled than before, half pony-tail's a quarter abandoned. ondine is on the seat beside me, swinging her blue-socked feet. her lower legs are sturdy and lengthening, she's got yellow shorts, an unmatched shirt. looks like she is choosing her own clothes now. grandma must be off (on a vacation?).

mother, can you take me to the office?

her lovely face has more and more the look of andrew's, angie's, matt's. angie's most in shape and in complexion, only eyes and eyebrows all her own. green eyes often folded in a question, even as she takes all in.

and it's good to have her, arms around my neck again, thank YOU for your tender mercies, thank you for this day, again. i'll call on mother mary through this whole long week, and try to live by her example. but YOU who put me here, you're the one i need. i can't lie and say i don't have questions.

you want me to work out — aborted daughter. you want
me to be brave, to pierce right through this skin of darkness,
this cover almost smothering my self (my soul), hovering most
everywhere on earth. but for that i'll need a pocketful of light.

put yourself, your love, and children in it.

31

i'll dig down here inside this place, with you, ondine, not
scared to face my own worst (demons), own up to the fact i
killed you... for convenience. no accomplices but fates, just me,

you had no light that time,

to say: just save her skin, don't throw that lovely child in the
trash.

she's carrying...

i only had the sense that i was wrong, a feeling sad, to mourn
a bit your passing. then later still, the decision: my renouncing
you was wrong, the loss will always be,

boundless, everything you threw away

with your lost life. yet how much dearer to me still than you,
ondine, are the children i let live.

they who are enough, are everything.

even so, my love for you is great. and now, as bearing years are
over, maybe i can — not forgive myself — but give you like the
shadow of a substance. something you might want too?

32

i'm no longer scared of death. but here with you, i really can't remember. how do you get dressed?

not sure how i get clothes, think they might be hand-me-downs. there's a pile — lost and founds — upon a smooth red floor.

that's the floor that holds the house among the thorns. the one my chubby knees knelt down to pray on.

i picked the shorts and shirt, you the blue socks, and now it's angie's picking…

saddle shoes. that's fine with me, your

childhood is whizzing by.

soon you'll be like others, passing eight. then things might start to add up easier. time will be less frenzied, wrong, too late.

33

see, ondine, i've come to you again, time's been granted free to me this fall. i'm even going to swim for you. (help, perhaps, to bring you to the surface), save us both from drowning in anxiety, build us solid lungs and ground for feet.
it's thanks to you i've made it through the summer. you said that you would help me and you did. you backed me up to death, and showed me how to live. to live will mean to live with this commitment, to learn to be devoted to my loves. the plan inside this magic world's impossible. i'll have to just let happen what will. but thanks to you i've lost some fear of it,

won't cower at each ghost or devil, can let them simply dance across my mind.

i saw my fantasies don't all come true, only those that i commit to, and which gather up support from you. i did not commit to madness, even though i felt its power coming. yes, i resisted evil in the corners of my mind, and now your light and love have flooded in. let me keep this "fire" burning. more, for more, than just an instant, let me build you something like a temple, fashioned out of letters in the wind.

> the shadows on the grass
> don't see your face
> but i can see them sparkling
> through the glass
> that keeps me from
> all forms of turpitude
> seeking only bits that last

34

ondine has a smile on her face, again. meeting up so soon with me, this morning. mother takes dead daughter to work again.

this time i'd like the air conditioned, next i'll turn the radio on.

so quick, my ondine, is learning worldly ways, i wonder, will this forward bent always swell and grow? or we will we just retract in winter, consort with just our selves down in the hole.

the problem is i'm too distracted, wanting always last things first.

if you do that we will never get anywhere.

i need to reverse my practice. this writing is in part an empty-
ing. but what if everything becomes that in the end?

and you never come to know what fills,

just because there is no outside pressure. okay, i have to recognize that i've become forlorn.
     so here i am, just writing what is present, and trying to
bridge back into the past. the story of a little girl waiting.

i'm here, i'm always here waiting. it's you who always go away,
you who never sit, never come to spell with your ondine.

     i don't come because i'm trapped. (that's nonsense.) barely
felt the warmth of our two bodies. ondine's just sitting by.
23 years dead — she won't cast me off, knows more than i
can know about patience. let's see, then, what could happen.
has anything occurred since i began?

35

15 minutes since i sat down. and i'm bored, resisting almost
to distraction. i'm thinking there is emptiness all around this
place that i could fill up easy with my junk.

not feel the end of morning passing,

not care i've got to write, ondine. that girl, she needs no ordinary story. she'll feed and grow on any kind of words (in
poems). happy words of hope and great redemption. sad words
facing evil too. no need to

shield the child already put to death.

no thing that comes from me can frighten her. so come ahead, you dark things lurking.

once upon a time: a woman, filled with hacked and evil parts. just her slivered will refused the night. tips of ever-shivering extremities were often searching, trembling for the light. the mass remained aloof, inert. if i could just articulate all this, give some form to all the blackness in my mind,

perhaps you could make room for something nice?

but that thought crashed into a paradox: chopped-off heads, rolling into wicker baskets, blood coagulating, dripping like sperm that goes to waste. spit from lips, squeezed by fingertips. wiped, the sperm that could beget so cute a baby, but spills out withered sack instead.

now there is one true fact of my distraction. the demon always pulling at the lower part of my head saying: why not go for just this kind of opening, the kind of space that's really just a gap, something like a blindness to step over, a thrill that you can get at, not through beauty, but just by staring down some "thing" or path.

is this then all there is to it? when i begin to think inside the nothingness, my mind fills up with gore and guts and trash?

this cannot be shown to anyone and is hardly any use for me.

what i began is not for anyone. if i can make a world for us to live in, we'll have to live there, daughter, on our own.

uncontrollable bird, which i took on myself to carry,

maybe for a flight, long overdue?

by daybreak, an annoying... blue jay — the loudest bird i've ever heard — by night, a bird that's pale and fears the emptiness. paralyzed by all that vastness, clutching all its might on my raw finger, it shits all kinds of things all over me.

but somehow through this whole ordeal, we've bonded. and i've agreed to bring it back inside, within my present nest and packs of relatives, visiting in this corner or that. and i'm not so much disturbed to see them all,

because your bird's become a brand new baby,

beautiful, in blankets, like the last ones.

innocent,

my arms are full.

36

ondine, she has become my duty to myself, but i don't really think of her in those terms. for me she's what she is today.

depressed,

she's sick of water falling on all sides, and worried that our story won't go forward. right now, i have to laugh at her, pac-ing up & down. i see i'll have to spend some time on editing,

see what's up if anything at all.

> should this have more
> poems or a plot line
> or should i just beat drums of tin
>
> how can i hope to get
> anywhere without a sense
> of where i've been

a mountain, the feeling of clutter,

trails of my worn-out sin.

37

right now, a harangue, from ondine:

nine months practically, i've been waiting here. i made you: a dramatic appearance. you promised: you would come and give me life. instead, it's just eternal coming-going. a regular revolving door. i'm not the garbage you take out once or twice a week. but the flesh of your own soul. the one you can come back from the dead for.
you said that you were scared, but you're just lazy... make me up some semblance of a story, use your sorry feelings & your head.

went swimming today, just for you, today. wondered as i washed and wrung myself dry if that could make you come up to the surface. immaculate conception, age 48?

bring back all that's left behind.

another round, a second chance?

death now,

my love's father, through the fall.

38

don't know if i have any strength to write today,

path on which to take ondine.

i could pretend something, very close to truth: that i could almost be that old goat herder.

devote yourself to watching.

contain myself in a few soft whiskers, emitting more benevo-lence than grace. let her take her own walk up the mountain today, set her own agenda and her pace? she hasn't the fullness that always brings me down, can snatch what's good for tasting with her own awakened soul, without the tethered burden of my weight. meanwhile, in here, in silence, i could try to make things better around the house.

cold, extraneous, not the way i want. the proof was in that screeching at my tenant, who dared so change the kitchen that i sued. i've reached the point where eyes (environment) draft up all the sense of who i am. extended now the borders of my body. perhaps that's why i'm mad for real estate. seems that passion's growing in my clan. think about my two sisters. not enough to make a base together. now they're setting sights on buying towns.

i'm more obsessed with time than space or money. but still i need a place to live. not just for me, ondine, my night and day dreams, but sure enough some room for my whole family: sisters, brothers, parents, in-laws too, those to come, those who've passed away. grandparents, especially, deserve a place to sit. all will need a frame who appear.

39

i'm ready to withstand some trials. ondine is out and scram-bling up the mountain. grandma, come and sit a moment in the "north wind," closest thing i have to an easy chair.

staring at the underside of piano, five or six, i knew you'd be my first "to death," my dear.

calculation, always, since childhood.

luckily, i missed yours. italy — nineteen. letter, much as usual, from your daughter, lise,

rationalizing,

mother, round and round about.

when i left, you were a whiteness in a nursing home. peaceful, i had thought, not depressed. when i returned you were: remains to see?

not even.

just some random comments uncle made on father's wild hair and something he said too about your laugh.

true, hearty laugh.

i think i do indeed remember that: wide just like your smile and (our) ass. remember how my baby jaws gobbled that cow's tongue? but your fingers, they knew pianos, playing, delicate and thin. how to smoke and hold their sherry.

and tea parties,

especially, with ladies playing brahms. that's the closest to your century i have been.

40

that frozen stretch of pond, i was glad yesterday. air moving in and out — my chest. on the left — inside — the whistle blew.

outside —

nothing but a smooth white blanket. on the right, the woods and water, splashing.

those brave ducks.

reminding me to read NILS HOLGERSSON, join my passion for the world to that held by my love, give this wrapped up presence to our son.

meanwhile, your unborn girl climbs the craggy tops.

you're out there in a skirt. happy, getting tan. one leg crooked, foot gripping on the earth — the other straight, just touching ball of foot. two hands pushing, pressing on a rock. and smiling, like:

mom, just take the picture.

when i get back from a walk, next door to dentist, i try to keep the doctor at bay. why not see if i need not go in? of course, this ends in bitter (dis)appointment. no clean bill of health. pneumonia not yet gone. much like incident of squir- rels left in the attic. anticipate a problem and you'll get one... that's somehow an effect of your delay.

the holes in my serenity are punctured by my health, al- ways, of late, or so it seems.

mind over matter?

should i go back to the shrink? apparently, that "science" grandma preached. but i cannot recall her ever teaching. only frosty glasses for ice coffee, see-through cups & saucers for hot tea. a stack of novels borrowed from the library. jack parr, then johnny carson on tv.

41

i'm looking for the tender spot this morning, but it's buried under mountains of paperwork and dirt. would there be a way to do housecleaning? i realize that this overdrive's illusion. something like a sugar rush. the one i got from seeking candy in the night. 6 to 10 kept popping in my mouth.

was she an overeater, hetna?

i never saw her do that but i did see something, sorry... sorry, to bring this up.

when i turned (sharp) the corner near her bedroom: a hanger. how odd a thing to use for that. i guess it fits though right into our story. heard this was the scalpel for abortions, when ladies used to do their own at home. the corners make friction on the lips. the hook yanks out the babies within.

don't let her leave, in shame, or anger.

grandma, sit with us, and make yourself at peace. it's true that i was horrified, didn't understand. now i know how deeply we're connected. or perhaps you never knew such brutality. maybe you were simply feeling... ladylike — at eighty,

trying to come to grips with something like an itch,

one that often drives me underground.

lonely grandma, frightened, in her pink sequestered room.

42

tina called and woke me from disaster. my sister, a great houseboat, people on the deck. a mansion planted in a vacant lot. but pale green slats, the wood, with moldings, style that i picture in the south. i know that fancy house is going to blow sky high, and i'm running up the street with my contingent. one, a student, who can't begin to read: a classic text that she will soon be teaching. not only this semester, but next. a beginning t.a. (already) hired as an expert for the summer.

this same student keeps on borrowing money, napkins, ladies' things. she's in love with a detective who comes to scoop her up and carries her around like she's his dolly. she's lucky, i think, to have herself a man like that.

yours is greater still, more faithful,

devotion that's like earth. but that's not how he comes off in my dreams. there, he's often undecided. last night, a little mistress, sleeping, on the side. blond, i think, or maybe japanese.

i asked him if he'd please get rid of her, stop and then be just with me? he really wasn't sure, as usual. so i rolled into this world to ask,

make sure your problem wasn't real.

then hours later, tina called, said she was feeling overwhelmed. but i knew she was mostly being "big sister," checking on my state instead. so i reported indirectly all my health concerns, but forgot to tell her all about the tacos.

her call's mysterious.

she's stuck inside her dreams, teetering on the threshold just like me.

the lines where your imaginations meet?

disaster and guilt. she, thinking we're short-handed in emer-
gencies, "got to get back in there, be a nurse."
    i've always dreamed about that caribbean trip. the one that
grandma took her on when i was 6. a parting gift because she'd
finished high school. floating off together on

a houseboat.

and i think that i was present when she told hetna to let go.
sent grandma from her room to the arms of death.

who made tina so darn helpful with brutality?

a kind and tender soul always set her off. but i'm reaching to
you both this morning. allowing for her telephone to yank
me out of bed.

and returning here to rock with me upright.

43

ondine, you know i've got a one-track mind, but time has set
before me fields,

distractions.

luke is right, when i sit down to reach for beauty,

it's got to be alone.

when i write things for money, nothing much remains.
i'm in the service of others (completely), and what i want to

say is just: no. so angry in my critical endeavors. i think that i'm responsible for truth out there. tension mounts up. muscles retract. snap, i'm shut inside the box.

ondine, i've long been stuck inside that quarry. the task was to connect the dots. what other people said, then what i meant before. nothing there to do with

us,

nothing of our own invention. only lines and shifts of damage control.

accompanying activity with sheets —

sheets to pull the covers off anxiety, forms to fill out, and linens not inviting. those in hospitals.

like those that wrapped slit finger's fate

on groundhog's day, allowing me to skip out from the jury

accidental slip and slide on ice,

yet making all normal duties just more onerous & vile.

then rhymes broke out in new protracted hives, intermit-tently: a streak, a patch. covering my belly, neck, and thighs. but now i'm home to make you into spring. my due or homage done to others, ready now to settle.

inside myself, an emptiness floats,

near, another one is waiting.

place where dearest dead come fishing too.

44

not a good scene, but a setting all the same. i saw you late last night inside an antique store, a half-boutique, half-ballet studio.

all my parts divided, reproduced.

a hundred jesus-parts plastered on the wall, mostly black and white with room to dance. no barres that i can still remember. then all around: things, in a surrounding sort of mall, fanning in a circle around the studio.

all those things i'd seen many times before and i still didn't want any: red leather bags, or cowboy boots. some with your motifs, some without. so i picked instead discreet "small black shoes," then walked right by, looking for more human interaction.

a child of yours was somewhere in this place?

yes, keeping the whole scheme together, which meant that i, at least, was not the babysitter. but i was briefly in charge of other children too, maybe overseeing others who were sitting.

whence, a doctor for teeth was beckoning me up the stairs. and i was wanting to flee his house (not mine) within this mall around an antique ballet studio, where suddenly there blew in a horrible mirage: doctor, fix it, i cried out,

for god's sake, screw that baby's head back on.

inching after me, a bowling ball. but the doctor replied, very nonchalant, not worried about his own kid's separation,

could you please wash your hands?

and i see now that i did have shit on my hands, which was somehow related to the baby. but i know i wasn't holding it. how could i, since i now can barely look at it?

so i must have done some tending to the baby before. i babysat before the separation, just like i tended closely to my body last night,

leaving your own head on hold.

45

europeans now think angels are preposterous, jaded or somehow askew.

dieu vous garde,

m'a dit la dame malade, pour un seul euro donné sans peine. quel bon retour sur mon investissement. hier le grand colloque, mieux qu'aujourd'hui. mais l'intérêt reste toujours "relatif." j'ai fait ma "solennelle" conférence de france. 48 ans, je me retire.

plus de tels élans vers le public.

and the little one said: "mommy, i'll make you a big heart, write on it, and give you all the cookies in the world." and the brave girl, disjointed by her disappointment, said: "i missed you, mama, take me, just till august." and the grown son: "i love you mom, how was your trip?" while i said to my own love's father:

tomorrow i will come to your grave
i've been resisting it your death

love mary

i imagine that you see me in this train
as i see you everywhere in the shower

everywhere you used to be
fine-tuned well-dressed gentleman

figured somehow you had caught
my number judging harshly till the end

big blue eyes listened better
heard more words before the birth

in the open space in the ground
from whence we absent ones

each pulled a stone

a small breeze blew
wanting to be near your body

46

    i can do better today on the writing front. don't try to wake
the wee ones or the demons. don't stick those furtive candies
in my mouth.

    time, today, even to sit or wonder

why i'm running: crazy,

    with ondine, a frozen moment on the mountaintops,

and me down here, always running, wanting to be: a good person, do my job correctly, always put my children first. of course,

your artwork isn't getting anywhere.

but am i really interested in writing? or do i only want to fuel life? i think it's finally just about to happen,

you can no longer separate the two.

that's the good news.

that's the good news.

even though i'm old and tired, i still have yearnings —

bring ondine back down to earth.

47

the young don't want to live past 50, a truth once nailed by thomas bernhard. and me, i understand the point. it's a young heart saying (seeing) there's an end, let's not have it happen-ing — forever. i also like to think ahead,

confront the end,

but then i also want to clear: my plate.
    so i am getting ugly from the overdrive, full of some es-tranged combustion, no longer drinking spirit's light.

squandered, one (of four) month's building.

    you who are in that place
    where death is can you
    speak to me advise me
    how to rush into the void

48

perhaps it's not for me to write, because i have no interest in publishing. the question is:

can you care about (or value) what is past?

this creepy body railing like a relic. i think today i'm hooked by an addiction — recognize the symptom and then run from it. that's how best to protect the void. fill it up with something, of substance, not to be so all afraid. sustaining me, a tug (that is the devil). maybe i'm just not to be (afraid).

it would have been good, if i'd had the time, knew what time it was when i laid down:

three hours left till olivier comes home.

then i was on the phone. then i laid down, my face exposed to sun (my nose becoming lots redder).

and when you woke?

well i was hungry, so i did what i always do.

you filled time up with this.

my belly. i filled it up last night with something too. last night i stopped the haven that was sleeping because unsettled feel-ings crept through.

49

ondine splits off — a life, her own? she's pretty in her climb-ing clothes. ashy blond. small yet overgrown, perverse, a little wily, like lolita. she wants to meet somebody and it's not an-other girl.

i'll save my moral treasures for a different time in life.

for now, she wants to try her sunburnt body, test the green
that's lurking in her salty eyes. at first, it seems there's nothing
on the mountain. a flower here and there, a smooth out-jutting
rock, and now and then a wiry patch of trees.

two things happened here last night, but there's only one
i can remember: the time i spent disgusted with that freak
george bush, not as a lover, mind you.

more like someone screwing up the family.

thankfully, at daybreak, nature still was free. a honey-
suckle carpet welcomed me. and here, again, today, there's light.

50

last evening i spent high in carnegie hall. so cheap the seats,

you had to put your breath on hold.

while fingers close to mine just clutched the program, others,
greater, slashed before (like mine), came back to ripple strong
accross the piano. it's strange how sounds familiar to the ears
return, but always keep their message secret.

leaving me suspended, on the mountain,

while i down here must strain to see what's up. we couldn't
push on further together, but perhaps our paths will cross at
dusk. then you'll return to tell me stories. that i can play, a ripe
old passive role, woman who makes time for others' stories.

of course, we'll have to cut the cord first.

51

i'm more than a bit interested in what angie says about the whole conundrum of listening, responding to a thing that's not your self. so clever she, so wise in weighty things. designed from the beginning for life. striking from day one, those dark and shining eyes that blessed me with: i still get a girl.

even though you threw away the first one.

but god's forgiven, given me a girl.
       boys, they seem to come from another world, miracles just passing through. andrew arrived panting strong from birth, gentle eyes with nostrils flaring, wondering

what good is there in landing here?

and then again, the next beautiful wave, matt. i was always truly grateful. gifts for me! running through the corridors, soon as i gave birth, cheering — let me ever hold and play — my baby. nothing ever poaches joy of that.

guess that's why your tossed one harbors sorrows,

carries all the weight of what i've lost.

52

so it's fine if i just dive into myself today, which is: this is not them,

this is me.

thank god i can't manipulate my children, get what i think they want.

a tight woven cord, one generation to the next.

fathers tend to redirect their energies, say they may not get just
what they want. best not inflict our hopes upon our children,

only pray that nothing tears or cracks.

let me focus then upon my own desires today, resist inflaming
toxic their ambitions,

or show another way, a different path.

    andrew, angie (two) now grown, still two to raise — matt,
who just needs love & discipline — and ondine, whom i must
lift from dust.
    listen then, you,

excavated daughter of the mind,

listen to this list — of all my failures.

53

first, i ended up too roly-poly short

with hole in baby heart.

and this was known from my inception. such failures felt like
permanent shortcomings, for which i still am paying (dear)
the costs.

first failure that was passing?

mathematics — no consequence or stain from that. then grade
and job catastrophes, rejections of all sorts. yet none could
ever stick on me. the bigger the failure passing, the better

the next succeeds, always like a rule: following. even covers
break-down of first marriage.

perfection nailed the second time around.

not even just for selfish me. second loves restored to first ones,
blessings raining families all around.

even you, ondine, your disastrous death (beginning) paved
the way to such astounding births.

enough of your crude gloating, mother.

ondine has come to call, plops her body down, rocks a bit
where erstwhile grandma sat.

speaking of what won't stick,

rejections were always — salutory. a. a. ammons telling me
to work: "sometimes the words we use... so we — all poets
— have to work at that." never could take no for an answer.
that letter burned a new hole in my patched-up holy heart.
bled out eye for something like "effect":

> that bird
> skipping
> is so
> hesitant
> to disappear
> all he wants
> is for us
> others
> to stay far
> away as he
> draws near

let's hear a word or two about nadim...

54

sorry to get caught in verse, my dear. can't tell you much about your father, except that he was gold *&* gentle and quite concerned with

pretty

girls. i met him very soon when i got to new york. we lived within the same student housing, but didn't sleep together for some time. first, we played some baseball on a camping trip, then were nearly friends a while.

you slept with him

while drinking on my birthday. nothing too ponderous for either, except that two weeks later i was pregnant. i don't believe i ever told him.

didn't think that he would care.

then once again we slept, some six months later.

as though i never were.

he had finished school, was working in a bank, apartment on the upper east side. can't remember why we happened to go out. just remember my own image glimpsed at through a mirror, looking somehow innocent,

like a baby's what he said,

even though just barely dressed... that's all i can remember of your father, except that he knew well my friend karima and languished for her friend, a pretty, green-eyed blond, from france.

in between the thrill of watching circus acts
sometimes hearing music
something powerful
tries to control my cough

55

ondine wants to come along. she always has,

but it's oh so difficult to take her.

trouble keeping things

closed in my own mind. don't even want to think about that
dream last night,

wrapped in finest sheets.

it was horrible, for certain. for sure, the middle east:

torture and abuse

on every side. one creepy old guy buying several wives.

and you had to be among them,

and somehow get through murder and disgust. people come to
fetch us. all with hoods, crowding round the insides of stores.
someone would come near,

and you'd know that was it.

you had to run and hold your breath, slink into another alley,
find a spot where you could hide. and the worst was in the
city, city underground, where torture wasn't something in the
future anymore,

hordes of murdered children up on crosses,

systematic death all around. finally, i made it to the old wom-
en's camp, where white-haired witches came to give you yours,
and i laid down to breathe my poison. whence i was petrified,
and soon woke up. clammy from this horrid, epic movie.

and then you asked your love,

this torture going on, the sex abuse with hoods, electrocu-
tions, off-heading that happened to nick berg, is it individuals or cultures? those people taking over the world? and he
said: no…

56

ondine, i couldn't take you on that (french family) trip, for
i could hardly go myself. registering, just barely any feelings. i
liked it when the little ones told stories: the chair sat on the
cucumber, and so on. and i liked what i could see as we approached lake george, especially the picture from the house.
the minutes on the dock, just sitting there, the children safely
playing on the beach. olivier's brothers playing poker, tenderness of dark eyes all around. but then, almost the next day,
i was sick. (i hadn't liked matt's pain when fear crept in the
boat, nor the mountain climb's fly picnic.)

but now i think i'd like to try a choreography — ondine
dancing to paco, bach, or hersch.

but how can we do that if i'm your flesh?

dancing leads to sex.

so, the girl's not real?

can dance and doesn't have to be my daughter? luke says that
asking for god's company's enough. he says

this can't be managed like the rest.

ondine,

> you were so beautiful
> spinning rocks and dirt
> your limbs upon
> the leaves and dirt

57

i'll send ondine for good back up that mountain today.

cut the cord.

she's not my daughter, not bound to me by moral strings. i am
but the author of this:

fantasy.

she's dancing up there crazy, just about half-dressed. and the
first creature she meets: whirls. water spurting, ashes all about,

she straddles every element in sight.

christianity, a step toward nature? spirit, as unnatural as
it seems, passes through the body, incarnation. somehow that
makes sense to me.

58

i need for just this summer to practice what i preach.

sufficient for the day is the evil

thereof — this work leaves me too much room to think. i'm
certain that i need to stack these letters, but i'm never sure
what for.
 no, i didn't scribble as a child,

except for poems you penned at 8.

somebody handed me a notebook, so i skipped and wrote:

 midnight blue midnight black
 creepy crawly on my back

only luke with dance and paints encouraging.
 but now, i see it's time for...

death once more.

twister, our dog, has cancer (his jaw). the pain's become
obedient & gentle, looks you in the eye,

with eyes that finally do look in.

59

ondine, i ripped you into shreds last night. at noon, the dark
began to set in. what, i thought, can ever be the point? if i can
never know what for. no interest, here, for anybody dear.

just you and me and this

hard life. another problem too, even more grave, what's going on between us in these lines. me, not thinking tender thoughts for you.

and me, for you,

well, maybe even hatred?

something like you cast on your own mother.

cloak of something like disgrace. never could forgive her own dispassion (innocence, except for lack of grace). think of how she looked on hetna, and then upon her own six

children, who she "didn't really want,"

just thought would make life interesting for father.

and yet lise was a girl,

much like you (your first apparition in the cave).
      whereas, now she's lost her short-term memory. forgot about my (own) birthday. got herself a smoking nurse. "we're tending to this part of me and that," she says. not an ounce of

how i miss you,

where she's aching.
      deeper than the well in which i threw you, where have all her feelings gone? father always said she had no feelings. that was why he slurred when i was 23: "we two... didn't you always think that i should love you? too bad for you, you turned out pretty. why not me with all those other guys?"

60

time to talk of ellen, other sister. sister who is always swelling tears. she slapped me hard.

well deserved

when i showed my cold-heartedness like mother's. decision to suppress... resort to something else, like

judgement.

i never want to be like you, i'd said,

wantonness, rough edges, all exposed.

better to be crafty — calculations. always playing hide and seek. shun all of that shallowness and drama.

don't give your sharpest instruments to others.

they'll operate and lay to waste. too many were my brothers and sisters, never could take stock of any one.

love, love.

how i love them all. all abandoned, much like orphans, each to each and others' fears. parents were preoccupied with building. we their pawns in facing games.

61

rest, long walks, thinking about ondine. why does she come off as surly? she doesn't have to be angry. she could be

happy just to be...

anyway, she's come along on this fast train.

invisible,

she pops in and out, crazy about the little one, tagging every-where with angie, goes to work with andrew too. she's flying really low, and running with the breeze, over the countryside of france.

she's discovering what it feels like to be beautiful. sixteen, mirrors in the trains to metz and austria,

the cold, the loneliness.

the need to snag the hearts of men.

i remember still the velvet jeans: gray, one pair, the other, peach.

you were always busting out.

and i can feel the strength inside the soft rust sweater.

heavy viking cross you got from luke,

gift from gudrun's iceland, where i landed from new york. with a growing cool and calm assurance: here on out, i've made the break.

no need to grow up smothered by the family.

62

ondine's out on her own and dancing. this time, she got to come to europe.

jumping up and down for joy.

whereas me, i'm with matt on a *bateau-mouche*. he and i were charmed about ten minutes. then we cut to playing ping-pong. that's when aleks first appeared, walking, toward us in the champ de mars.

a pretty polish girl,

in the flesh, disguised. trying to make a buck from children's pictures. "her drawing style's close to luke's," matt said. how could i refuse my budding draftsman? 20 euros cheaper than all others, taking me for tourist and good sport.

but it was more those bare brown legs (her gait advanc-ing, weirdly like luke's daughter's) that made me say, well yes, maybe... sure, come around again in 10 minutes after we take leave of this *&* that.

and so then she came again

to draw your boy,

who said to "worthy" ping-pong partner: "you can keep on playing with my mother. me, i am going to sit for a portrait." whence she,

aleks, went straight to work

and did catch a likeness. something of our matt, just older. proportions were elongated to make him look 13. so i was not aghast.

much better, i advanced, than what i've bought before. what happens if you just charge more? go up to where the business is — montmartre? i can't, she said, it's legal there, they're paying taxes. whereas me, i'm illegal,

calling it a tip.

ondine, if not aborted, slipped into the world? no way she could have ended up in poland. but that frowning, timed with pretty deference, brought to mind my long-lost girl.

63

ondine, you have been present on this trip,

accompanying,

in the weirdest ways. i saw you at the start through airport glass (not the fancy tube that crashed on people's heads) filling air that waits for us in france. then a bit more moving along the tgv, looking at us hovered through the window (bracing for a hundred obligations) — taunting:

look, ma. i am free. wind that comes and goes and dances.

you found your way to this world, made me bring you back

sucking in sweet air just as i please.

crazy about the little one, darting in and out, she's popping in on andrew, angie, checking out their studio, saint-germain-des- prés. work, and play.

happy to be back

and yet your roots did not spring up from europe. lebanon's another continent: eastern mouth of méditerranée. then all that crazy mixture in america. maybe, though, it's europe where we all wish to return.

europe's genes and ashes spread on far-flung earth.

trying to get back to plant new cultures, take a stand, claim
a little history for our dirt.

this explains your own ... obstinance.

trekking over here at age 16. from no-man's land in barren
arizona to here i am in everybody's paris. looking for the opposite of spaniards' gift or gold, come to find and test my worth.
european:

scot-irish jew with polish huguenot.

chicago mix made mexican at birth.
 anyway, it's obvious ondine has come across, become a
savvy city-dweller. doesn't draw from me alone what happens
at 16, has even hooked tangential stories. found herself a real
character? aleksandra wiencek,

de pologne ou nulle part,

first drawn to paris too at age 16.

64

thank you for this dream, fantastic clairière. i'm really in another place in time. white dress, with lacy borders,

trimming hails from france?

no way i can know, although the gates appear to be wide open.
maybe further back, or east,

roots are deep in grandfather's country.

what's important is i'm sitting, still in the back (seat). a woman's body (dressed) is lying over me and other children. then, all at once, a favorite nursery rhyme, presented in an actual theater setting.

large field of grass, with southern dresses,

european but american too, with flying machines strewn all about. a lovely yellow fan and fiddle too.
    and the next thing you know, it's happened: projected into the atmosphere,

a giant jersey cow

is crashing through a picnic table. and that pretty woman lying over children in the white dress,

the belle,

is all at once me and not me.

she stays accompanying, but transparent.

and somehow we think we're stuck inside the *clairière*, though the gate turns out indeed to be wide open. so we don't need to call for help after all. i know we have everything we need.

65

ondine, i saw you on a poster. upside down, swimming, stark naked in a pool. bright blue, except for big red flippers.

your own lost girl,

pretty, diving down. pasted up at austerlitz station.

your pretty living daughter saw me too, was "weirded out"
almost as much as you were.

it's strange your name appears on things i've never read:
including stuffy works of french theater, making much of hesitating borders. can't make up my mind if i should read it...
how fitting for a play by giraudoux.

meanwhile, it's matt

i am picturing at camp:

blue-ringed neck, your yellow boy scout.

spotted on the back. how hard to let his sweet face go.

out there in the world with other faces.

so attached (my given three), i can always call them back.
despite the ever clouded strips of memory, my eyes get rest
and drink upon their faces. now, yours is growing stabler too,
something more than plans, intentions. even though it often
changes form.

> that cat face
> neat in a round
> gray body's shrine
> brushed against
> my ritual legs
> two times
> as the cheeks
> of newfangled
> europeans
> reddened with the
> flesh of wine

it's capital for me to cast off... this tendency to throw my hands.
i can learn to do scenarios, re-capitulate slow start, weaving
in and out of intermittences, time that i experience in prose.

66

ondine's skipped through her adolescence.

— appeared at 5
— stepped out of the cave, went with me to work, then flying
down the canal at 7–8
— spent her whole life mountain-climbing 12 to 13
— then came (with me) to me in france
and there was reborn as: aleksandra, august 7, 83 in the
poorest suburb of warsaw. mother: kasia, a pillar in a glass
factory. father: mikhaïl, a russian painter.

and she also had a little brother.

jan.
kasia's parents lived three hours from the city in wojnowo,
a small town on the road to krakow. grandma julia cleaned
and sewed and played the piano. grandpa józef liked to cook
and paint. kasia never left the city, but sent her children to the
country every summer, soon as they turned 6.
there beyond the river, summers on the run, aleksandra
discovered

how the sun brushes the earth,

calling all those sweet sounds out of morning, offering up
honey with its hay. she'd felt

how light receives you when you fall back in the pond

(keeping you afloat even as you plunge through), and how it
flits about framing what is good, bright reflections in the glass.

her room was small and dark in warsaw. messy in there.
nothing ever came out as it should. she thought a lot about
her father (who'd never even come to see jan). left, only the
vaguest memories: fine words, brave looks, dancing (she knew
her pa was good at dancing). the last time that she saw him
she was eight.

mother was her anchor and her footstool, attachment she knew
least about.

small, green-eyed, pale and tired blond.

grandpa said she too had been a dancer

right around the time she met misha. she posed for him in
paintings when she was seventeen. then stopped all that soon
as aleksandra came. couldn't find her footing in the city, threw
her whole life down like a sack. crushed early into something like a doormat. settled once for all into the grind of life.

let her own hopes fade like summer dreams.

school was hard for aleksandra,

hard for her to pay attention,

always getting lost or falling in some current of hot water. but
finally she got tough, did sports through middle grades, played
the clarinet in marching bands.

then grandpa gave her paints,

the day she turned 13, & so she took to reading stories, novels telling tales of artists, models. she knew which she'd rather be.

to train herself she started tracing faces in the mirror,

then shut her eyes and learned to draw.
aleks didn't want to be like kasia. she didn't want to care for children (despite her tender spot for jan). she wanted her own light, a big white room. dreamed to be a painter like her father.

she tried from very young to flee back to the pond,

or make her way to find a brighter city. that is how she ended up in paris. the first time that she went,

she traveled with her band,

the summer that she turned 15.

67

ondine, exhausted, i'm reporting to my desk. insomnia with sore throat, aching.

worried about being, sick.

and now i see it's all my fault. it's the devil that is trying to make me slip.

but maybe, ma, it's not...

it could be just a sore throat from anxiety.

you do the best you can to feel better, try to get some sleep. and when you wake again, two hours later, that's not just the devil either? even when you eat the last pepito?

well, that pepito is a bit the devil, for it does something that blocks the light.

what would you prefer to hear about? the real-life crimes of my mothers-in-law? or more on aleksandra's trip to paris?

aleksandra set out early in the morning.

had jolka (her best friend) beside her. their band filled up the sixth car on the train. no one could afford a sleeping berth, though the trip to paris took two days.

aleksandra didn't look at things in detail.

not on the trip, not even when she got to paris. everything slid by, like passing through a well. reservoir for drawing a future. only pictures saved with expectations:

getting off the train, moving to the bus,

arriving at the student pension, tucked between two crosses on the right bank.
first stop, sunday morning, mass at NOTRE DAME. second, visit to the MADELEINE. it must have been that evening, six o'clock, her first walk from the *bateau-mouche* to the EIFFEL TOWER. that monument she still saw shining,

behind closed doors and eyes,

in the blue room (shared with jolka) down the hall.

68

beautiful clairière, clearing in the alps. heaven sleeping on that ground. birds calling, in the distance. loved ones very near. face at rest under big red hat. comforted by sleeping bag. blue voices, visions all around, singing yellow cubscout songs.

that red hat's horrible
when firmly
pressed down

on head upright
for fashion
intervention

but even
round and full
of stomach bugs

touching
muddy earth
bleeds protective

green blades
offering a thing
like mirth

who knew what was breeding underneath?

69

by your grace, alone, i am real today. and i have proof of this on my computer.

last year, i was struggling. just like this, to make my life adhere. and again, by your glory, i have matt today, who makes

his papa cry with french and cubscouts. andrew is tending to
his complicated strings, and angie's flowering too. so me, although i don't know who or what i am, i know i didn't

waste a minute, writing.

for sure, i am fed up — with this scratchy throat —

something maybe lurking in the water?

and yet i think i've made some headway. ondine,

i am here.

appeared to me in air, then brought forth aleksandra and a
story. then greeted me again through that garden cat. and
clapped for my fine efforts with matt. jumping up and down,

with those little birds,

all along our daily walk.
    now she understands i lose my sense of who i am each
time i have to

take a shower.

how hard it is to be like water: clean, transparent, brimming
pure as fire rinsing earth.
    one thing i learned while telling stories:

in the future, your hang-ups with the past go away.

so i ought to start, like poe says, with an ending. it's possible
things still could happen.

hope and space for truth remain,

which means i need to sketch fast.
  but it's hard to work with discipline and feelings, the passing moment and the plodding way, which brings up an abiding
problem.

can't have your cake and eat it too.

thus, i remember best the times of great restraint: clearly,
eighth to ninth grade. the running

time

early in the mornings: then peace beside the cottonwood.
a building up of happiness till tina's nicolas was born.

the hotel and the hospital,

the border. like confirmation crossing for my own birth. running there too, chased by a lazy bull. my beloved tina,

following, monitoring each risk

beyond her belly, neatly packed behind the wheel. exercised,
she was. swimming countless laps a day, in a polka-dotted
dark pink suit.

*you're waiting on the border for her baby, whose father wasn't
noxious yet,*

who'd just caressed my knees,

when you were six.

70

i'm not even guilty at age fourteen. i remember that i feel well in my body. green-flowered suit, lodge-on-desert pool. happy wet or dry, getting dressed to go. sometimes with steven, my playmate (from birth), who now long since has died of aids. i remember too going on a trip, with fishers to the beach in mexico,

feeling lit and airy like the sand beside the sea.

thin and gold instead of plump n' pink. something like i've earned "beautiful."

those days i even sewed a dress, with tina. wore it to begin high school. some boy remarked: "too skinny girl." by the time that school got going i was underweight.

5'2", three hard eggs per day,

90 lbs attained for halloween. then candy, gum, and cigarettes till christmas. still, i became the (spanish) dancer, though i soon shot up to 110.

you couldn't have been fat.

but by fifteen, i was good no longer.

i'd worn miniskirts before (ugly backs of grandma's knees), blue & white checked things, and finally had a taste of being (thin).

and you had been touched

by music

many times

as well as family (papa, siblings), children and old men. must have been 13, for my first french kiss: a mexican, who took me to the wall to dance. pecking lips — a few, since age 11.

mostly time was spent with older girls. all beautiful: my sisters or my brothers' girls. chaos must have happened late in 1969, or very early 1970. i'm thirteen. papa's drunk and jump-ing beds in search of women.

tina had come home, claiming her old room: pregnant. but left some space in there for me too. that's when papa reached for me,

by accident,

i thought. we'd changed around the beds since i'd shared them first with gudrun, luke's fiancée, who'd landed in our desert from iceland the summer before, the evening our first man walked on the moon.

71

sore spot in my belly, bird-park yesterday. the ground be-tween the leaves called, just the bare earth, not the red ibis, nor the parrots' dark blue. much more sensitive today were eyes to furtive glimpse of delphine, olivier's ex-wife's picture. swiftly, deftly covered by jacqueline (*mamie*). no one wants to show her to our son.

in july 68, you must have been 12,

but i don't remember much of anything from then. it's possible i had a maroon-colored suit, babysat and cleaned houses, was heavy friends with other girls, dancing. maybe at that time things were boring. papa making wine, going lots to mexico. i went there with him after christmas the year before. we two in an old train: me, in a blue and white jumper. he, in the bar-car drinking,

when you climbed back

to bed from peeing,

strange men found you sleeping

in the wrong berth.

the summer before that, an airplane. chicago, with my other grandma, edith (stout like me). learned of things like skyrises, carpets, powder-blue, riots, cold water, and dead fish. there i saw my first great movie, *KING OF HEARTS*: geneviève bujold, alan bates.

english, french, and pretty ballerina,

sheltered from the war,

living in a crazy whorehouse too.

it was all about ballet in those early days. tina and ellen were gone back east. a quiet time with just two brothers: theo, joe, and me, left with nothing but my girlfriends. my best buddy steven had gone to japan. when he returned he was an other (got himself some boys, a band).

so by 11, though still girlish, bearing polka dots, i was preparing for the battle of the bulge, often with a dull gray boredom (same one i fight today). watermelon, mashed potatoes, gravy paved the way. i was taking care of kids from 10 years old, playing hide-and-seek with cupboards, sleeping through the day at school.

no teacher really cared for me in those middle years. the last one who did was from fourth grade. fierce but sympathetic, bright red hair, made me "doctor" though i wasn't popular, worried lots about my tiredness, concerned that i had too many "irons in the fire." and my (texas russian) ballet mistress was a royal bitch. one day she'd say, "you look like little lotta," the next, "that irish actress named maureen." other girls looked better with their go-go boots, though i knew they had no class, no less ensembles like my flute and drum.

only truly loving teacher was in third grade: mrs. de passe. i was happy when she came for dinner, though i knew it had to do with all my spaciness, lying down in front of cars on my way to school.

school for you, the child?

mostly boredom. still can't believe it's good for kids today. second grade was empty science. first grade even worse. i was really shaken by the teacher, her blue-white hair, enormous, flapping boobs. boots and saddles, kindergarden? not so bad, except for nap.

things were pretty good at pre-k,

attention still was coming thanks to surgery.

although i did once get a whipping with a fishing rod, for going to my neighbor's off the bus. that was from my fearful (sadist) father,

too scared to deal before with hole in heart,

but always there to teach a cruel lesson. angry and scandalized,

yes, you were.

perhaps that's why i wet my pants.

still, i was proud to have survived my operation, wore it like a flag. collecting funds with mama for the HEART FUND jar. mama lise and tina helped with all of that. tina making pjs, mama dressing me in red, singing out my bravery too.

lise going with me, though she wouldn't, "couldn't" stay, came back to fetch and see me through. suitcases and all, no wonder older kids were jealous. they had to stay at home with father,

mom all to yourself,

even if she left for christmas. 3 going on 4, 1959, that means joe was barely 6 (also born in mexico, 1953), theo 9, ellen 10. luke, 13 (would soon be sent away). tina, sewing sister, just 15.

1959, december.

don't know why i must fill in these gaps.

72

15 was horrible. thin to "fat," must have reached 120 pounds.

or perhaps you were "fine" all that time.

but what a deal was made about my figure. or maybe i did creep higher? or maybe i was just too short. i remember looking ugly, next to sisters, tall and thin. i was squatty in my dress despite those pretty blue-gray drawings: white stubby roundnesses, exploding.

trip to europe was a way to feel better. champagne and cigarettes, wealthy greek-mexicans, a mansion in the richest part of paris. the trip, pearl diamond ring (i lost) & cool gray london cap: all tina's gifts, and the *beginning of your lifetime "love for france."*

for there i met denise again, luke's french friend from san francisco (who'd shown me small was beautiful eight years before). got kissed *&* necked again at *bal musette*, then seduced by denise's husband in the car. such fine attentions made me see.

even short and stupid, you were pretty.

so i could get my shit to work inside the big wide world and evolve some plans for my escape. by the time i left for france again (age 16),

you'd been taken by a dancer...

BALLET FOLKLÓRICO passing through my town (his tender spot for virgins wrote me afterthoughts), and chalked up three affairs (one with the husband of our family's... maid).
so though neither tall, nor thin, i felt powerful again, not dependent on my family's whims. i crossed the border with my girlfriend in my dark blue shirt, worked at our cook's new restaurant, drove myself to pool. eyes cried out on the plane, escaping to new york, but liked the feel of cold in iceland. hit luxemburg then paris,

threw yourself into the world.

happy to be thrown (in). lise and father let me go for good. the tv i won (in color) paid for ticket. for sure i could babysit, maybe go to school. "papa" told me not to sleep with other (married) guys.

73

at 17, i came back home, armed with year in france. sporting
with my eyes, a tiny cadence in my speech.

both sisters, they had babies now,

luke and gudrun too (home from frankfurt, texas, army drinking zoo). and theo back from munich (crushed by girlfriend
killed in crash), drafted only by resemblance to our father's:
do just what i do. drink to math and make me solid houses.
painting, dancing, music aren't for you. confused, he couldn't
think his thoughts through college, had to follow first, then
stomp out luke, make his own way out to texas to be true.
   in choosing relations, ellen messed through tracks of tina
too. only joe, the youngest before me, ever did his own thing.
sleeping round the house (like i did), falling into ditches with
his daydreams, then found his way upright through law school.
but then he too got caught in family drama, eloped with

tina's… maid?

— catalina.

74

nose flare-up has brought morale way down, stuck here in
these patterns with my e-mails. all signs putting pressure on
my ego. but i guess

you could keep trying to remember.

i've combed through correspondences,

timed this year and last,

and found a *décalage* of just two days.

difference?

olivier's father was alive then, now forever passed away.

july 23rd, martin got his bad news, we all knew on some level. he was dying. but then, like now, i had to go home, check out fresh fears implanted in the hospital, rays in breast detect-ing maybe cancer (not at all like this year's operation, one more slight adjustment of my patched-up nose). ekg and blood tests on the 31st, then free from worst of waiting by august 15. this year could be earlier, lucky 13? all this silly bean-counting? calms my nerves, though it doesn't mean a thing.

still, if you can't think, you can remember.

proust says remembering's creating, as long as things brought back are mixed with feeling. and that is where my struggle is today. i'm getting all my times unscrambled (more yesterdays to reach toward than tomorrows). but my body still resists. maybe just because i'm tired?

remember, mother, sleeping is allowed.

yes, last time my nose flared up was just like this. i went to see the clinic on a tuesday. papi brought his bad news back on wednesday, which i remember perfectly this monday, as though it were just yesterday.

walking up the hill, unfettered father that he was, with his cell phone working in his hand. and then he was well, jolly, on that evening, glad to get the bad news over, because the waiting's always worse. and how full of joy he was months later. after brush with death, when we last talked by phone, i sat in a potted plant, toppled by a true sense of thanksgiving.

happier than ever in those last days,

surrounded by his sons, when the knowledge of the worse was all behind him, before the fact of worse became.

75

yes, there i was, the devil, with my snout to heal, when the first scent of what was to come to pass came. playing with my little matt, cards and such. holding close, though wary, my mother-in-law (jacqueline) who couldn't figure out martin's game. "il y a mieux à faire quand même qu'à mourir," she said. then turned her tears of panic into empty call for prayers, even as i voiced objections, fearing that her stubborn will was lame.

but can't you stop the devil if you gather some blind trust?

track back whence all the darkness came.
i would say eighth grade. that year was most chaotic. it was an early (winter) morning when my father laid with me and i thought he must be thinking i'm some other. he was in the crack of where our twin beds came together. so tina, then my roommate, where was she? (gudrun and i slept far apart.)
i knew he was drunk and thought he wasn't after me. until that second drunk proposal nine years later. mexico's proposal, when i was 23, put negligence before in different light.

progress, you thought, deliberate abuse,

a bit more flattering to me.

thank god, you got away, each and every time,

from his groping hands as well as those of others, sisters, brothers. no sex with any dear one till i married.

spent your crimes of lust alone with strangers.

76

the summer of '68 was melancholic, despite some rays of light at camp. someone said that i could write

poetry

drawing long-haired smiles from the bookstore. was it brian or his brother bobby?

who sang and played guitar beside the fountain,

who i weirdly watched for many years. when i finally did get brian to come over, he got fully smitten with joe's wife-to-be.

story of your life at lise's house.

no one was impressed with me.
   so, starting seventh grade i became downright depressed. looked for ways to somehow get distinguished:

wouldn't answer anyone who spoke to you at school,

which worked for weeks — till rocks were thrown — and it was decided: i was cool.

beginning of your social strategy,

peculiar little maverick *(personality),* shortest-cut for climbing steep hills.

77

i didn't have a sister near till i turned 13, and gudrun crossed the sea. sister-in-law to be landed in my room, in late july.

that's when it all started happening,

when i went to tina's, visiting boston bars for several weeks, and got propositioned in the commons: 50 bucks. then back home went riding bikes with gudrun, whose long viking legs wanted mine too, after crashing into clubs and bowling alleys.
that's also when i got that first french kiss,

a mexican french kiss at your first dance.

and when carlos from colombia got a crush on me. and me and my pal steven (back now from japan) fixed up toilet-paper rolls for smoking pot.
it was 1969, and i loved HAIR. was careening now full blast through adolescence, though the blood had come before. two full years before when i was just 11, quietly in summer '67, when i was first molested by mr. mack, dear old dirty "grandpa" (neighbor, friend).

78

so now we've circled round again to nearly age 14. tina's come back home. we're happy that she's going to have a baby, and it really is chaotic for a while.

so it surely was that winter when your father... in your bed.

there he was when i awoke, sleeping (?) with his hand inside my underpants. i sat up quick and out i slipped. wrote it off to "papa's drinking."

surely he was looking for someone else's bed.

must have rolled by accident between two beds. i still find grains of truth in that today,

even though he later duly made a pass,

asked me in slurred english nine years later: "why not me with all those other guys." drunk then too, but cheerful, childish, and with me wide awake, saying "papa, you're not thinking, go to sleep."
whereas back in those grim years, it was tina who gained control, and reigned over our house, while father slowly slunk away,

sliding deeper into mexico to stay.

79

note from a former student: it's with... pride... that we announce

"the birth of... ondine."

what a ghastly thing to find on my computer. our problem must be this

dis-continuity.

can't seem to see where you and i leave off. that's why, i guess, i'll never get ahead. can't figure out what to fill in, nor can i invent for you an ending.

what you want for me is just to live this time.

but maybe i can plant a flag somewhere, claim some sort of ground? since you're

sending cryptic messages through air.

80

you surely got to me through aleksandra, who draws pictures in the parks of france. i told you days ago,

you thought i was her,

and i was taken with that whole direction. walking up to meet me with those limbs, that face, merging me and you around that portrait. tracing with my youngest, matt's "older" face, something like your own eclipse.

i thought if i could give her time and substance, radiate that present back toward an anchored past, there might yet be some fire for your future.

why not use that girl for fodder, do it for your daughter,

ondine.

81

projection 5 years hence, july, 2009. matt and i were tired,

in paris again,

settling in to watch some late t.v. olivier was not with us in our *pied à terre,*

as you prepared to sleep,

inside the dark, by staring at the small light-screen.

look, cracked matt, behind wide feet,

il n'y a que la vérité qui compte,

look who's showing what on tv.

what kind of truth reunion would this be? sister meeting brother, long lost twins, friends estranged or secret cyber lov-ers? it was

another daughter

meeting father.

i recognized the woman walking down the hall with the game host, sam.

small, ash-blond and tan,

smug instead of shy, very much at ease in front of cameras. as if she knew exactly who she'd come to meet (which was against the game-show rules), someone she herself had meant to bring there.

lexy was from warsaw but lived and worked in france. the first two months were difficult, hand to mouth,

ate on tips she asked for childrens' portraits,

then she got a break. city lights' supportive framework. odd jobs in the gallery for vincent, babysitting weekends on roxane. she made a trip to poland every christmas to see kasia, julia, józef, jan,

but she hadn't seen her father in more than 20 years.

where can someone whom you've lost come back to find you? ask for your forgiveness through a silky screen?

she thought that this was weird, american.

and of course that father could be me (who's so long-lost her own ondine).

for it's you who're mixing paint with blood and water,

beginnings of a wasted future with the trash that's being served up on tv.

while i am sitting scratching in this hole beneath the screen, to see

if i'll accept to give you contours,

and show how what was not must be.

82

meanwhile our family (drama) closing out the scene in france. something like i never witnessed.
andrew's stormy tenderness, emitting dark clouds, wracks angie's sunny goodness through with guilt. all in tears, as little matt (in tune) cries out in alarm advisory: they too have to learn

to live and love

like me.

we all have to brave the fear of death.

then everybody's tears clear the air for good. a fresher day with jolly humor, still dotted through with dark asides (to me).

witty transitions moving fast.

83

time collapsed. at home i had a dream. i was trying to perform or some such thing, but my speech ended with eternity

on the blackboard,

which was green. i read it back and forth, right to left, swinging my poor head to and fro. side to side at least 10 times. and
then i closed with something simple (like "bonsoir").

yet no one really knew the show had ended.

awkward silence, not a person even clapped.
  i sat down at the back disappointed, but was still not sure
the problem was my acting. for no one knew the spectacle was
over.

nor could discern what the story was about.

84

impressed, you were, by the little girl's dance, a totally fantastic clown act, by luke's friend, denise, but who looked here
not a day over 9. a bubble mask was sitting on her face, and
i clapped heartily for that and purred.

how great it was, and brave, her fight against time,

and she was funny with her stomps and tumbling runs, defiant
to the crowds. i was even glad she picked on me:

two pints of water thrown on your right breast.

freezing, it was, but with no pain. the intention was good,

attention's always good,

who cares,

no matter what the kind.

then i settled down to watch more numbers. the last an in-termingling of the singer and the *salle.* a sweet swaying tune started to be sung by a man who'd finally found his

"someone else kinder,"

and safer still, by far, than family.

85

and after that: two poems. the first one, marking efforts to get back on the path, was pointing toward luke

> *fire*
>
> yesterday the silence
> of the stark
> november trees
>
> reflected in the dark water
> circling in
> the form of geese
>
> suggested there's no harm
> in being stripped
>
> time has come for holding

the second one still weirder (not at all me) recorded a colloquy *with*

father thanked me graciously
for gifts back given
through the years
letters, tasteful presents and the like
which he claimed
never to have answered

so i also seized the wire
to thank him for sparing me this life
at which point we both were
happy till mother lumbered in

two important men (longest in my life) caught inside the
coldest (war). no wonder i "relate" with difficulty. whenever
any current of feeling comes, tail between my legs, i head for
cover. don't want to brave the strong winds. ondine could help
a lot with this. she's laughing at my small predicament. scraped
myself at last some real free (time). and now i'm all afraid to
think on it. she's laughing but i know she'll help me in the end.
that's why she's come:

to help you to an end.

help me not to run, settle down with her within the dark
cocoon. the hole, the dark where i am going,

the whole from which we all burst through.

86

now it would be good to spin... love stories. only mine or other people's?

i don't care, i just want to hear.

it's hard for me, because you are my pure lost girl, and me...

you're caught inside the box.

the flesh box i ripped you from?

yes, the clear flesh box.

but my flesh right now is falling, sagging to its knees. creases are horrible, just like grandma said.

you used to love the lines up top.

these days i barely eke out mere approval. now i feast my eye more on how much others please. want women all around me to be beautiful. vicarious, i guess, desire comes.

then let's see you stage some other womens' boxes,

other people's semiotic flesh.
but how to fall in love through others' thoughts? never could articulate my own true love. that path to safety's wrapped tight in a mystery, blanketed forever like you children, delivered with no strings attached.

tell me then about the "loves" you had before, or others that you might imagine. how they all went wrong or could have gone... right.

*like the kind that could have been with my father, if your own had
not reduced you.*

i'm frightened to drop down, crawl around those lands, bleak
and dingy emblems of the past.

    but that is where i want to go, mother. do it, gather fodder,

for ondine.

87

    *perhaps then we'll need other "characters"? the twine of con-
tradiction's lurking still in me.*

    perhaps we'll need a blond (woman).

your father, nadim, yearned for only those (with me i think his
lust was faint). i think that i would too…

    remember when we saw that tall blond girl?

last summer, in the beauty shop. really big boobs, thin otherwise. that is my idea of what is beautiful (as soon as i am not
in the picture). let's give her a good name: poldy. after molly's
moving plea: "give us a touch, poldy, god, i'm dying for it." yes,
poldy's a fetching name, even for a man, and perfect for the
woman stepping in my head. or if that name won't stick, then
maybe: sarah.

    *sarah? that's a bit too serious, but maybe she could be inside
there too.*

why do you want to hear such rubbish, you who fly about, you who see the world, you who freely mix with air and space?

it has to do with you, becoming me. you know how i missed out on family stories. i want to know those feelings, all i should have had,

all those years my eyes were closed.

your mouth was shut.

all right, i'll try to think about sarah. don't have to think too much about poldy, because she hasn't any point to her except for big pink... and a very pretty empty face. she's nothing but a surface for desire...

that makes all creatures choke

with fire.

88

my love says pornography's a "fausse piste." but i can't just stay focused on

what's happening today?

the big strips of shadow laying on the lawn, the grip of that uneasy

all this time...

waiting for me here to fill it up.

one sick child, on the well path.

that's matt with me, walking slowly toward the stop. "i'll drive you off to school," i said, "don't worry if you miss the bus."

he made it at top speed nonetheless.

but i don't feel like wandering into narratives today. not interested in poldy or sarah. it's just the nameless real that keeps me afloat.

but me?

it's true, my love, there you are, you too now have become commitment. so now i have to write you...

a story,

o.k. o.k. but maybe one that sounds more like a prism, or quartet.

start with poldy
she's a vacant
shiny surface
story can't be
told in first person
poldy is an idol
in the mirror i
saw her in the
shop window
had never seen
someone like
that before
and she wasn't
doing anything
special was just
fixing every
one's chairs
and exposing
different angles
of her body
which was thin
but round in
amazing long
curves going
up and down
except for the belt
of here i am
right around the
hips and then
protruding really
full breasts
clothes nothing
special the usual
these days
jeans black
t-shirt showing
glimpse of belly
skin and under
wear the crazy thong
more or less
matching the
slinky slides
insolently
shuffling along
none of this
for sure would
have mattered
if it weren't for
poldy's face
god is it
fair a woman
like that with such

the i who's
seeing this is sarah
it's me who's
watching poldy
strutting i'm the
one who's
writing here
the one who
thought of this
quartet it all
came on one
day in august
when i was
sitting sweetly
as usual dealing
with the fact
that i have
hair in the
corner at the
beauty shop
when you look
close you'll see
i'm beautiful
but nothing
about me stands
out except for
very often my
hair that's soft
and brown and
messy curly
everybody likes
it just like they
like me and
wonder what
i'm all about

i live in
an apartment
in brooklyn
i'm trying to
figure out
what to do
for now i am
still going to
school trying
to become
a writer studying

there's a man
across the aisle
johannes who's
looking both at
me and poldy
he's a customer
i guess of poldy
in any case she's
fixing his chair
he's struck for
sure like i am
by her beauty
and wondering
what she's doing
shuffling round
the shop when
she could be
a top model
making millions
in a deeper
hall of mirrors
johannes can't
help thinking
things like that
because his job's
about exchanging
values you
guessed it
he's a kind
of banker the
upscale kind
that's always
wearing suits
to no one knows
just where
anyway he's
thinking poldy
on his shelf
that would be a
nice trophy
but at the same
time there's a
nagging thought
nipping at his
sandy brown

i'm tom i
am afraid of
hairdressers
but have decided
i should cut
my hair i've
come here 'cause
it looks decent
calm composed
concerned with
only form
removed a
bit from all
the frenzy my
hair's too long
to be a real
composer's
everyone will
think i want
to look the part
of someone
really dreamy
when that's not
what i want
i just want
to make things
sound right
stand up to what
i need to know
but can't express
or find another
way i don't
much care how
good i look
except i do not
want to look
flaky or spaced
out the work
i do in life is
serious i care
only to look
clean cut move
through the
world so i
can make my
music within
i hear things
but i can't say
what they are
i only can
identify their
timbres their
notes then i
assign them

pale skin pale
lips pale eyes
smiling teeth
and strong but
messy long
natural looking
silver blond
hair eyes
blue of course
thick shaded
and set off
by ashy lashes
perfect brow
and cheeks
well somehow
opposite to
body's shape
more roundy
open than long
drawn

poldy lives
in a small
apartment
on the upper
west side
around 86th
and broadway
carpet powder
blue a queen
size mattress
on the floor
mirrors on
the wall
lots of closets
the kitchen's
in the corner
it's a studio
with not much
light but a
big white
bathroom
down the hall
it's paid for
by her boyfriend
marc who lives
in rome an
older guy a
record producer
he's married but
he's mad about
poldy (everybody
is) but he hardly
ever gets to

to get a phd
i teach english
at a great university
that makes
me feel both
big and small
i'm happy
i've a job
i like but it
doesn't really
feel like the
right thing to
do i don't
connect with
the person i'm
supposed to
be and i feel
like i'm not
following my
destiny instead
it's like i'm
always putting
everything on
hold waiting
for my right
moment which
i realize might
well never come
and my life
will be a big
wasteland
the desert
the emptiness
from which i
sprang instead
of a delicate
monument
a whisper of
comfort to
all who come
saying yeah
this life is
worth it not
for itself like
my mom once
said but for that
something which is
magical singing

hair what good
to me is all this
money?
what's the point
of all her gold?
that's when
his gray eyes
get glimpse
of sarah
who sits there
like an answer
to all questions
he's decided he
should put on hold

johannes is
in fact from
germany i
heard him
saying that
to poldy
when he
first struck
up a conversation
that first day
when she sat
him smiling
in his chair
he noticed that
she had an
accent even
by the way
she said hello
and figured
she was
scandinavian
gorgeous blond
more delicate
than girls in
germany far
prettier than
most in usa
he thought she
didn't realize her
own worth and
set out from the
first moment

my rhythm
my dynamics
i guess those
are the parts
that come
from me
i match what
i am feeling
up with what
i hear and
what i hear
well i don't
know where
it comes
from but i
know that
it connects
to me and
makes my
life make sense
worth living
i never have
lived without
music i didn't
always think
about it in the
same way
at first i only
liked to play
it repeat on
the piano
tunes i liked
to hear and
could manage
with my fingers
and the notes
my teacher
taught me how to
play i guess
i was a kind of
monkey then
but i was always
a monkey
with feeling
everybody
noticed my
light touch
and that made
me feel happy
and alive the
rest is kind
of hazy
i don't like
to think much
about the past
i'm afraid my
decisions

new york any
more he's got
too many irons
in the fire so
poldy who's
from denmark
lives her own
life got a job
at the shop for
something to do
doesn't really
need the money
just needs some
where to go
people to see
so she won't
be all the time
alone the first
time she went
to the shop was
just last year
she was herself
a customer
wanted to get
her hair cut short
but frank the
owner wouldn't
do it said he
couldn't do it
it was just too
gorgeous
he'd pay her
not to cut it
off to come into
the shop parade
around take people's
coats sit them
in their chairs
get them something
soda or coffee
while they wait
to get their hair
done poldy thought
why not? she
hadn't anything
to do just liked
to see herself
reflected against
the backdrop of
the city and to
check her silver
face all day long
make sure it still
was there making

in the air
something
unforeseen that
can't be touched
but holds
everything
together
sometimes in
great moments
it comes to
me in words
sometimes i see
it all around
trees sometimes
for days i forget
sink into fear
obsession with
details and
warding off
death but then
i'll get a break
somehow open
up and that's
where my hope
and my heart are
my writing
is a witness
that's why i'm
here to keep
track of everything
that happens here
in this shop
where everything
like poldy is
materially firm
shiny hard metallic
or soft and pink to
touch where the
magic is well nigh
invisible but the
world we can
grasp looks so
shiny and real
that we can't help
abandoning the
other i guess
it is this idolatry
that brought

first appraising
glance to win her
for her own sake
more than his
he never
really clung
to property
had less the
urge to own
than to close
the deal the
thing that could
lead to something
better something
that might grow
that's why he
was a good wall
street banker
everything he
touched turned to
gold but the gold
never really
stuck to him
he never had
to figure out
what to do
with what he
earned just poured
his all and every
thing into the
next deal at work
at home and
in his love life
of course he'd
had a lot of
girlfriends
usually the
prettiest any
one could get
all shapes and
sizes all
nationalities
with some he'd
been entangled
more than others
and when he was
fourteen

haven't all been
right but i decided
to stick with
music to make
it my life and
go to music
school of course
i was admitted
to juilliard i'm
good at what
i do and i have
worked hard
practicing hours
since i was twelve
impossible
to count them
all day long
i worked on
this and that
kind of music
till music was
my whole language
hardly said or
thought anything
else but i was
never a child
prodigy i didn't
have a special
image of myself
as someone
artistic a genius
or even as a
person with a
special gift
composing-wise
i started rather
late i just became
so full of music
so good at handling
the instruments
and notes that
i began to
translate simply
the things i
heard in the
time when i was
not playing music
i liked that and
started playing
less and less
and listening
around me more
and more and
the music somehow
just came to
me and comes
as long as i'm

people feel
surprised and
happy that any
one could be
so pretty and
just be kind of
standing there

it's been some
time since
i have lived
with jo i'm
working for a great
photographer
ten people want
to be my agent
i've shot more
than a dozen ads
and even played
a small part
in a film but
nothing really
is happening
except i'm
wearing thin
i want for
something different
to be happening
and that is why
i'm leaving him
i think that things
were better back
inside the shop
someone else
i should have
looked for
something better
not the same
reaction to my
pale pink skin
but something like
a transformation
i shouldn't have
gone in for
multiplying mirrors
i should have
tried to make the
mirror thing stop or
blocked it so the
world could turn to
something else
a place where
i could be inside

me in the shop
looking to be
more like poldy
trying to include
something in my
life like what's
going on between
johannes and her
a measured
and controlled
exchange

i wish i weren't
always noticing
thinking what are
other people doing
i wish i could be
centered on myself
but ever since the
first day i came
in here i realize
that i hardly
fill my chair
i'm too busy
watching thinking
staring and then
trying to be
nice cover up
the fact that i
hear every word
that's said and note
each look like
i was jealous
it's like it's not
about me but
if ever i'm to
be a writer the
world will have
to turn around
me more for
now let's say
i'm just taking
notes trying
to develop my
hand so it's
okay if i just
ogle poldy and
write down all

he thought he was
in love but
then the girl
he wanted
moved away and
he started on the
path of choosing
substitutes better
than the one that
slipped away
that's always what
he told himself
as soon as he
got free and
started working
on the next girl
deal that's what
he thought when
he saw poldy
and planned her
future starting
from his loft
a very nice
place in soho
the third place
he'd lived since
moving to new
york the first
was a kind of
dorm uptown
for all kinds of
students
from all over
the world
he lived there
while earning
his mba then
had a small
apartment on
the upper east
side while he
worked for
a while at a
city bank then
moved when
he switched to

not anxious and
when it does
my job's to
write it down

not everything i
hear is dark
you know it's
just that darkness
is easier to float
in to get your
bearings in and your
grip it feels well
more substantial
and deeper than
light
that never really
shines from some
thing within you
have to get empty if
you want to feel
light
so it's always kind
of permeating
chasing you out
of wherever
you have been
that's why we
musicians like to
linger in
the dark it's
easier to walk
around down there
pick up sticks
and relate to other
people's...
sympathize with
others' beleaguered
lost souls who
just like our own
have been
rummaging
not knowing
where to go or
just not wanting to
move forward
in time darkness
is a place to stop
i know when i
feel nothing
perfectly okay
it has to be an
overcast gloomy
day with some
thing really bad
threatening

there was i think
i saw one man
in the shop
who didn't ever
really see me
no matter
what time
of day it was or
how many times
he came in
it was weird
like he was
blind didn't
have eyes except
maybe to worry
about his hair
and shy away
from what that
small woman
thought with her
dark and judging
eyes always
hiding in her
fluffy bangs
if i could maybe
go back make him
look at me then
perhaps i could
start something
begin to step away
from surfaces
think and feel
i'm real instead of
only standing like
a statue happy
just to be projected
never thought i'd
feel so hollow
would need
somebody else
to fill me from
inside but now i
think i do his
name was tom

i wonder how
i'll make him
notice me
i've dressed
myself in
simpler clothes
today hoping
that he'll see
inside

the moves the men
around her make
i knew that when
she quit working
at the shop it
had everything to
do with johannes
they started going
out the first day
they met and
now i know
she's back here
looking for tom

i can't believe
she wants to
get under his skin
he doesn't care
a thing about her
beauty i thought
at first he had
a crush on me
but then i figured
out he was just
worried wondering
what i thought
about the way
they cut his hair
he smiled at me
shyly that first
day when we
crossed the street
and invited me to
hear a concert
tell him what i
think of his
music which
he says he's writing
just for women
like me
not for experts
nor dummies not
for artsy types
nor hicks just
normal feeling
people who like
things that sound
good so i went
and i did think

wall street to be
closer and to have
more time air
space

poldy she was
great but she
was boring
i would never
hurt a girl like
that but i don't
mind that
she left because
in fact there
wasn't much
between us as
soon as she
began to make
money on her
own there wasn't
much for me
to do we ate
and exercised
together we
made love out
of habit more
than happiness
she was pretty
everyday really
gorgeous but
never any more
or less than on
the day we met
so there wasn't
anything for
me to look for
or watch it was
like keeping
track of weather
where the sun
always shines
and that's all right
but can't go on
forever once it's
been established
that it never
rains

giving the horizon
an edge only
then can i cough
up a comment
on the world
and it's only in the
dark within where
the folds meet
that i am sure that
i myself am really
something as
opposed to maybe
nothing at all
that's why i tend
to shut the good
times out and have
not spent much time
with women i'm
afraid that one of
those or what she'd
make of me could
undo my carefully
fingered knot turn
me into something
regular a space
in which the sun
might shine and then
i would be nothing
but an interval
i've always thought
it best to keep that
one truth veiled
conserve the world
of complex layered
forms but at times
i get the courage
to be honest think
ahead or maybe on
a somewhat grander
scale and then
i know enough
about dust the
pain that every
creature sinks to
this is enough to
keep the shadow
world connected
no posturing of any
kind's required
it always cinches
end of tragic plot
perhaps a greater
depth then and
something true
could grow if
i myself would

i need for
him to make
something out
of me something
that's not
tangible firm or
real something
that will float
and carry him
carry him into
my arms i
heard his voice
his throat pained
me i wanted to
clasp my hands
around his neck
i saw the shifting
darkness in his
eyes i wanted
to fix them with
my own i can't
abide his looking
elsewhere any
more i need for
him to come
to me supposing
that i risk everything
tell him with my eyes
how i'm feeling
why i came back to
this bloody shop
would he reject
me for some
other plainer
girl who he
thinks would
have more heart
or will he always
simply want
to stay aloof
loving only
shadows god
and music last
night i listened
to his music all
night long and
pictured him
beside me years
long gone a
father to three
earthly children
he was gray
and all those
coals burning in

it was beautiful
and i kind of like
tom but i think
he's too caught in
himself for me
he never even
noticed poldy
so maybe he's not
really interested in
girls anyway he's
got to be strange
i wonder what
has happened to
johannes
i wonder if he's
found a new
girlfriend
he smiled at me
the last time i
saw him in the
shop and once i
thought he had a
question that was
meant somehow
for me but i really
do not know that
guy from adam
maybe i'll ask
poldy how he is
and why she's
back here working
at the shop

she could not
believe her good
fortune the day
that she was going
to ask poldy he
was right there
standing in the
shop giving poldy
her messages
and mail but he
didn't seem to care
about poldy no he
kept turning his
eyes toward sarah
looking at her
smiling at her

that everyday can
be as productive
as the last even
poldy noticed
this and wanted
something else
to happen i guess
that's why she
went back to
the shop it made
things look like
she'd been
through a crisis
a depression
or a spiritual
awakening of
sorts at least
if she moved
backwards
she moved
somewhere
instead of always
standing around
i think i'll go back
there tomorrow
look for her and
ask her how
she's doing
give her all her
messages and mail
maybe even cut
my hair and see
if i can buy some
pot off frank
maybe i will
see that small
brunette
who was always
staring hard at
poldy i wonder if
she ever smiles
her little body's
interesting
i think she's
there a lot
she always looks
mixed up like

let the sun in
let my whole
insides be gilt with
gold forget about
containment and
dark spirits and let
my body live in
light that's when
his eyes caught
their first sight of
poldy who had
helped him many
times before to
settle in with
milk and coffee
he saw that there
was milk also on
her lips that parted
in a tiny brilliant
smile

he was minding
his own business
yes he was
when he saw
her at the shop
that morning
those clothes
those shaven
eyebrows milk
drops on her
lips at first he
thought she
must be there
to clean how
else could
someone there
look so unkempt
but then he
couldn't keep
himself from
staring she
looked familiar
standing there
but like no one
he'd ever seen
she smiled just
a little when
she wiped her
mouth and looked
at him well kind of
helpless her hair
was weirdly pinned
and her big black
shoes were clunkier
than mother's

his eyes
were gone
their fire faded
with my beauty
they became softer
and softer and
softer till at last
all the shininess
was gone we
were toned down
to nothing together
there was nothing
to us left but smoke
we had turned inside
to something other
than ourselves
together we were
ashes we were gone

and when she
left the shop
he followed
asked if he could
drive her home
she didn't want to
say yes to that
but did say he
could have her
number maybe
after all i'll get a
life she thought
but before i
ought to write
it down

there's a problem
something really
messing with her
maybe it's an act
or maybe she's
got something
on her mind
i see her there
writing in her
little black book
i wonder what
she's writing

but that look that
she kept giving him
was so intense
her pink-rimmed
eyes were pale and
flecked with gold
he wondered what her
body looked like
tall he guessed and
thin in that big sack
he never saw
a girl look so strange
and beautiful yes
her image got seared
inside his brain
that night he didn't
feel like working
he went out walking
late wishing he had
poldy at his side

89

ondine, i'm having trouble reaching you, no less the whole
world waiting, and am feeling very

stuck inside your flesh,

conscious of its bumps and bruises,

horrified by points, and lines, and folds.

i know that i'm supposed to be detaching from the mirror, should have long ago moved beyond that stage. but i'm
paralyzed today by wry reflections, windows in the car, shiny
doorknob plates, mesmerized by white spot turning into bump,
rising on the tip of my nose. surely, this is punishment for all
that badly

misdirected energy in youth that kept you clutching

to the who,

what should i be?

instead of lifting floodgates to emotions.

90

while we're waiting, i'll transcribe

the dream.

we were purchasing something, my love *&* i. it's possible
it might have been a car. in the middle of negotiations, the fax
went off, wild, like it had something urgent. olivier is brave. he
fumbled for the light, and adjusted neatly plain white paper.
but it turned out

there was only noise.

this disruption in the midst (the heart) of darkest night reminded me how much this year is different from last.
    then upon this very day he called from france, early christ-
mas eve (thursday morning). just like that

a loud disruptive ring

with a message, not so urgent as definitive.

that's it, he's dead,

he said, nothing re-collected in his voice, just a very loud and
clear announcement.

something like a strange bugle call,

articulating what must be accepted. martin, gone.

his father, dead,

his body, dressed. leaving only the horror of witnessing his last attempt at breath. the whitening face, the clear crossed line, moving slowly up the chin. then all the paperwork, frustrations.

you were numb, but stayed awake.

consoled my sobbing angie, wondered how to put it to our matt? woke up andrew, then took time to light a candle, look at pictures

papi, mamie, you and he with your living… three.

whereas this year, olivier and i just fell asleep again.

time works

better in dreams.

91

then walking in a forest park. olivier's grown young again. me too, and i really want and need him. i'm distraught because he says he's going to leave. he's decided that he cannot marry me, pleads to keep his options open, see or be with other women,

but he's still olivier,

so kind and sweet that deep down i can hardly believe him. at the same time, i have my pride. so i tell him go ahead, and then i leave.

soon after, he follows, searches for me in the park. hiding in a corner behind trees is where i am. but they hardly have any leaves on.

whereas you, you're wearing shiny pajamas,

so he sees me and he comes to me and i'm so glad. but then i say it once again: if we're not going to marry *(c'est pas la peine),* it's better if you just go. and for some reason he can't yet commit or doesn't want to. so, he does leave and i am very sad. then the scene cuts to some months later. and here, at last,

you have your youngest, matt (the one who used to be a baby).

i've even fetched his diaper in my dream. i'm glad at least my hands are grasping that.

and you have your older sisters too.

tina and ellen, and they say to me, forget about italy, don't remain dependent on that renaissance man. this year do your research in switzerland. and i think about it, yes, turn over the plan, but know i shouldn't follow their advice.

love them, but resist their guidance.

so in the end, i join up happy with my love again. and this is how the story (in between) goes: first, i come across him when i'm looking for a job, slinking through an eighteenth-century glass shop (that also guards the history of voltaire). i'm lurking in the trinket aisles and very much aware that olivier is searching for something too. he's in the archives, and my position still feels insecure, so i

remain out of view, in hiding.

but after a while, i relax a bit, wander through the shop, which (once more) turns out to be a complex of stores: cafés, parks, and even some contrived scenery. it's a wonderland of sorts, not just the brash, bald commerce of the mall. so i ask two women if they'll hire me. they say they will since i speak spanish. and the next thing you know

you're doing what you're supposed to, deep inside the mirrored park.

i'm sitting pretty (in the splits) with smooth dark hair, a win-ter hat, and a face that's turning younger, japanese,

and who walks by?

all older-looking (now), and dignified, but happy with our tall, dark, curly-haired boy, gentle & handsome by his side.

it's olivier with matt, now a teenager.

and they have come to fetch me.

he's decided that it's you after all.

he doesn't want another woman and we walk into the world together,

me lagging two paces behind.

92

perhaps, i'm just afraid to write

something that might push into the void.

with this feeling of an emptiness before me,

there's the need to fill it up.

should i borrow things perhaps from other times to plug this new and gaping hole? this photo out of which my own father peers at me? the one that does indeed carry death.
    it's normal, i suppose, to be afraid of it. i'll need your help, ondine, to carry through.

well, here i am, mother.

and smiling. i see your head is bowed to pet. you're sitting gentle, quiet in the rocker, waiting for me, not inside the house, underneath,

inside this hole you've dug for us.

you've come back to meet me in this warm, dark cave where there's nothing ever lit but fire. this place where we can hold each other.

all else that comes and goes are apparitions,

but you've come back in time with all your glowing flesh. and now i see you've grown as old as angie (just about 18).

so i'm asking you to hold me.

we sat and rocked about an hour.

93

ondine is real and beautiful just like before. she's 5 foot 2 or 3, her skin is golden brown, her hair is long and thick and ashy blond. it's falling to her waist and wavy.

has never been cut.

it's clear out in the world, she blends with nature, or tries on clothes that living girls cast off, fuses with a wild cast of characters.

but today, she's put back on again that 1920s dress, though is also wearing something different from before, a petticoat i bought for her god-sister (another girl of mine who can't yet walk, who'll never reach her stride). now, the tulle slip's neatly blown just to ondine's size. sitting on my lap, she's thrown her arms around my neck and plants a tender kiss instead of surliness. all the wit and irony are gone.

please mom, let me cross the desert.

there'll be time enough to write when i return.

just hold me tight before you leave, and try.

try hard to live?

so that i won't die.

if you can stay alive walking through those thorns, even just a spark,

we'll gather such a store of kindling.

the fire will be bright when we get home.

94

so better get a move on with the story.

i hardly ever get to

describe the dark canal glittering against the pink *&* setting sun, or

detach

my shoes from muddy tracks, to talk about confusion settling in the night.

which lover's left the one i see?

is singing just an act?
or should i simply sit
pump out air
with still crossed knees.

95

the need to write some things

about luke.

wonderful he is and spiritual, but indulges in a lot of posing.

and you are taken in by that.

how can such a painter think in time to pose? like learning, i suppose, to keep the sabbath (helps draw lines around who we are), except his framing's all his own.

you need to learn to see mirages while there's still light.

but nothing waits for me in arizona. a "complete dose" every single time, no matter what i do or how it goes. always out-of-body experience, have to leave my body far behind.

so you can no more take me there than elephants?

it's just not possible. there's no such sturdy plane and once i land... there's no security.

does this mean you don't love the ones who call there?

no, it's certain that i do. and i keep them in my mind as follows:

your father?

just a little, lost inside his smoke, coughing up... some kind-ness with his cancer (operation). he's said a few good words with mean ones to this child and that to assure one and all that he's okay.

and mother, lise, you love her, don't you?

lots. but she makes me hopping mad, and her wounds cut fathoms deeper than father's.

what the heck, you'd wonder, is wrong with lise.

how could she be so crude? manipulating, even? think of that remark she made to her old friend (flame?). so mean and quick-planned: "i see that things are good for you," she said, sizing up his new "fling." and right in front of the poor woman. showing she's still tough and in the game.

though for us daughters, she always had: compliments (over and over).

tina,

she'd say, "you've raised your kids just right." "maia" (to me), "you know best how to divorce." but the link from her to

ellen?

was a little more direct. there was something almost personal between them, perhaps because she (her middle child) dared to show unruly sides, and play the sharp loose cannon with emotions, whereas tina and i (the bookends of her brood) always kept ours safely under wraps.

anyway, i'm sad that lise at 85 felt still afraid to die, fearing just that non-existence, which she'd always claimed (was not so terrible) though down it swoops to take us all.

like last year when we drove her to the airport, and she told the same joke uttered the year before. "parking that is terminal? how scary." thoughts like that kept her up at night, broke her reasoning down, enough to go and see our family shrink (dr. fox). she'd sink so low as to blame no god on "pop": "he's the one, you know, who says there's no such thing," back when she was smart and judging things.

so pop? he…

well, just used whatever he got (in hand). i've never known a man quite so self-centered. "if i don't know this," he'd say, "or can't do that, then it's simply gotta be ain't."

whereas your mother's

singing i rang empty: its tiny shrunken heart in a heavy armored bell, only peeping out to play the piano... but there she

always held the sweetest touch.

makes me want to cry. help me to forgive,

maybe really call her time to time.

96

but for now the need's to build a fire. see, ondine, it's blazing just

for you and me.

a sign of peace i'm lacing deep inside this place,

though we're here to talk about family, right.

and why it's been so hard to begin. very hard to take, my father,

who was always so there's nothing but me,

and mother,

who just couldn't be found.

siblings, they were different, very moving.

love, love, how you love them all.

but it's hard for us to get along.

tina, the rock,

tireless worker, so always ready to proceed for everybody else, also rock-headed, and controlling (like mom). can hardly stand it if she's not in charge (but she knows how she is), while her emotions rule more like pop's (without the drinks): ever clinging to the baseline of instincts, feeling only what she herself can do. now she's living well, and

selling houses with ellen, her opposite,

my mercurial second sister, who's sharp and witty, cries and laughs, says whatever crosses... her very busy mind. they've inverted all the qualities of "ma and pa," my two imperious "realty" sisters,

yet they strangely make a good couple.

yes, and now live together like "maiden" aunts, though they're grandmas both, with brightly checkered pasts, in a house that is peaceful and welcoming. even i don't feel too far out of the loop. see that picture of us three there,

you between the two of them, each bending your ear.

"i know you have that on your mind," says one, "it's true i go too far the other way," says two. they're riding now in tandem on their christmas bikes, pretty, graceful, into old age.

and luke?

the artist? he was tired. his stone carvings were gorgeous though (the paintings too). his politics, more like: posturing. the songs he hummed (like mine) came from tender, missing spot within. i wonder if that last one was for me.

still, the only thing i learned was captured on his wall: "a clever man can always strike a pose." i hope that's also true for women.

act as if.

i really like that. could help keep my integrity together, ensure my devotion be ongoing, gather better kindling for our fires, so we can figure how to move from b to c.

and theo?

the conqueror? he wasn't there.

and joe?

for justice, the sweetest of the lot, and the youngest (next to me). i liked it when he said about his teenage daughter, telling him she'd give away her baby of two months, "you could have knocked me over with a feather." joe took that child in, yes, he did. now he has a son, with his four daughters.

a solid, loving man, that one is.

never struck a pose in his life.

97

but there are two more things you need to know today, ondine.

one, i should have written yesterday, connected to the joke about the panda bear who goes into a bar: eats shoots and leaves.

you mixed the panda bear with a koala

and had him in an outdoor restaurant, like the ones we used to eat in on the beach near mazatlan, where there was joyful shade beneath the wide thatched roofs, and open air that hid away the "classes."

getting you even further off track.

yes, because of two.
    for it turned out we weren't in mexico. but instead found ourselves diverted.

stopping by the hills around l.a.,

staying for some reason at my friend's house, on a beach that now was owned by cathleen. the one she got herself when she divorced (this house does not exist, she never got divorced). inside (my dream) it's been... abandoned. it's empty and i'm not sure she even owns it anymore, but i'm staying there a bit with my parents, so i feel i ought to call her up.
    i do and this is true. it turns out that, yes, the house still is cathleen's and of course she'd like to see my parents. her love for me remains intense.

i'm sure you were at her place

when i'd just turned 24,

after the phone call from tina

telling me to put you quick to death, though the abortion was some four weeks later. "you think you want this baby but you don't," tina said. "if you do, get rid of it, and go get pregnant again, you can have another one instead." fool-proof reasoning for floundering in the dark.

and cathleen, what did she say?

well, it seemed she was struggling with same, though she was more stable, more grounded in her thinking. but what she said was of the same general persuasion: everyone was, saying all around you at that time (and by "you," here i mean "us," the women raised to bear this brave new world), your mother, sisters, brothers, and even (if you had one) your man:

babies, a matter of expedience.

they should come only when you're sure you're ready, with all your ducks lined up in pretty rows. ready for them, focused on them, living just for them. and my ducks weren't even squaggled in a circle,

perhaps that's why you wanted me so much.

my ducks are hardly straight today.

and finally when cathleen let her own kids come?

all the rest, she just let go: nine years of school, the books, the thoughts, the cigarettes and pot.

all the rest, she just let go…

98

so that was it. that is how it goes. and this dribble that i'm writing

in the light of death,

means perhaps i'm trying something "like montaigne," my love said, but without the help of avid letters, and

more preoccupied with kids than death.

but the snow has a rare sparkle today, shining with everything i need this day, extending something

    like a branch straining
    hard against the wind

it's trembling but it's really there

    with a frame for it
    of higher leafless things

less tender but still swaying

    and a backdrop of snow
    brought on souls within

seeping through some random gusts

    but me i'm salt
    and sand begins

with sin of sitting steadfast

99

JE SUIS MAINTENANT IMPERSONNEL, ET NON
PLUS STÉPHANE QUE TU AS CONNU — MAIS UNE
APTITUDE QU'A L'UNIVERS SPIRITUEL À SE VOIR
ET À SE DÉVELOPPER À TRAVERS CE QUI FUT MOI.
— s. m.

now there were words that meant… something. kept me going through some pretty grim years, while i was waiting for
my love to come. they were the balm that helped to cure the
atheist, as she was sitting around my room (age 23) the spring
before you came to "pass," when poems began to pour and
things seemed suddenly, strangely in control, waiting for
something like manna to fall down, instead of braying hungry,
empty, out or on the prowl.

   i began to think in those days (and still do at times) that
i'd be better split in two persons.

we could manage better in that way.

person 1 would be in charge of person 2, make her brush her
teeth and take a shower, do discipline and not ask questions.
2 would be the one who felt her skin, could sense the world,
and answer to the treatment. a clear division then between: i
think/i feel. or would that be the ego and the id? never could
put those two together, still can't do that trick today.

   and i was thinking just this morning i might need a mythic
me, a stronger image, something to grab on to, a stabler point
of reference to return to, and help me make it through each day.

your hero made that reference: emptiness.

nothing lurking, tarnishing the glass. but what a dandy presence he could whip up on the side, a very kind, mysterious
demeanor, saluting other marchers on the way. he was stylish,
fully mannered on the outside, whereas e. d.,

she, your lady poet, was a seamstress.

always stitching up herself within. she never really dared ex-
pose her image to the light. and i take more from those two
than from montaigne,

but what have you to give to anyone?

only you, i guess, for i am ever dizzy, choking on the stuff of
life. better part of days spent tending to children, or padding
all my nothingness with this new chore and that, hoping time
itself will float away, or behave like something crossed out on
my calendar (passion i have always had for lists).

when i first realized i could write... poetry, the hole backed
off or at least began to fill. my regime became as though stabi-
lized with water, calm and clear (i need a sure environment to
write). i found serene hours for nothing but myself (without
which i'm still not).

yes, i got myself together for a time the spring before you
were, and that fall accumulated something like power (de-
fended my m.a. in november, was deemed the "queen of hearts"
on halloween).

100

and gathered strength (as usual) from two strange men. one,
mad, pale, and thin, romanian. the other, blond and portly,
french.

the first was in the lunch line, with his hair on end, truly scared,

of static electricity, while i was

drawn to him for fear of chocolate milk.

always staring, green-eyed handsome, that one was, and following me around. i asked my cool professor what to do with him (he, the expert of literature on the edge): "wondering if my friend is schizophrenic?" i muttered. "maybe he's the healthy one," he said.

but you wouldn't have become entangled

with that troubled boy, were it not for my sorely needed balance,

were there not, on the other side, parisian prestige.

that coddled fellow, plunked down by a famous, rich family, trying to find adventure in new york.
   i guess i might have looked adventuresome, flanked like that between europe's finest always forging west, and storms fleeting through central europe, since i always held my own

arizona cowgirl mexican,

stomping best i could true otherness,

decked with ivy leagues for height.

   one night we three walked arm-in-arm down claremont street and the plump blond did his best to sing SANTANA. at that moment i felt all together, equiped with everything i'd need: madness on the left, legitimacy on the right. the dark boy and the solid source of light. didn't last long.

you threw it all away?

or maybe let it run its course. i'm trying, really trying to remember…

   i know i made a phone call to lise late that fall, telling
her i feared i was losing it. she, not understanding anything
at all, except i'm having troubles with "men." and threatening
to come see me with her lover, she lectured against acquiring
"notches on my belt." men, they're innocent, that she always
said, and can never help it if you're pretty. repeating things
she'd maybe learned from father? or maybe that she'd figured
out herself.

   anyway, my balance was totally destroyed. i found myself
cast down again by winter, and stayed low and lonesome till
i drank with nadim,

   sleeping through wee hours with he who gave me half,

and who months before had almost been my friend.

   and it was shortly after that my warm professor died, the
one who flagged some tenderness for me. a heart attack the
night before my birthday (24th). when i got to school, they told
me he was dead. and it was four weeks later on the very day
you died,

   the ides of march, 1980,

that we marked his passing at the french house, with a delayed
but very classy service. i climbed out of the cab, shaky from
it all, because i thought i ought to…

   the only show was black and white photographs,

his, of manhattan, very tasteful, hung up all about. and i was
oh so sad.

there was no remnant of me.

buried with him, you were, or so i thought, as was the way
i'd dodged his gentle pass. but not the story of him taking me
to dinner, amidst a flock of all his cackling colleagues, who
might have dared to think that i was crass. i remembered to
tell people that.

so, i could always say i showed them. they didn't get me
then or get me ever. though maybe that was thanks more to
the meanest of them all, saint-yves, who sensed i was hungry
with a flair. still, i shouldn't have gotten myself entangled,
nor let myself be challenged to one too many duels. that's how,
no doubt, i lost my haughty footing.

succumbed to the sin that finally broke you down,

it must have been that — sleeping with your father.

why'd you do that?

what was there to gain? no doubt the pull of some desire,

something to fill your horror of the void.

but it added up to nothing, nothing in the end, and started
up a long chain of episodes: empty acts just like it with others.
beginning with the portly frenchman, though now it was too
late. for he'd summoned back his own "virginia" for settling
in new york (they'd been betrothed from childhood or some
such thing).

next, a tall, extremely handsome actor, who asked me why i
laid there like potatoes. then, worst of all, when i moved from
the dorm, that sad conclusion with a colombian from yale, a
nice boy who had really been my friend. the night we slept
together, he was helping me to move. his reaction the next day
was: guilty. never spoke a word to me again.

then, i really lost my bearings through a string of one-night stands, and hours of wolfing down, then puking up, the doughnuts, staring at green bathroom tiles, till a gluey neon light went on (signaling) above: maybe what i need's a proper shrink.

meanwhile, i received a gift. a pretty shirt from jamshid who was missing me back home, the beautiful iranian i'd loved and left for years: a gentle soul, a soccer player full of pot, cocaine, and beer, writing now to recognize my birthday (with all the mounting tenderness of one who's been betrayed), threatening to come to see me in manhattan, ready now to ask my hand in marriage. but news of that came way too late... and news of you sure rained on his parade.

101

so let's not even think about the dreams spun last night. i'm pretty sure they weren't pleasant, though i'm sleeping hard these days,

regathering, i hope, not alone.

and perhaps when i am done reading this and that, i ought to

read that book about heaven.

it's incredible and sad, how slowly i proceed, but that is how i take things in. and i have no idea where to start today.

perhaps reflect on that summer when you worked.

that summer when i should have been pregnant?

bleak, it was, an awful summer.

well, i just got myself a job and then maybe three or four more, winding toward the world trade center, answered ads, went to agencies. first got hired, then fired at a record company in queens. couldn't get the names of bands or labels straight, which made me want to work in restaurants. but nobody would hire me.

you walked too slow.

heads would shake as soon as i came in. till i finally broke that pattern at THE MAGIC PAN. i bought myself a uniform, excited, but then realized i'd be needed in the kitchen too. so i quit that job, right around lunch.

couldn't make it through the first day.

the agency had two ideas: the first was... nothing much... except "help" a man. when i met him and his wife, she asked me what i liked, which made me break off all communications.
next and last stop was chambers street. far steadier, that work was. i stayed two months, "training" for a german freight company. greta, my tall, blond, clipped lady boss was patient with my awkward letters, while

the office boy took off your glasses in his dreams,

and said he thought he knew that i was beautiful,

not made to play that part or join their team.

only one bright memory all summer long: ellen almost naked, wearing hot green pants, leaning on her husband's hippy van, with two tired children scuffling in the back. what a sight that was against gray wall street steel, striking out the sobriety of dull new yorkers.

my people, they stand out in arizona, always make a splash for color, throw their whole flesh beings in your face. by the time ellen arrived, i'd thought: i'll quit my jobs, tell 'em after all, i'll be heading back to school.

and greta didn't bear me any grudge. she invited me instead to her apartment, and tried to hook me into another sales scheme: something about pyramids and soap. but ellen told me that was cheap & common, saying also that i looked the "faded flower" when she stayed with me one night, in my first and only solo apartment, a studio bay window on 106th where

shortly after, you received a lawyer.

the first of three. the second was still in love with a woman from brazil, and

the last put an end to all these series.

jonathan. he saved my life and gave me andrew and angie. today remains the dearest of my friends.

but the first?

i never knew much about. i'd just heard he was interested the year before. and then amidst candles, almond chicken, moving boxes, something in my heart began thumping, while my pen began scratching toward these dreams of you, stories pushing forward unborn daughters. one began: elizabeth and henry…

but back then it seems my love could not begin. i was just groping to be rescued from my blooming thighs (that had shocked my moving helper back in june).

you shouldn't have jumped the gun,

should never have let that first guy come over. son of a wine-
importer, he wasn't really shy. he was a wily, almost weaselly
lawyer, cleverly harboring a french girl, while sending me a
postcard from spain.

he simply put you in his pocket

as he went about his jobs. though once he nicely cooked for
me at his house, and we must have gone out three or four more
times: middle eastern stores in brooklyn, paddying around his
mom's place on the upper-east side, and a summer weekend
partying in the hamptons. we ended it sublimely at strauss's
SALOME.

then he went to israel and stayed.

202 Nights

OUR LITTLE LIFE IS ROUNDED

— Shakespeare

1

what a horrid night. went to do some business at columbia. the secretary told me in an off-hand way: they couldn't give me my diploma till i took the last exam. a take-home it was, and i didn't recognize the passages, except for one,

molière… or maybe marivaux.

but the names were somehow based on PHÈDRE. i decided any-way that this might be okay. theater. familiar territory. then i forgot, didn't get to work, until it would be due the next morn-ing. had to be turned in to the office before noon. i panicked a bit, then settled down, began to write — contrast & parse the language in the first *réplique*. but then i lost my way.

doubt crept in.

i started to consider other passages, and explained all this to olivier.
    he suggested that i choose a comic strip, something about a clever fox, said that we'd have everything i'd need. but some-how i felt stuck with my own passages, though less and less clear how to go on. i noted then the faint trace of a rooster, which grew into the jacket of a book. as i considered what to do next, tried to read deep into the text, my stare revealed a glossy cover. a date appeared, 1569, and everything except the author's name, delicately framed in script.
    all these things i'd found, yet was no further than before.

and time,

well, it was still ticking. i still would have to cough up the exam. i awoke uncomfortable, shared my fears. and the ever-gentle one beside me said: none of that is real, but i had awful times with my computer

lost when hit upon the wrong button,

can't believe i didn't save.

2

ondine, i've got good news for you this morning. angie's weighed in strong on your side. she wants me not to let you go. she who always has good ideas, thoughts for what's most meaningful in presents, bought me something sumptuous for my birthday (49th): a pouch to keep your papers in.

like the one she gave you last year to carry in your purse? some-thing from her that goes with you, related to the passport pouch?

yes, the pouch means you are precious, the red means i won't lose you, the leather, i can take you with me. now you have a sacred space,

a haven partly guarded

by your sister, who's long had thoughts of lugging me about. on the prospect of my shrinking, she, aged 5 or 6: mom, when you get old, will you be small enough to fit inside my book bag? wise, so wise, and such a wit.

mom, say thank you to my sister.

3

there's a story i must write, begin right here. but i'm not sure how to do it. i never could step up to this event before, though i've been trying for twenty-five years.

why not? you've never minded much revealing…

the problem is it feels like fiction, although each point in fact was real, unfolding something structured and coherent. every-thing so full of portent, pointing toward an end, with me still wondering what the meaning was. if only i could get inside.

tell the story in the third… person. give yourself a name.

extract myself a bit from who i am today so i can feel the *ac-tions* of the characters. see the girl i was as though from with-out. the man i met more from within.

make all this be present though told within the past.

yes, i guess that's how it's done.

4

maggie schmidt leaned out her window on the rue saint-charles, the market smells and noises were just rising, the café customers clanking down their coins and cups.

one wave (of all this clamor) reminded her,

she'd thrown up mussels in the neon-lit bistrot down the street. no more mussels, i'm allergic, she thought. i should stay away from cafés, or maybe just avoid this street. but all those things were last night's dilemmas. this morning was a new... day.

on the other side of town,

reuben meyer still had not rolled out of bed.

he wasn't so tired as hung-over, so hung-over, as sick of heart and head. he'd had horrific visions all night long, felt forever trapped,

caught

among the screaming dead. this inner struggle showed in signs of chaos: dishevelment, his ruffled blond hair stuck out of the sheets. his cigarettes were tossed upon a newspaper, with ashes strewn along the carpet, toward the saucer, where a half-drained coffee cup (crookedly set down) was teetering six inches from the bed.

rrrriiinng.

he was awakened by an old black phone, plopped down side-ways on its cord, stretched along the floor from the kitchen. the call was from alberto.

"¿cuándo vienes hombre?"

"esta noche. el tren sale a las once," reuben said.

gare montparnasse, onze heures du soir.

5

meanwhile, maggie prepared herself more consciously than usual. she straightened up her sparsely furnished studio — a lamp, a chest of drawers,

a mattress,

a wooden desk and sturdy chair — washed the dishes in the *coin-cuisine.*
she even showered and dressed, more like a college girl than usual. neither jeans, nor high heels. a dark red corduroy skirt, a light pink sweater, tan leather boots. dark blue over-coat with gold buttons. she had for some reason

the feeling of a… start,

marked this with a hair wash and eyeliner.

why couldn't life begin anew?

she was (only) 21, wasn't hooked to anything, could al-most choose her own direction, instead of always wondering (wandering),

gathering so much emptiness each day.

6

maggie had a job teaching english, a degree: in french,

a fellowship,

as though she had a future.

but she felt like nothing

ever happened to her, or rather like

nothing ever stuck.

and yet within a few weeks, all sorts of (lasting) things would start to happen. she'd puke her guts out two streets over in another café,

burst a hole

in her appendix. be hospitalized a spell inside the town where she taught school. then hop around some cities, and clinics,

to freshen up her wounds and see the sights.

boucicault, a fine hospital in paris, then one in london, one in cork, then kerry county,

biding all her time in bed

and breakfasts with bread and milk,

bandages and sleep.

then, just about cured, and no one back in town when she returned to school: a frenzy for february break. she'd go ahead and take that train for munich.

7

accept that invitation from karl, joe's friend, a curious aristo-
crat farming with his mom, who never really pushed his own
interests. there she'd get a first taste of

bavarian wheat beer,

then be swiftly transported back to paris, plunked on the back
of a big black motorbike, wrapped like a cocoon in yellow
plastic, driven 14 hours

through the rain and night,

dropped off sharp at dawn at her apartment, so this senseless
weekend could be over (germans like to work).

then back to work herself again,

around mid-march, maggie would get

another fellowship

back home, and to boot (or to go) with it, a new fellow,

another fiancé to

carry home from france. then

drop inside the dry dirt desert,

just in time for moving to new york. honorable means, then
she'd have, and the appearance of "things" happening.

nothing to be bored about.

8

but on this january day (gray — paris — 1978), she didn't know all this would happen. nor was she busy with her past or future. she was instead

suspended in the present,

in touch with what would come to pass.

what put her in that state?

i think it might have been a movie, but i'm not sure because

the road forks here.

it may be all

the boredom

that weighed on her (for weeks)

just gathered up and lifted,

a moment, so maggie felt:

why not just take charge,

take some brief possession of her body,

open up and take things in.

this being the case, against all odds, she might have bought herself a magazine or newspaper, record of

what's happening in the outside world.

for, on leaving her apartment, she walked straight to the latin
quarter —

>   not wandering aimless through the streets
>   nor casting sideways glances through the subways
>   not loitering in pizzerias
>   nor stuffing bakery shops
>   but attending to a classic
>   IPHIGENIA —

tell me, what is that about?

a myth, an ancient story, here told in modern greek by cacoyannis. agamemnon, a king, a really big shot, is told to sacrifice
his eldest daughter...

9

and here's what lise wrote in 1982 — IPHIGENIA'S THIRD SONG

>   Mother, it is time,
>   oh it is time,
>   the moment is at hand
>   to quit our tears and grief,
>   to lift our heads and stand
>   as rock-rooted hilltop trees,
>   bent, not broken, in the storm
>   yet stripped of every leaf.

that's a pretty song.

light, the touch, and sweet. trailing, yet firm,

and searching,

like her fingers on the piano.

10

but notes discovered by maggie from 1981 explain her earlier

presence

at this movie by the rain.

hesitating in her choice of language

and approach,

caught between the telling of the present and the past,

resorting to the... third person, and to the shallow trick of changing names,

she was trying to account for what had happened

in a letter, to her roommate, a dear friend:

~~Ma chère Bri~~, My dear Brig

Knowing your taste for extraordinary moments and the romantic side of life. I thought

I heard an extraordinary story the other day. This happened to my friend Merin who's spending the year in Paris, thinking about studying she says... but mostly ~~eating~~, studying pâtisseries.

She told me that one dreary afternoon she???? decided to go for a walk in the Latin Quarter, take in an afternoon movie... to fill up her afternoon. It started/was raining, so she took refuge at the movies...

Iphigenia, was the war, greek, got her tragic — just the
sort of film my friend adores. tragic but meaningful
with an ?? epic "soufflé." After the movie, she was
walking to Notre Dame. Thinking all the while, that
Paris was like the movies — that life doesn't seem very
real / so real. ~~Out.~~

so, what actually got maggie

to the movies that day, and

primed to greet the mystery

that followed, remains something of a blur.
   but we do know this: she ducked her head inside the dark
theater right on time, as though she knew what she was doing:
a bright, young american,

intersecting with the world,

heart of paris, 2 o'clock.

11

and while maggie was preparing, walking through her day,

reuben cooked eggs,

ate them scrambled with the left-over coffee, and two dried-up
pieces of baguette. looked out his fifth-floor window (on the
rue de rennes), to see if he could find montparnasse. showered,
shaved and dressed — black jeans, blue shirt, brown sweater,

put on his leather jacket and went out.

he walked briskly to the station, bought his ticket, browsed through rows of books, then slowly ambled toward the lux- embourg gardens, where he read two works: *UNA HISTORIA FANTÁSTICA Y CALCULADA* (g. marín, 1976) & *SECRETS, SPIES, AND SCHOLARS: BLUEPRINT OF THE ESSENTIAL CIA* (also '76, by r. s. cline).

next, he bought himself a *QUICK* hamburger and headed for the kiosk on saint-michel, to buy some spanish press. and then, because it looked like threatening rain, he

sat himself down

inside a small café, just beside the cinema maggie had gone in,

and read his papers through

till 4 o'clock.

12

he'd arrived in paris just three days before, seen some sights with miguel and rosario, before the couple left for new york. those two were documentary filmmakers, old friends of adam, reuben's cousin, whom he'd just been staying with in london for three months. it was rosario who'd set up

reuben's next stop,

the journey he would take that very evening: to begin a six- month stay with alberto.

barcelona

would be beautiful in spring.

13

reuben was from argentina, he'd never been to europe be‑
fore. he'd read a lot of european history, was well‑versed in
its literature and philosophy, had studied french and english
throughout high school, learned some german from his par‑
ents at home. but he'd never been much interested in traveling
before.

now he had no choice.

before he would return to argentina (1984), he'd come to know
a vast network of latin americans scattered in cities through‑
out europe.

he was looking for a place to settle,

find a job.

why not spain?

and though he might like barcelona very much, he thought:
better keep moving for a while. he'd need papers, books, more
documents, to work anywhere. and those would have to come
later. he'd left them in buenos aires, in secret, on the run, along
with everyone and thing he'd ever known.

14

reuben's parents were jews, had come from germany as chil‑
dren in the thirties. he'd grown up in the ONCE district. his fa‑
ther was a well‑to‑do lawyer, his mother taught school. most of

his friends were marxists,

some had become MONTONEROS.

his wife had been active in leftist student groups. she was chilean, two years older than he, had moved to buenos aires after the '73 coup.

reuben met her in a class on spanish poetry. she tried at first to make him join the party. but reuben didn't like groups, had always kept his distance from politics, preferred to think historically, or talk about art,

take things with a long view.

reuben and lidya married in '75, when they found out they were expecting —

manuelita.

soon after she was born, reuben got a job — dropped his studies and all thoughts of highfalutin writing. in '76, he went to work for his uncle's newspaper. that's where he was when the generals took over, and why (i guess) his troubles began.

in early '77 he was

detained by the police, a number of times, and yet well treated,

questioned courteously, then let go.

he felt guilty about that. people all around, no more engaged than he, were being handled in more brutal ways. his uncle's business partner had been kidnapped. colleagues at the paper were being threatened and harassed every day.

still, he thought, better not to dwell on suspicions. just try not to pass information to the police. he warned lidya to do the same, to drop all talk of what she had been doing.

always assuming that the worst was here,

reuben kept a low profile, which fit the flatness of his feelings. history, he thought, could turn itself around,

things would maybe right themselves...

15

and within a year of meeting maggie, reuben did settle down. he worked for a leftist newspaper for five years in madrid, then became an investigative journalist,

reporting

all over the world on the ins and outs of political events, finally returning once more to south america.

and somewhere, i am sure, today (graying, balding, wrinkling) in a whitewashed room with ceiling fans, he still is working on the details of his own most urgent story.

what does this entail?

weirdly, the retelling (in a slow and probing way) of things long past, which he was still somehow experiencing

things, what things?

those that happened, with people and in places that had ravaged his life.

16

the ABCs of Argent   's "Dirty War" (–1983)

Argentina's National Being: this is   the "generals"
and the   wing claimed they were trying to protect,
the   spirit of their nation,   happens to be
    eighth largest country in the   , second
    country   south america, occupying most of the
southern   of that   . the republic won its
        from spain   the early 1800s.   chief
natural resource is   .   main
products   meat, wheat and maize.   population
(97% european) dwells   towns and cities.

Batallón 601: this   intelligence unit,   charge
of repression   torture,   also involved   domes⁻
tic   international business   : arms   drug
trafficking, extortion   laundering.   1978,
    managed   extra⁻territorial task force   florida
(authorized   cia),   helped fund   train
    nicaraguan contras.

Buenos Aires: this   city, the   of argentina,
located   province   close to uru⁻
guay,   a population of   11,000,000
    the largest jewish community   south america
(about 200,000, mostly of   european descent).

Campo de Mayo: secret detention center   a
buenos aires army base   run   task forces 1 and 2,
made   military, police,   gendarmerie, under
    control   commanders galtieri   suárez mason.
        1995 *la prensa* report,   particular
center detained, interrogated, tortured

2000 prisoners, 20 to 300   a time. when
too crowded, prisoners   disposed   .
    other   centers, campo de mayo
internally   -sufficient,
funded   supplied   the military government.
    with prisoners' cells (both 1 by 2   "tube"
and communal "lion's cage"   ), the space   in-
cluded store-rooms   stolen goods, dormitories for
guards   members   task forces, lounges, bath-
rooms, kitchen, dining-room. administrative, file, and
documentation   . laboratories. torture
  , and   infirmary   tortured
detainees   interrogation   ongoing.
    ensure   isolation   keep
    whereabouts unkown, prisoners   *not allowed*
to use   *names*, nor to speak to   other nor
to   young   low-ranking military personnel
      guards. these   performed menial
tasks   the prisoners   food, walking
   to the bathroom,   to the torture
in handcuffs   hoods. they were also   (for
entertainment) to abuse the prisoners   will.

CIA: while it is   known that   u.s. central intelligence   backed   pinochet's 1973
      salvador allende (democratically
   president of chile),   no sure evidence
   officially   assisted   argentine generals   coup. many   , and documents
  those released   u.s. embassy, suggest that
   supported the *junta*'s   goals, but the
  is still contested. perhaps   because the cia —
despite   appeals — has to date
to refuse   release of its own   documents.

Counter-insurgency operations: military actions
other activities — summary executions, torturings,
kidnappings, extortion, money   , blackmail
—   chief commanders, task forces,   para-
military death squads engaged   1974
rid   country   insidious leftist
terror.   these operations   aimed
guerilla fighters,   also targeted other
enemies: students, workers, labor-union leaders, jour-
nalists,   , doctors, mothers,   , and priests.

Crusade (the):   argentina's "national
being" was laid   in the generals' "directive 504/77"
once   succeeded   eliminating   bulk
terrorist threat. replacing   military action
sectoral campaigns,   military government
     last few years,   consolidation   coherent
lifestyle,   eradication of all   methods
used to teach   encourage subversive (that is, "com-
munist")   ideas.

Death flights: stripped, heavily drugged,
still living bodies   many "disappeared"   loaded
   army cargo planes   helicopters to be flown
to sea   dumped. leaving   campo de mayo,
unregistered   conducted   very low alti-
tudes   pilots   later bitterly regret
what   forced to do.

Declassified documents: interesting,   not   hard
   read. see,   example (partially   below)
ATØ17, released   u.s. embassy   2002 — summary of what   well known   the   government
   1978. or CU132 —   straightforward but not

graphic account   one tortured american   experience   october 4, 1976.   she   a
boyfriend,   in the process   divorcing a man
         marxist literature,   left *partido comuni-*
sta rosario leaflets   a parkbench (given   her   a
friend),   lucky   managed   escape the
nightmare. she   rescued   embassy officials
    returned   u.s.

Disappeared: this is what   , on the other   ,
to 10   30,000 people   argentina: one day   were
there, going along (   ) with   ordinary, everyday   .   day, they were   ,
and no one around — loved ones, friends, co-workers,
neighbors — had   idea   . now people know
what   *los desaparecidos*:   executed
    removed   corpses or abducted still alive   the
government, they   dispatched   secret
centers   processing, whence they   then quietly   , without trace (burned   buried
mass graves, or dumped   atlantic ocean).

Galtieri, Leopoldo Fortunato: graduate of   u.s. army
school   the americas, this   commander   army
corps II (rosario)   third   president
    de facto   . within   context   po-
litical infighting   divided   *junta*, he   supposed
    a "moderate"   opposed   "hard-liner."   he
    led to the military   downfall
    falkland islands   march   82.

Guglielminetti, Raúl: colorful thief, low-
life political henchman, journalist (*sur argentina),*
    ultra-right storm   bahía blanca

early   mid-sixties,   a nazi.
                    argentine anti-   *alliance,*
          -wing (paramilitary) death squad   kidnapped,
tortured,   killed   activists, he   charge
of selling victims'   . according   juan gaspa-
rini (*pista suiza*),   especially good
extra money   kidnapping   (many
          jewish)   large ransoms, and   blam-
ing   kidnappings   leftist activists.   late 70s,
he   key   laundering   lords'
money in miami to   anti-   paramili-
tary operations   central america.

Hill, Robert: ambassador   argentina (appointed
          nixon   1973),   accused henry
     giving argentine general   "green light" for
tactics   76, reassuring   foreign minister,
admiral   guzzetti,   the generals would not
          trouble   u.s.   long as   could "fin-
ish   terrorist problem quickly." hill, a republican
          "yanqui imperialist"   extensive interests in
          america (who   served   ambassador   costa
rica   1954 cia   coup   guatemala),
claimed   tried   to oppose kissinger's flexible   regarding   *junta*'s methods   the
atrocities committed   human   .

Kissinger, Henry: germany   1923, natural-
ized   u.s.   1943,   widely (respected   )
hated harvard-   intellectual served   secretary of state   to 1977.   received
peace prize   helping to negotiate the end
viet nam   1973,   time   was instigating
          coup against   allende.

Marxism-Leninism: political   philosophical
                german   marx (laid
out   *manifesto*   *capital*),   inter-
preted   implemented   lenin,   russian
         who brought   bolsheviks   power
1917.   doctrine   belief   dialectical
materialism and   determinism,   theory
labor   value.   class struggle
   history   ,   ultimate estab-
lishment of   (achieved
     seizure   power and   period   dictatorship
      proletariat). throughout   century, devel-
oping   looked up   marxist   ideas
         soviet union   viable alternative
   capitalist   society   government. cuba
        fidel castro and argentine   guerilla hero
che   led the way   marxism-
leninism in   america.

Montoneros: armed revolutionary   formed
around 1970   left   peronist   to
fight for   justice   return of juan perón,
          exiled   paraguay
    1955 overthrow.   montoneros broke with
other wings   movement,   rejected by perón himself in 1973,   return to argentina and   presidency.   perón's death (1974),
     went underground,   "columns" of guerilla
fighters   major urban centers.   peak,
          primarily above ground,   profu-
sion of magazines   communiqués, and organizing
massive   estimated cadre of
7,000   .

Mothers of Plaza de Mayo: mothers of the
"disappeared," 14   protesting

presidential palace   buenos aires   april 30,
1977,   demand   account of what
    their children.   marching around
    plaza, donning white   , every thursday
        . Several   "disappeared" in turn: azu-
cena villaflor   others   abducted, tortured,
murdered.   international acclaim
        several hundred people (including
men),   role, after the fall   ,
        prosecutions. *las madres*   still
marching   plaza de mayo   thursday,
3:30   4 o'clock.

Operation Condor: covert   cooperation
        1975   intelligence   six
south american   (argentina, bolivia, brazil,
    , paraguay, uruguay) working   terror-
ism,"   eliminate   -wing groups, activists   others   countries.   any
shown   u.s. government   crucial, silent
"sponsor"   ,   intelligence
and training,   facilitating
involved agencies   telecommunications
    panama canal zone.

People's Revolutionary Army: *ejercito*   *del*
pueblo was   the 1960s   armed wing
    communist   workers' revolutionary
        . although   group's   trotskyite,
    erp members   ties   castro regime
cuba. despite the generals'   to the contrary,
    guerilla   never large   powerful
argentina, counting no   than 500 to 1000 fighters,
    concentrated   tucumán. the group in any
    wiped out months before   1976 coup.

Perón, Juan: charismatic   politician, fas-
cist-populist   ,   crucial role
military take-over   1943, and   elected three
times   president   argentina,   ousted once
(army, in   )   sent into exile   18 years.
    originality   not just anti-commu-
nist,   reformer   fervently anti-british
    anti-american.   second   , evita (of musical
fame), helped   progressive policies,   support
    labor, women,   poor. isabel,   third wife
    vice-   succeeded   in office
he died (1974), led   corrupt   started
"dirty war"   crumbled   76 coup.

Pregnant detainees: hundreds   babies   born
secret detention   . some say   mothers
        taken care of until   birth.   babies
then used   leverage   torture, killed, sold
black market, given   adoption   childless military
            or   added to   *junta*'s   children.

Richard Nixon —   **— Jimmy Carter — Ron-
ald Reagan**:   american   held power   the "dirty war,"   distinct talents.
        ideas   apparently little impact
unfolding events.

SIDE: *Servicio de Inteligencia del Estado*, was (still is)
    main intelligence   argentina.

Suárez-Mason, Carlos Guillermo: primary
    junta, an   "hard-liner,"   rival
videla,   controlled   aires province   commander   zone I. by   own account,
signed,   a long period, 50   100 death warrants

per day. (died himself   june   , 2005,   day
before yesterday.)

Tactics: harassment. isolation. annihilation. torture
(in   forms: burning, near-drowning, hanging
— right side up   down —, body part
    mutilation — finger   , eyes, genitalia —, electric
        ,   expert administrations   different blows
).

Timerman, Jacobo: jewish   writer and
        , born   ukraine   1923. founder   liberal
newspaper *opinión*,   arrested   1977, held
        tortured   two years, ultimately released   the
junta,   banished   israel (thanks   carter).
    lived   write   ripe   age.
    1981,   a best-seller   expe-
rience   detention, *preso sin nombre, celda*   *número*.

Two French Nuns: bodies of sisters alice
        léonie   along   those of   others
(including mothers   )
dumped   allegedly   dec 8   dec
10, 1977,   found   later   atlantic shore.
        disappearance   two people   particular
"poisoned" argentina's relations   france
        last years   "dirty   (american nuns suf-
fered   fate   chile). thus,   curious
        one document   jan 20, 1978, u.s. ambassador
        castro (first mexican-american   governor
    arizona   1974, tapped   jimmy carter   replace
robert hill   argentina   '77), claimed
        following both   example   french gov-
ernment and   the church   not demanding
accountability   president videla   these and

disappeared victims. ultimately,   french did
bring the matter   justice: navy commander
astiz ("blond angel   death")   convicted
     condemned   life imprisonment   role
played   *"madres"* group   achiev-
ing   nuns'   other women's capture, torture,
murder. astiz, however,   not   go to france.
       stand trial   argentina, where   also ac-
cused of   navy mechanic school   a torture
center,   cleared.   may 7, 1995,
   buenos   (reuters) report, astiz   put up
promotion   enrique molina   , head
     argentine navy. pico,   days before
publicly repented   torture   murder   leftists
in   70s,   astiz as possessing "all the moral
qualities needed."

Videla, Jorge Rafael ("the   panther"):   october 27, 1975,   brigadeer general,
     , trained   world   II and   pillar
military   60s, authored   signed "the struggle   subversion" (army
404/75),   would become   war's blueprint.
         took power   march   , 1976,   videla be-
came president.   remained   chief (despite
challenges)   resigned   1981.

Zones of Defense: argentina   divided into IV
these corresponding   army's corps commands.
army directive 404/75   each commander
expected   "exert constant pressure,
time   space"   guerillas   own
region,   decide who   what   subversive
harmful to the "   being."

17

now reuben, thanks to life and reading, knew all of the above,

spotty, shot-through information,

instance of a gathering, which also slowly came through national security archives released (in 2002)

for all — including you — to see.

so, it's not hard to imagine why, after living and commit-
ting himself to retelling all of this, he never could go back to
writing with a "long view." he couldn't anymore write poetry.

no emotions recollected in tranquility,

nor fiction, nor play-writing, as he once thought he might like
to do. but at times, he still thinks he could or should have hung
his hat on such meanderings. and when he does, he remembers
maggie, and wonders what she's doing today.

blowing up this story, trying to begin.

she's still doing that, as she was back in those forgotten days.

18

i've found these strange writings from november '79. my first
stupid poems, "columbia collegiates"

trying to impress your father,

and all that. i was turning 24 and kept writing... poems... through the death of my warm professor, including one for you, ondine, in march 1980.

that one you must have lost,

though i still somehow had it two years later. for i remember hiding-showing it to jonathan in the spring of '82, the father of my (first) children to be.

  i had started writing stuff beginning in '79, though apparently had lost

just one (lost) poem (for) me,

and also tried (with no success) to capture and convey maggie's story. i have remnants of that and also of a few verses from the summer when you were no longer, scribbled in the apartment near broadway at 71st, while living with brigitte the next fall and spring.

  all this before the trip to israel with father and lise,

after which you wished to kill yourself.

  then the writing started up again, fall '81, once i moved in with the "bridge" into the "hearst" apartment on 101st: fancy, with a river view. then i stopped writing again, winter '82, no doubt to study (hard) for my orals, after which i met then married jonathan,

your first true...

and then with him, i really stopped:

put all your thoughts and troubles on hold.

wrote nothing but note cards for my thesis (26 to 28 years old),

and then?

well then, i wrote the blasted thesis and was transfixed by the love of andrew,

your first baby.

have you ever seen his gentle, shining eyes? i saw nothing but those till i was 30. but then it seems i took a break again, a break from

putting me on hold.

yes, i wrote again, reached out for you once more, one after-noon in the black apartment, i did do that, once i was done with writing my thesis, when andrew was a toddler, up and about. one june afternoon at age 30, the year before

angie came.

when my braces all came off, that summer in the black apart-ment, before i was (named a professor) and became promoted to the blue... and now, even though i've lost your tiny body

and the poem,

it's good to have records from those years before,

from the time i almost was...

and of my life as it unfolded then.

at first, so bleak and lonely in the studio window (106th), then slightly brighter in the neat one-bedroom (71st), around the time when reagan was elected and the corner where john lennon got shot. then on riverside and 101st, where i found myself perched above the hudson once again,

the water, the same, that breathed through me before

(when i was living before near GRANT'S TOMB). and i'm not sure what those final "first" poems were about, only that i was starting to get help, at last,

trying to come to terms with ending,

beginning to sort through the mess.

19

i'm guessing that this fragment was from august 1980, three months before you...

should have been born,

before i left 106th and moved to 71st. but it could have come somewhat later. written on the machine that wrote my thesis. mallarmé (mind and body) and only emptiness in between. here it is,

the first version?

of what we're writing here, transcribed

with slight corrections only.

Mariel's Home Journal

This is only the beginning of a record of a journey not yet taken. a venture into past and present, a projection of the future... who can say?

A recognition of my own responsibilities, a late and longed-for journey into the night with hopes and dreams accompanying, for a day and sunlight's witness when i will say and softly (to my little one) — Oh yes, I've been through times of revolution, and then I fought and conquered and I came into my own, whole as you see me before you, ready to love, give and receive, prepared as well as possible to live and to let live and prepared my darling daughter to pay the price of your priceless life. In order to give you life, I live, in order to give you room, to give you space, and for no other, diviner cause, but it is enough, I die.

And now, she backtracked into the present and the lingering thoughts that had come on her just the night before as she prepared for all the hardships of the journey.

These are bits and pieces of the thoughts she entertained, they seemed to her not unreasonable as they persisted through the day. Her fear of undefined death was by far the greatest, and most haunting that she knew.

If i sit and allow it to seep into me, penetrate my mind, it paralyses me absolutely. Only then, am I aware of being alive. Death is my dauntless enemy, but now for the sake of my life and yours to come, I'll look at it with a squarer eye… Oh! but how I shudder at the thought of it. But then a voice comes to me, a motherly one saying —

Little woman, do not do yourself such an injustice as to be cowardly and to refuse, by one mean or other of evasion, to look into black night and feel its horrid chills engulfing you, and touching into your bare little bones, unprotected, indeed. There's no putting off until tomorrow the nature of things which are unchangeable. Your recognition of this is a simple matter of bravery. You will not be the first to note this and unchangeable things will remain unchanged. But, take hope and courage to your side, for each man and woman is exactly that to the extent that he or she feels it to be so, and awful pending pains can be at will converted to extraordinary joys. Ask the one beside you if he has ever feared the dark. Own up to who you are: a living, breathing, fearing soul, you may find yourself in comfortingly good company. (here's hoping he will be beside me soon). *The superstitious evils of this world can be conquered and pure heaven is only the reflection of pure hell. But beware of this and learn it fast and well… No doctor, mother, priest or lover can save you from your fate, it is yours, lying in wait for your embrace… Pick yourself up and go, child, but carefully. It's better to be safe than sorry, haste makes waste.*

Ironically, procrastination was the sign post that Mariel most often came upon. Ordinarily, it read Turn Left, Road Narrows here (temporarily under construction), Danger Ahead. And one could hardly blame her for wanting to save her head. So, she lingered for hours, months and finally years, on the brink of construction, not wishing in her deepest heart to take the wrong road and too nervous and worn to forge ahead. She knew that any further step on firm, if not unfaulty,

grounds would demand a stark assessment of the present, and some measure of a backtrack as well, a brief
return neither loving nor nostalgic, to pick up some
necessary pieces. heal the wounds of the beginning, so
she could have the illusion of a freshness at the start...

As sleep glosses over night fears, changing altogether our attitudes, yet never changing facts, when all
that goes, goes as usual, and the sun rises personably
in the early hours of the morn... A new day, the next
one, demanded for Mariel, a semi-conscious diges-
tion, a recollection in dreams of the events of the old.

"Where exactly should I start this reverie?"

20

yes, that part was surely written well before these two,
dated december '81:

This story is about a story about a story that had
great difficulty in taking place, but which finally
(thanks to tradition) agreed to come to be. And the
first lady (in no way related to the President's wife)
was an airy-headed female, a vaporous creature of her
own imagination. How do you solve a problem like
Maria?

Who bothers these days to take a walk in anybody
else's shoes. The preceding are asides... The point, of
course, is the story about the story...

Born into the thickest of ambiences, Mariz went
mad with the lack of her own imagination and set out
to develop it by practicing other things.

To my sister on the eve of her 3rd born, with love and envy from me.

* * *

Merin dropped her book and ground her jaw. There was something about reading that left her feeling high and dry, so she decided to go and drown herself in the movement of the city streets below.

Her absent-minded musings on other people at other times, that exercise she was learning from *books*, didn't leave her disinterested or passionless for the present. She wanted to try out all those formulas on the world.

Dressing was a two-minute affair. She was lovely with no particular feature standing out, no definable traits... just sort of blankly pretty and always postponing the definitive stamp of character for the day she'd make her mark. This lack of specificity in her physique... was troublesome at times, made her feel vulnerable and insecure. but it gave her too an air of eternal possibility and youth.

This was useful, for the phone never rang at the right time. A penchant for superstition... made her take this as a sign — everything has meaning for an available mind. So, nothing keeping.

and then, of course, there's the end (?) of the straining fragment we began with —

that odd letter to your friend —

trying so hard to say what happened as opposed to

fending off what's not real.

it proves that maggie met reuben on a bridge… everything is there except the dialogue.

what sort of dialogue?

if it wasn't him throwing out crude lines, and i'm certain it was not,

he must have asked her a polite question.

this indeed seems confirmed in the text, for he opened on the subject of a building, and told her

HE WAS MARRIED *from the start:*

(~~something like out of the corner~~) A (~~beautiful looking~~) curly-haired blond man slowly made his way into her field of vision. He opened the conversation with some vague open-ended comment about Parisian architecture. She responded coldly. But seeing that he was ~~very beautiful~~ very fair and pretty cool, and relatively innocent looking himself — She also put in her / let slip/ slipped in a little smile. He introduced himself… Rudie with nordic eyes and a latin smile and asked if she'd mind his company for a while. Rudy was a refugee, a jew from Argentina. He looked ~~and sounded li..~~ so she had taken him for German. He claimed to be in search of a resting place for his *family,* which he had left behind. Looking for a ??? city or country to live in. And after the initial (and familiar) disappointment, on learning that this charming boy was not her ??? magic Prince… Merin became curious about the actual man. He was leaving that night for Barcelona. 11 o'clock train, he said. Would Merin spend the evening with him just for dinner? They two were strangers in a strange land.

21

reuben spotted maggie on the bridge. it was windy and the sun was just

beginning to fall, to set.

and full of all he'd been reading, he was beginning to feel ill. for here and now at last

the evidence was sinking.

his world, before, orderly gilded frames of mirrors, high wooden bedposts, sea-breeze blowing through the dark and polished rooms. now, cold metal, torn hands, pink-rimmed eyes, chaos spewing lungs and blood, till

something like a bubble… popped.

this is what was coming together as he stared down in the gray and muddy river, then cast his clear eyes upward toward the buildings, catching only for a moment on the patchwork steel.

maggie, meanwhile, had again that far-off look, projecting on the seine those vast golden seas, the waves that had engulfed her through the movie.

she was running in her head —
through the curtain of her hair,
the veiled screen of her eyes —
the beauty and enigma of free images

when reuben broke the spell

— *cuan preciosa... ¡esta arquitectura de paris!*

introduced himself

— *soy reuben de argentina...*

and asked her name

— *maggie... ¿margarita? ¿norte americana, verdad?*

and she

— *nací en mexico. mis padres son gringos (judíos americanos, polacos, irlandeses) pero mi papá sigue viviendo en sinaloa. ¿y tu? no me pareces sudamericano, pareces más aleman a mí*

and then he

— *mis padres eran de alemania*

back in the 30s they were refugees. now it was his turn... he had to leave, had come looking for a place to live in europe with his wife and little girl,

manuelita,

one year old. that night he would be leaving for spain.

— *¿has estado alguna vez en españa, margarita?*

yes, maggie had. with alba, a friend she'd made in france, a colleague from the basque country. in fact she'd just spent new year's eve there with alba's family, in vitoria. and she'd traveled around spain also the summer before...

— *¿quieres cenar conmigo esta noche, margarita?*

it would be nice to eat together, go somewhere nice, and just talk. reuben had to leave that night, had just a few more hours to enjoy the city in the evening. he was so happy she could speak spanish.

— *para hablar, nada más. sería bien para nosotros... hablar.*

22

they walk a while in the twilight, find plenty of things to say, then go inside a little restaurant: a simple, small, old-fashioned place, with few tables, a colorful waiter, white lace table-cloths. reuben orders wine, smiles a lot. maggie thinks he's super handsome, truly nice.

too bad he was married,

that crossed through her mind, too bad he was going away,

but she doesn't really mind,

just kind of goes along with what's happening, as usual, but in an unusually receptive mood.

they talk a lot about this & that. he asks her if she's in-terested in soccer, following the line-up for the world cup?

not at all, she says, doesn't know a thing... about sports. he asks her what she's doing in paris.

she tells him a few things,

a little about her job, teaching,

about the courses she's not following,

the university. mostly she talks about alba, her friend, from spain. tells him also all she likes about that country, especially the north, though she doesn't say a word about her travels there before,

nothing about the two-day lock up?

in a strange hotel,

the balding radio producer who hid her passport?

gathering her into the film festival in san sebastián. nor does she mention what she knows about the *guardia civil.*

nothing about the turkish jewel thief?

the gun to his head nor her nine hours sitting in a barcelona jail. she just tells him that she really likes spain. and after drinking a few glasses, reuben begins to talk a lot — about politics, something she's not yet figured out, saying (in span-ish) stuff like:

> *— margarita, did you know your country is backing the murder and torture of people in my country every day? the cia overthrew the president of chile in 1973, and now,   ar-*

gentina,   all over, americans
terrible corrupt things,   money   power.
      horrible regimes,   stop... com-
munism.   they say.
stopping democracy,   nothing to stop murder
and corruption — good,   people   killed
every day, murdered   thugs...   your
government   human rights!
talk   all the time.   ambassador   president, and   other clown,
all talk   all the time... and then behind closed
doors,   the other side —   people who have
taken over my country.   cia   taught
      knock people off,   steal and hide
people's money. and   american politicians?   give
other countries' corrupt leaders   money,   get
rid of   elected leaders,   leaders   the people want...
maybe you don't know this, margarita?
      great country, right?   believe me   not good at
all.   people   running
    really bad.

and then she...

  — i don't doubt it. but i don't... follow... politics.
      can't stand republicans,   i   like jimmy carter.
      against   death penalty.   other than
that? maybe   things   get better
true, i don't know   don't like to read
   news. i believe   what you say   but
it's not like you think   america. everybody   here
french especially, always telling me   my
own country,   what   americans are doing and
why. i heard about the coup   here in France

                got lectured   all the time,
by kids in my school. and i never doubted   bad
things   happening.   wa-
tergate was going on. and everybody knew our government
was full of crooks... but i   hate being lectured about
america, even latin america... that happens   all the
time. maybe that doesn't make sense to you.

                                                mexico,
        i was born there and i feel close,
            closer than   europeans.   same with na-
tive americans and blacks.   close to them, they're
of me, so i hate being lectured here. the french love to tell
me what it's like   be black in america, how we make
"indians" live. they don't know what they're talking about.
i know more about this than they do.   blacks in my
own family, reservations all around   that
for me is the ground...

and then he...

    — well, me, i'm not french, margarita, and i know what i'm
            about... maybe i should tell you   stories?
        what happened to some people who i know?   uncle,
        owns a newspaper,   whole neighborhood blown
out   a bomb.   friend of mine   tortured,
        tongue cut out,   because he wouldn't talk
        . another friend of mine,
got home from work,   found his wife   his
baby girl shot dead. and all of these people
good   , margarita, just like you and me.
trying to live their lives,   my government decided to kill
them, your government showed them how   now
        killing more   every day. i know you don't want
this, but it's happening,   margarita.

*— i know, i'm sorry. but what can i do? what am i supposed
to do?*

— just remember that it's happening, i guess.

23

maggie never changed her politics. she hardly even started
reading the newspapers, couldn't change the shape of her own
blank mind, but something still began to happen on that day.

something like a new emptiness,

and in that hole a new kind of feeling settled in. she felt sorry
for reuben, felt sorry with him, and didn't think: what did he
think about her? those stories of his must have

cracked the mirror,

established a bridge between them.

*— won't you stay with me tonight, margarita?
walk me to the train? wait until i leave?*

24

they headed slowly for the station right around 10, had a beer,
a few cigarettes. then maggie walked reuben to the *quai,*

to wave goodbye.

and she decided she would stay until he left — liked to see him
happy just to have her standing there...

but the time passed heavily.

so, now MONTPARNASSE, which had often seemed to maggie like no place at all (she'd trampled through the station many times before, pacing to and fro, running up & down to catch the escalator), began to take on air and depth, a heavy volume more and more steeped in silence. conversation dwindled to gentle, awkward words.

— *here we are*

— *what time is it?*

— *where's your seat?*

till finally reuben bid a quick goodbye and stepped into a moving darkness.

but the train stayed poised a few minutes more. so maggie fell back down,

sank within her stare,

looked hard inside the old, familiar emptiness.

she tasted what is bitter

on the surface of things, the flattening of all that happens, the settling back to lines and planes.

no fullness anymore,

no silence, no contact, no feeling. everything adjusted back into its place, *where nothing's ever left behind,*

nothing blurs or overspills the edges. but still she didn't wander off, nor absorb the boredom into her small bones. no, she
waited for the scene to change of its own accord, because she'd
made a small commitment

to be there, nothing more than this.

when lo (i guess), the fact of joining up her mary with her
martha (for a change) to stand for just a moment as a witness,

hold the space that shelters moving darkness,

but still attest to light through which we pass — this small
devotion — jerked poor reuben back outside his train. through
the corridor of tense and mounting time, he straightened in
his seat, stood alert, then bolted down the aisle, through the
open door, and took maggie by the shoulders on the platform:

> *— remember what i told you, margarita?*
> *the cut-out tongue, that friend,*
> *who found his wife, his baby girl shot dead?*
> *that's my story, margarita.*

a kiss, a leap, and he was gone,

gone with all that happens on the train.

maggie stood still, eventually sat down. began to measure up the time and all the weight of it. travelers scurried
by, carts with many bags. sometimes when they beeped at her,
she moved.

25

reuben came from argentina, not chile. he was 26. blond, curly-haired, and jewish. i know that now, but did i know that then? actually, i did, but i forgot.

his wife and daughter were cut off at the root.

and i'm guilty of that too... for being american and clueless. but why did he have to tell me in this slanted way? so i'd take his story on the bias?

that's what you're doing here?

yes, trying to figure out maggie and merin, mariz and mariel, as though they'd help me bring you back to life... it's like for once i felt that i was almost with it. like maybe i could help another leave some "demons" behind.

move aside impediments, get a brand-new start.

yes, reuben and me, we could have come out of our dream worlds (where we weren't in control) to a place where we could make connections. but then suddenly we found our-selves alone again. awake and empty-handed. ten times more bewildered than before.

but then instead of settling down

and thinking, taking time to clear a pathway through the mess,

you both just went on blindly with your lives.

since i was maggie, dumbfounded, waiting on the *quai*, i just

sat there stunned

till my usual ways of coping came back. and he, since he was reuben, he just

got back on that train,

because the train, at least, would be moving and was supposed to be his, though he didn't know where he should be going, nor why.

worm rotting from within, long-suffering without.

maggie and reuben were opposites. i knew that even then, and wanted to do something about it, but it took me forever, because

time works like this.

march 3 comes and goes. people live and die, shit happens, and we're left to interpret.

26

when it comes to maggie's story, one thing is clear, i should have tried to understand

the whole thing on the spot.

on that very day, i could have asked reuben for an address, written him a letter, learned to be a friend.

the road not taken.

proust said it all, faced with his madeleine (no doubt because he took some time to eat it), how we always shrink in front of any task. and me *you've shrunk so long from all our stories,*

there's hardly any meaning left. they might as well have never taken place. and yet, i'm glad i have

these remnants

of my fears.

proof of what you're trying to put off.

they show that

you've been struggling for a long time.

i have pictures from that time and

your memory's both good and faulty.

right on about the "jew from argentina," perfectly precise, the "11 o'clock train" (maybe i was wrong about the rain). and i got the movie right, IPHIGENIA.

human sacrifice.

what was that about? this girl was to be killed by her father, so the world could carry on with the war that was their lives. i've tried to look at that from both sides now, take the long and short view, but i never could make any sense of it.

the greek actress was beautiful, i remember that, as was the gold light pouring from the screen. some sort of tragedy, that was clear.

and layers of revenge.

for the butchering, i guess, of other children. and these trag-
edies go on,

that's for sure,

but the movie didn't seem "realistic."

you never found out much about it

cacoyannis '77, not distributed anymore.

why should you have?

it wouldn't have helped a bit with my exams.

27

the date of racine's play was 1674, molière wrote a play in
1659 (*LES PRÉCIEUSES RIDICULES*), marivaux we need not
even mention. 1569 for french theater? that's 32 years before
HAMLET, 35 before *MACBETH*.

perhaps i should try to see the greek film again, but who
knows when i'll track it down. what's important in the story's
only this:

it's a tragedy that ends well.

agamemnon, the king, hesitates. he's supposed to sail for
troy, avenge his brother, menelaus, get back helen, who was
robbed by paris.

but the winds won't take the ships to war.

so artemis, the virginal goddess of hunting, and

destroyer of mothers in childbirth,

asks for iphigenia's sacrifice, that is, the death of agamemnon's daughter, who was supposed to be marrying achilles,

who finally would be killed by paris.

meanwhile, clytemnestra,

iphigenia's mother and the daughter of a swan,

who eventually would slaughter agamemnon, and be butchered by orestes (their son, in return),

she and achilles are enraged,

don't think iphigenia, whom they love, should be the chosen one to die.

but the girl herself, she knows her destiny,

concedes her father can't do much about it, even if he tries. so, she lets him go ahead and hesitate, try but fail to revoke her sentence.

luckily, the fates finally do intervene

to provide a few good endings for the story.

28

in the first version by euripides, iphigenia was supposed
to be sacrificed, in order to keep things real, but then

euripides died.

so the play remained unfinished, till his son decided to complete it, with an original, mythological good solution:

artemis herself swoops the girl away
and leaves for the sacrifice — a deer!

racine's solution seems almost farcical by comparison,
though it's modern, both modern and realistic.

the verse is beautiful, flows throughout,

like an ocean or a never-ending river,

but the play has to end,

so, a strange sub-plot is built, one whose unknotting

borders on the dérisoire.

mirroring the miming of the tragic that happens in molière,
our poet shrinks the story down to something very human,
very petty,

a lovers' quarrel,

mixed-up identity, with a name switch for

another victim.

ériphile, the jealous lover and

slave, turns out to be

the not so good and pure iphigenia,

the one

who's meant for sacrifice.

she saves the day for all

(behind the scenes) by rising up to kill herself.

no end like that to help us with our story,

we're stuck here with your sacrifice.

29

i've learned my lesson as you're about to see.

morning of march 1st.

thank you for this day and snow,

storm that keeps you cozy with your children.

help me to see, feel, and understand that what's happening is just what always happens. i've been off track for a couple of weeks, but i can get back on. i've been way off (for at least three days), but i got back a bit yesterday and can do better today.

so there i was, perched at the end of february, like my usual self, having just swallowed my 49th birthday, but ready to go on, when i was

thunderstruck, again, and by the telephone.

9:00 tuesday morning. "it's very upsetting," our secretary said,

lee is in the hospital.

"i know he's close to you, very close to you and to your husband.
they don't know exactly what the problem is, but they're saying
it's something in his brain."

and you?

right away: "oh my god, yes, thanks for telling me," marching
straight upstairs to tell olivier, who then was tired and still
sleeping.

the poor thing, the poor dear.

"it's hit," i said, "lee,"

something in his brain,

his wife is with him in the hospital, and we must go. "we'd better go right now." so, we dress and i tell our little matt, who
says,

why does it only happen to the good ones?

and angie, she takes over caring for matt, for the whole day,
while olivier and i, we head straight for the hospital, like
i guess we always will have to do, with

you praying selfishly the whole way,

thinking: let it please be over, or please, god, let it be okay,
because i don't like facing

more bad news.

and i suppose you'd say my prayers were answered. because the minute we get inside, lee's wife is howling: "do you know what's going on?"

he's dying.

"and i have 15 minutes to decide."

have them do a surgery?

that might save his life, but will leave him paralyzed and speechless forever.

never again be able to eat or walk or talk.

completely paralyzed on the right — "and i've got to get the children to come…" and, oh my god, indeed, inside that 15 minutes, we too must take leave of our friend,

as his body, it really is twitching,

and while his wife is telling him we are also there, and asking him "what should i do? […] honey," and telling him again and again that olivier and i, we're beside him too.
 well, it looked like he was answering, nodding to say "yes." but then, for sure, he began twitching again, and the doctor said it wasn't possible, "he couldn't have been saying *yes*," and then he hooked him up to something serious: "a sedative," he said.

and then we never saw him twitch again.

for when they finally unhooked the life support, late on the evening of the second day, when all decisions finally had been made,

the surgery not taken,

to leave our friend, in what was painted in clear strokes to be
a nightmare,

full paralysis, and no communication, no food,

and ever the threat of it happening again.

any time, impending death might strike.

and what's the point of body once the brain-life's gone?
    well, then we were all told to get out of the room, if we
didn't want to see lots more twitching, to be left forever with
images of that... rather than with feelings and memories more
like this: reflections that i wrote the day after, the actual day he
died, after finding one second to mourn a bit and remembering
that we both wrote poems.

30

first, one of mine, inscribing just this date, the date of lee's
death. but written 41 years before we met. i wrote it in my
mind when i was 8.

    march 3

    today i will
    always remember
    said the child
    to the cold
    brick wall what
    ever transpires
    will not wipe
    away this mark
    that your name
    calls

and then i found one of lee's (from april '93) — a pretty ditty,
written just for me:

> stronger than a backbone is the green reedy stem
> when spring fills up tired winter's husk.
> when flowers' bright heads seek the rising sun
> troubled haze melts into perfect dusk.
> then right will redress every wrong
> and surety banish doubt.
> then every bit of emptiness
> all will be emptied out.
> — r. l.

a response, that was, to a few lines of mine (from march '89),
answering a "query" on grace.

> you ask my dear what
> is this thing called grace?
>
> it brushes daily
> colors on my face
>
> and whistles to
> the wind fantasies
>
> worlds of thought
> reshaped in boundless space
>
> feel the softness pouring
> that is grace

31

all questions felt like answers then. which isn't to say (now)
i understand why, when i was just about to write your story
— say, why not lock down what was meaningful

about what happened long ago?

— lee shoveled his last snow, and then died.

just like that, to call me back,

out from the past to today... where small and selfish, faced
with this computer, i still have to say:

LEE

i long to see you again

even if it must be in nightmares

in dreams beyond light

even with your baby blues
rolled back inside their sockets

your slack chin and everything
lain low in your gawky self

all your spirit so readily transcended
yes even in that last false form

how i long to see you again

32

if i'd only had the courage, i'd have seen lee through. stayed to see his body twitch its last twitch. i'm sorry that i didn't. amen.

but, LEE, you should also know that i don't regret, even though i might have been terrible (and god might punish me), leading the way (with my big mouth) in letting it be okay for your wife to let you go, so that we,

all of us,

could actually let you go, not have you hanging around here (forever), in that horrible state, the hospital bed. that's what they were saying: you could be lying there for years, just lying flat,

with nothing ever more, but maybe just enough

to feel the kind of pain you'd be in. miserable and paralyzed, and never able to speak, to say, or communicate a thing.

so, yes siree, i opened my big mouth and said, if it were me, i'd want to

go fast,

and thought that's how you'd want it too. and the way it went was

pretty much like that,

considering, from the minute the phone rang, praying:

let it just be over or let it be okay

what else was i supposed to do?

maybe you could have just let it be,

or kept my big mouth shut, which annoyed lee more than once... but, oh well, i didn't. amen.

33

LEE,

THANKS FOR CALLING ME.

TWO WEEKS AGO. NOT FOR THIS OR THAT. BUT INSTEAD JUST TO SAY "HAPPY BIRTHDAY." I REMEMBERED ALL YOURS TOO. (53, THAT'S ALL YOU HAD.)

AT LEAST, YOU WON'T HAVE TO WORRY ABOUT DEATH ANYMORE (THAT REALLY STINKS) CAUSE YOU'VE ALREADY "GRADUATED," LIKE STEVEN, MY BEST PAL FROM CHILD-HOOD, SAID, WHEN HE WAS GOING TO DIE OF AIDS (AT 39).

HIS NAME WAS REALLY P — THE WAY YOU CALL MY BOY FOR LAUGHS — WHICH BRINGS ME BACK TO THE *NAME* THING AGAIN, AND TO WHETHER I SHOULD USE REAL ONES, FAKE ONES OR INITIALS? AND WHEREVER THE COAST'S NOT CLEAR (BECAUSE THERE'S NO CLEAN SLATE) DECIDE IT'S O.K. TO WRITE FICTION.

HOW TO SORT IT OUT? THAT SOMETHING SACRED IN THE NAME. A STUMBLING BLOCK, I'M RESOLVED TO TWIRL ABOUT.

GOODBYE MY DARLING LEE,

I'M GOING TO GO AND REST, REST NOW WITH O. BUT YOU CAN KNOW WE BOTH LOVE YOU TO PIECES. LITERALLY. WE LOVED YOU TO PIECES.

34

yes, i'd have rather been killed off or just left to die, than be saved to stay a vegetable (forever). or so i thought the day lee died, but then matt said,

nuh-uh, mom, you wouldn't,

and added "if you or someone else were about to die, you wouldn't want to give your life either. you might want to give *some* of your life for somebody else, but not all of it." and maybe he was right but today

you don't have to deal with it.

and yet, a question i (still) have is: whether or not, if i were (as lee was), would i have wanted to be saved by an operation likely to leave me paralyzed, speechless, unable to feed myself? the answer is: no,

you think you wouldn't.

not want to be made to live at such great cost... to myself, ol-ivier, and my children. that (i think) is my honest answer and my conscious (most courageous) will.
next, would i have pulled my life support so quickly?

no sense in prolonging the misery.

and paid so little attention to the lingering body?

there you might have done things differently.

yes, i would have wanted things done differently for me, and would have liked for somebody to stay with lee,

to help him pass through living dying.

35

will someone stay with me till my body's laid to rest?

would you like it to be burned or buried in a box?

i'm pretty sure i'd like it burned,

turned into ashes and to air.

for what's the point of hanging on to bones underground?
i wouldn't want my poor wrecked body to have to go back
out and be smothered in that form, alone and in some lonesome prairie. better

ashes, dust to dust, express.

and i hope lee (like later pop and lise) didn't have to watch,
or feel, or dread in any way the burning... as happened in the
awful nightmare i had (a few days ago, months after lee died)
waiting to be cremated at the hospital, when scared to death,
i was, by marco's death,

another friend's death,

and the handling of his dummy dead body at the wake, when
it was laid out, pumped up, for all to see,

dummy in a box,

which we then escorted to the crematory chapel. but a good
thing was: my flower dropped on top,

a touch of yours to mix with his,

to send to heaven with the smoking box.

yes, waiting to be burned would be terrible. but the burn-ing would be over pretty quick, whereas that rotting under-ground would last for years…

i'm sure i'd rather not be a body, than be stuck six feet under in a box.

but a spot to remember in a field of green?

that sounds nice to me. maybe like we did with our dog mis-chief, his buried box of ash (next to: lise's purse, her purse inside of mine), or maybe also a little sprinkled, and a little buried, better yet…

a sprinkling of your dna to mix with olivier's

on someplace marking all of us were mingled here, so that our spirits (once gathered)

will be happy to come back.

36

so it seems, despite reservations, lee's wife, she did the best she could. i heard the doctor say: "you don't really want to see the agony," the reflex twitches of the body. and for sure, i could see why she didn't. and me,

it wasn't your place.

and maybe i couldn't do that either for my own most dear, but guess i would want someone brave enough go through that for me.

olivier is brave.

he tended to his own, tender dressed his father's body.

i'd have wanted him to stay with my body at the hospital. and i'd also want: my children to see the difference between me, living, and my body, dead.

but lee's children didn't want to be beside his body any-more. if they did, they would have asked. and this was not (in the end) about lee's wife. she was not alone and she did all she could. she loved him. (yeah, yeah, yeah). she said so — and painted him so truly at the service, pointing out to me what only she could know,

LEE,

she said you thought your hands were beautiful. so, i kissed them at the end, like

I KISSED YOUR DYING FEET.

couldn't figure out what else to do.

37

if only you could take some time to mourn. i'll do that again by looking at lee's poems. if anyone should ever miss me, i'd want them to read my poems. a remembrance of me, of the way i felt, and of something i thought worth remembering.

ondine, when you first died, i wrote for you

a poem

but then

you lost it, just like you lost me.

and when lee first died, i thought, i'll take care of his poems, that could help me *tend better to your own,*

but in truth i just recited two (for others) and instead spent my spare

breath writing messages.

sputtering:

DARLING LEE,
WON'T YOU PLEASE COME BACK?
IS IT POSSIBLE I WON'T SEE YOU AGAIN?

and around that time, often waking in the night, i was visited, at first, by

that loud ringing in his ear,

and the fear he had of death, and so on.

later he returned more like himself,

living and loving in dreams.

38

can you learn from this not to be afraid? even if it did scare me. death is part of life. can come at any time, which is scary. but once

death comes,

it's not at all (like father used to say), "that's it. you're dead, you're gone," it's over. instead there are aftershocks,

for you and everybody else.

and so, it's not right, as father always did, to just go furiously onward.

when i spoke to him about his brother's death (my one dear uncle, ron), he was hurting still, and he was angry. he didn't come back east to mourn his brother, nor to comfort the wife he'd left behind. and yet he still had the nerve to be furious with me because i'd dared years before to

tell the truth

and did it in a way that hurt him: "a surprise" letter, he said, that arrived on his 70ᵗʰ birthday.

i didn't foresee he could get the message that way, but it was the month of march, and during a hard time, when mainly

you were thinking of yourself.

but then the pain, i guess, of losing his closest kin, first his only brother, then his mother too, eventually softened that anger up a bit. for it was after i wrote to him one more time, telling him my sorrow for him when his mother died, that he finally wrote me back, and said this time

he was sorry for the troubles he had caused you,

and hoped that we might work things out. so perhaps i should find that precious letter...

mom, forget about the letter.

it's pictures you want more?

pictures, i want pictures.

39

o.k. i'm remembering wide streams. there's me, brother joe and catalina, joe's wife, and together we're receiving

"pop"

even as we're planning (once again) a swimming-pool sur-prise party. and we've all decided what would be best: a kind of festive breakfast, which we thought should be at 8 or 9. and though this was organized near an outdoor pool, we were also somehow here

back east

talking amongst ourselves and on the phone. whereas pop, well, he was sitting in the corner,

kind of sick,

saying that he had to fly to italy.
    and he was asking me to get him water, or some such thing, and starting to cough up a lot of blood. so i knew he was dying, and i wanted very much to help, or

love him,

and perhaps i really did. for i threw my arms around his neck. and at first, it seemed

he'd love you back.

but then

his hands went

again for my underpants, so i was furious (in turn), and

you slapped him very hard.

so he coughed up lots more blood, and was left with bloody
gums, but no teeth. so, then i

went to tell

the whole thing to joe.

40

and what do you know, on my way to see joe, i again crossed

pop.

but this time he was looking younger, a very lean and handsome man, sort of blonder than i think he ever was, but
otherwise

he looked… like you.

and he was holding joe, who was back in the size of his
second- or maybe third-grade picture.

pop was holding him

close, and hugging him, inside the truck. and i thought, wow,
him, he really loves.

look how he loved his little joe.

41

and then i found myself sleeping in a strange house. and i had a lot of blood, my period. i walked down the hall because i had to pee,

behind a stand of trinkets

that the host was selling. a nice blond lady, the mother of three girls. and there i tried my best to

get rid of the blood,

and the lady, she was really kind about it, hospitable in every respect. but still i decided to leave, began

leaping and flying

through the neighborhood, house to house (through fancy lower floors and finished basements),

trying never to be seen,

till at last, heavy, i sat up.

42

and here's another picture, quite negative, that i took of lise last night. i can't remember where, but i know she too was younger. about 40, i'd say, the way she looked around the time they fixed my heart.

when you turned 4, she was 39.

there she was, young and pretty, and looking straight at me,

lise wanting something with her pretty gray eyes.

she was suggesting something, or maybe asking me for some-thing. but i just couldn't

do it,

and that made me feel sad. i wish i could remember what she wanted. but i can't.
      must be time (again) for me to think about lise.

why do you resent her so?

is it because of the neglect, or

the betrayals?

when she always seemed to take the "other guy's side"?

your father's side, or that of less familiar men,

that of jonathan, of any of my exes' or whoever's. or was my resentment for her own sharp judging? you shouldn't feel this way or that, she often said, which i apparently dosed up to angie last night. and yet, i think

it's none of that.

instead, it's just i'm angry because

you can't be sure she loved you.

she never threw her arms around me, held me tight, nor said: dear, darling, honey, i love you oh so much. never said: you're the greatest, i'm so proud of you. you're so beautiful, so smart, and all that stuff. and she never got angry at me either, never said: how could you hurt my feelings in this way, or how dare you do that terrible... yourself.

and yet you think she might still love you,

because she showed a dogged attachment, and i know that she approved of me,

in such and such a way.

but i never felt outpouring affection, nor the calm trust that i would be enough,

that you could mean the world,

just because i was her little girl. what i imagine it is to be a mother,

what you want that to be,

she never was to me, nor i think to any of her children. whereas father, he, with all his stupid crimes, shortcomings,

pop who was mean and who always spat on love,

was perhaps a bit more like other fathers,

despite all of her efforts and devotions.

how can such unfairness be?

43

"she has no feelings," father always said. how ever did that come to be?

maybe you should ask him,

if things keep moving as they should, if he keeps growing kinder with the weight of years... in the meantime,

work with what you have.

lise, she was: beautiful, powerful. also, very smart and am‑bitious, a devoted, hard worker. how else could she have raised six children while holding down a full‑time job, and catering to the wreck that was pop.

other men, she told me, liked her. one wanted even to marry her, but she didn't (younger) want to be with other men.

your father, from the time she was twelve.

it was later in life (around 50), when father left, that she (out of vengeance?) looked to other men, but she

still put father on this pedestal.

always held him high, and lowered herself compared to him. she told me once, she did not like sex, and gave the feeling off she didn't want it, including with father, or maybe especially with him. but perhaps there's something screwy in that story. maybe instead she did like sex, and maybe even with father. but perhaps they went about it in a wrong, humiliating way, with feelings that they somehow could not mix.

maybe they were incapable together of good feelings, feelings of love for each other and for sex,

and

the miracle that comes from

children.

lise didn't want those, but he did.

they had six.

so maybe sex became a nightmare, but she decided that it
wasn't, so everything could be okay.
    whatever the problem, lise,

she hated her own body,

although she was beautiful and knew it.

she had the same mind-body split that you have,

but maybe even worse. to me she once said, and i remember
this, when i look

in the mirror,

i hate who i see, i know there's a

beautiful

woman in there, but somehow

you can't get to her.

44

maybe she needs help to find her beauty. or maybe i need help to get her back there. why not look (a moment) at how she thinks,

study a couple of her poems.

okay, i've read a few, with ellen's too, and it's hard because of who they are, which leaves me thinking... am i me?

pictures — i want pictures.

okay, if you insist, a scene from... chad.

one for all,

a nuclear explosion.

express yourself,

get in touch with

who you are,

am i lazy or just too frightened? today, perhaps, afraid of what some dr. says... even though

it's not a test.

i'll show you how i hate the feeling of expectant fear.

powerful last night,

like literally bursting from my sleep, but i remember. the scene
was chad:

that feeling underground

of an immense, developing explosion. that was coming and
the sense that this was *it*.

this the end, an old fear that.

and who knows just when the other shoe will drop?
    why should i be at peace this morning? i mean, it's not like
all is right in this world. so how am i supposed to

give strength off to your children, gird yourself,

in the midst of this dangerous swirling,

whose natural life now seems at risk.

45

well there's no making do, as far as i'm concerned, no hope,
except for

loving, god, and me.

yes, there indeed is where i want to go. the way to go, the only
help. and such a thing is here caring for our souls.

whoever wished us ever to exist

will help in our hours of need. who knows if i'll be jumping
up to heaven one day, or am just making room for

all your children,

you, who i destroyed, and my grown ones left behind,

watching over us, that's what you think of heaven.

and when i picture paradise, it's just that teeming place,

a place you've felt at times on earth, in nature,

which i don't understand, do not have to understand, just am

connected through the universe.

that's when i'm happy to be yours and all creation's and know
that death is not a threat.

for whether the body rots

slowly in the ground

or burns to ashes

in a sealed box,

it's not the whole of us

that goes by the way, but

just an old part,

the dead part, making room

for something new.

46

here's a picture (poem) lise once wrote. i like it, for it shows: feelings.

> *cremation*
> *(to bob & dr. josie)*
>
> it was a clean picture
> and one of hard surfaces,
> enamel⁄white, with bone chips,
> and an altar rock for worship
> against a hard⁄edged hill.
> hard edge on the beleaguered heart,
> hard clarity of will and act,
> hard line between our shadow and her light,
> and no deception.

the poem is quite upsetting and frightens, although

it's beautiful in its own way.

it says what lise always thought. life is life. death is death, and there is

nothing but hardness in between.

was it about the burning of bob's (adoptive) mother, dr. j? or about the two of them (bob and dr. j) burning,

with your mother as a witness,

a pet, the dead body of another dear one: "her"? perhaps in a makeshift, backyard crematory?

if the poem's about a pet, then there's just the fact of death, and love, and burning life. there aren't any images, nor figures.

everything is what it says, nothing else.

but if the poem speaks of the burning of dr. j? then lise felt life and death here somewhat differently, even though she'd not admit that to herself.

the poem presents itself as an offering,

which means the poet felt there still was someone she could give her feelings to,

a spirit that could linger,

and inspire lots of metaphors. the altar "rock" for worship, and the hard-edged "hill" evoke an ancient, natural space, replacing the awful, modern oven.

and where there's metaphor there's magic,

because despite their double truth, they still present "no deception."
one thing for sure,

your mother, just like you,

felt the burning of her loved ones to be hard.

the word hard?

full fathom five. five times in this little poem. so here we have proof, mom she always held

a hard line about death.

and that made it hard for her to be so near. i wish somehow that i could have helped her. helped her with the hardened horror of death, her bitter, repulsed attitude toward the hard-edged end of life,

which is infecting your own body now.

47

lise always frightened me terribly in truth. but i remember

as a child,

when i would have my usual nightmares (axe beheadings and the like),

you'd be allowed inside her bed, beside her body,

to go and snuggle up behind her, as long as father wasn't there.

her big, safe body, with its back always turned,

just like i do mine. i turn my back when sleeping with my children.

so that you can breathe?

the children cling like cubs, the mother bears. contact, close contact is needed. but somehow,

mothers too have to breathe.

so now again my mother's back... she always comes back. that's why

you're still attached to her somehow.

48

and here's a picture from my own dark past. when i woke up this morning, hovering over me, céline's face,

the same that gazes out of that old photo

where eugène, heavy-lipped and heavy-lidded, is staring at me, fixing on my eyes (or lips?).

ionesco, the playwright,

drunk and tired, with tremendous bags under his eyes,

looks like he's considering your thoughts.

whereas, i am just a profile: pale, flat, roundish face, dark neat brows with speaking, parted lips,

a lit-up face,

confronting this great man's sea of shadows. my hair is goofy, curly, cut. my clothes quite seventies-ish, but

your questioning eyes have brought his to attention.

looming over us, céline, pretty, sultry, is giving him the *look*, and grabbing the attentions of all viewers. "who's that?" each one says, while another puckish face, peeking from behind, smiles on with honest admiration. no question then we all had spunk.
and the scene?

an emblem of your youth,

mixed with confrontation and resentment. this photo, where my name's replaced (cathleen's on the back), was hanging in

lise's kitchen, gathering up the grease, till i grabbed it back
and claimed it for my own.

typical of your place in the family.

ionesco and me, the one photo of anyone that had historic
worth, till grandma edith found her beef & theo signed his pat-
ent (behind bill clinton), shoved as far as possible from view.
it was taken early on at columbia — perhaps within the
first two weeks. i arrived through the back gate of the great
divide: squeaked through with a fellowship despite math g.r.e.,
landed before sunrise near laguardia, then lined harlem in a
yellow cab.
once i dropped my bags inside the house on 123rd, i entered
through the service gate, the driveway that leads behind the
substandard gym. and i was sooo happy. i had the feeling that
i'd made it then.

49

but fields of darkness tracked you there.

the same that had always been. desperately alone,

your eyes were still half-shut,

no correction of my vision... till i was 26, nor sense, precise,
of just what i was

missing,

but now it all comes back

inside

my dreams.

50

how i wished i were céline, who was

never alone like me.

no, she was married to an american actor. so, when she got
divorced, in the second year, everybody felt... sorry for her.

and it mattered when she dated

cathleen's lawyer-friend, not the one i liked, but his best friend,
a twin: cool and smart and funny, and not interested in me
(too short, too fat, too much from arizona?), the lawyer

who made the sharpest cracks

on the garden state: newark's power plants, its finest flowers.
he always went for europeans, finally marrying a dutch girl,
i think. i felt decidedly inferior in cathleen's law-school clan,
because i never had a normal boyfriend, whereas cathleen
(like most) had one all along.

you were lonely and "so pretty,"

but couldn't make things stick.

and all the ones you had

wore strange stripes.

renzo, a 28-year old italian teacher,

when i was 16, to help me out of my affair with my "père au
pair." then back in arizona, at age 17,

kadir, the first boy you brought home, from libya,

who raped and beat me two years later, when i rejected, one
more time, his last proposal. and then,

*jamshid, who you loved, that gentle soccer player, drinker, smoker
from iran.*

with him i also tried cocaine.
    we stayed in touch at least three years, but he dropped me
when i asked him "please don't come to live with me quite yet,"

or perhaps because he learned you killed me?

yes, we broke up over your abortion, when i told him

my father, he was lebanese.

still, i managed to feel jilted when jamshid finally called it
quits, even though we both had always "seen" others.
    and there were other transitional relationships,

*ray, you'd dragged from france, and madison, the preppy, chinese-
speaking banker.*

yes, a waspy american, that one was (with a father killed in
vietnam). but mostly i liked european (french, italian, greek),
north african, and middle-eastern men,

with lots of latin dates between.

only kadir for a single, "steady" boyfriend, till i married jonathan,

a perfect match,

father and husband rolled in one.

51

maybe something cursed in my appearance? pretty, but flawed, the gap between my teeth

  not for keeps.

or perhaps, the way i behaved? anyway, the faces of my grad school friends, who had all glommed onto a better half, were looming over me this morning, making me feel rotten, reminding me of times

  even worse.

like when theo'd dated all my friends in college, and finally married ruth, who he met at nora's place.

  the girl-who-said-she-loved-you?

yes, and ruth was only there because tod, her date, had wanted to be with me.
  but tod was just a regular american boy, way too nice for sliced-up me. i wanted to conquer strangers, or mean or married men, let no one ever touch me who was "nice."

  but your sisters?

they had boyfriends, everyone did except for me.

  short-circuiting with boys?

that started back in high school, i guess, around the time i was leered at and pawed by

  drunken pop.

the first boy i blew it with was a senior in my school, a hot shot in the same ballet company as me. he asked me out when i was 14. if i hadn't let him touch me where he wanted on that date (or maybe if i'd acted like i liked it?), he might have called me up again.

boys i liked, i'd hurry up and give them what they came for, then be sad, and watch them run. if they didn't, i stopped liking them. so, all would end up losers or abusers.

something in there still hurts.

but miracles occur, somehow all that changed when i got married, though the underlying fear and

feeling's still the same.

give the other none or too much power. whoever i look up to can trample on my heart. that's why in dreams

you're always losing

olivier.

52

let's have a shot of dry earth. i felt something there,

you always feel,

when moving from the cold-conditioned airport to the hot blast of the parking lot. the ground swells up and bakes you.

home again,

where everything strikes right on the skin. the desert makes you peel, then penetrates with *shocks of heat, caresses of cool breeze,*

that treat you from the outside in.

so, heading down from phoenix on the empty road, in the giant suburban, with bare land all about, it was great to stop and go, not in the usual highway spot, but inside a true pima or papago store. despite all the poor corralled in there, abused, obese for lack of means. it felt better to confront this scent of poverty,

a close-to-the-earth, yet clean scent,

than the grimy, rotten, cockroach one that lines the east.

and the desert got more interesting as we approached the ring,

the mountains that surround,

till we finally crossed to tina's and let ourselves in, where (minutes after) ellen pranced in, with her usual big splash (sexy heels, silvery hair, and flowers on her butt). there was no one there to greet us till she charged through the door (to where she's now increasingly at home).

tina's house is beautiful,

commanding quite like her (statuesque) with luke's and others' colors, shapes surrounding.

it's wide open like its own majestic desert.

come on in, it says, even when there's no one around. as though

what's here's been left behind for everyone.

the ground, the sky, the toughest plants.

53

doesn't matter if you walk all over tina's house, cause what she has (a lot) was bought for everyone,

whereas ellen

has a different attitude,

carves her own small space,

california-style, closing off a room that is her plot. trying to control the borders: "me, i'm growing too," she states, "so this is also mine, and you may or maybe cannot use it, at least you must consult me first."

they really are opposites, your sisters,

even though they're much alike.

did you touch the earth a moment?

yup, on the second day.

running up and down the street.

though it was way too hot to run. the sun beat down, harder and then harder, with andrew and angelina accompanying, splendid, one ahead and one behind, my own two feet finally trodding native dirt between.

and the first day, or the night, before?

nothing. but sinking into tacos and refried beans, except the fleeting pleasure of *hearing berta,*

who took me on her bicycle to my first dance

the daughter of ana-laura,

the restaurant owner who used to be our cook in mexico, and
wife of father's foreman (on the ranch), saying:

maia, you never change,

"look at that face." and the even rarer pleasure of

seeing marisol

(berta's younger sister), who still seems

nobler, prouder,

than her older siblings, more ethical, like when she was a kid.
and heartening too, in that happy dinner scene, there was

kano,

my handsome nephew,

the long-road-taking

violin teacher. he came in late and ate up all our

leftovers.

for some reason, that felt nice.

54

no memory of greeting parents, except that lise looked cheerful, happy, while "pop" also acted... nice, suggesting we "step
back," so he could see us better.

and the next day?

after running in the morning, there was the business of getting
a computer, and also of copying

my picture,

you in the form of the five-year old that lise was once.

mom, be honest, if it weren't for that, you'd have forgotten...
me, you always leave behind.

and yet, i'd packed you in, had you safe with me, ondine, took
your papers there in the pouch.

but did you think about me, ever?

not much, you're almost right, and i know it's not enough, but
when copying that photo, i did think of you. and also when i
saw you in luke's painting. i even bought you in that form. let's
have a look at our new painting. you see, ondine, it's beautiful
like you.

hmm. oh yes, i like it. a portrait by luke of me. and i like it even
better since andrew said it looks like... you. i'm glad you finally
told him about us. see, he got the whole situation... even pointed
to camille (who made and sang LE FIL) as another who could be
my father's.

yes, for i also found and showed him a picture of nadim, who's now a big-shot banker in the middle east.

55

and the party out there? sure, i'll tell you about that. it was… something,

> *fine.*

the hugest storm, the streets were running high, with rivers from

> *a flash flood,*

like the ones we used to have in august, hitting now before the first of june. after all-day heat

> *the swimming pool, breakfast in the shade, then helping out with cooking,*

all day long, looking like i'm holding to the task. kind of going through the motions with catalina, olivier, and joe, cutting, thawing out, and rolling: burritos, tamales.

> *your body was there, your arm moved back and forth, while orders came from someone else's mouth.*

my face in an accepting smile, saying, i'm not into this, i'm not good at that.

> *thank goodness you were not in charge.*

but i wanted to keep my end of the deal. i could be doing this, or maybe some of that, with equal ineffectual skill.

it doesn't really matter what you're doing,

since i was only there to do my time.

    one thing sure: without my passive, petty preparations, the party would never have taken place. and it did seem to

please the parents in a way.

they were surprised, and yes, perhaps even moved, that lots of people cared for them, appreciated all they had put out.

two brothers missing: theo and luke.

they didn't want to play, which means forget about yourself: punch in, pitch in, submit to family rules.

and tina, and ellen?

they weren't in charge, and not yet used to that. so, though they were there, their clocking in was minimal. they just showed up, a little bit before, and stayed minutes after. that was all they had. whereas we,

you and joe, you brought the whole thing off.

we wanted to do something, that was half the game, with our true spouses for support. and the party like the trip was short (which was good).

the heavens were clearly for it.

the big storm: an hour or so before, though nothing much before that or after.

blam, kaboom, the rain poured down, and the family house fell apart,

water racing around the floors, fountains piercing through the walls. a flood,

and then a kind of… miracle.

everybody drenched and wondering: should we really swim around and decorate? or drudge through just to cross the street?

eighty people came with all shoes off,

and the whole party staff: soaked to the bone, especially joe, olivier, and all the men folk.

then the sky cleared and lise showed up,

according to the plan, tentatively stepping through the (back) front gate, and we all said

surprise! we got you, mom!

and i guess she was surprised, for she looked really confused, even if she had suspected something.

and pop?

well i doubt he could ever be surprised, and am sure this time he wasn't, because he

stopped on the way to pee like a dog,

as if somehow on cue.

so, you all had to say "surprise" twice…

since, as usual, he was tending to his body.

water spurting through the walls, father pissing on trees.

these, the stories of my life.

56

did anyone say something special? sure, father did,

pop, kind of drunk,

but not so drunk he didn't mean it. a weird look of gruff sat-
isfaction in his eyes:

*never thought that you'd amount to anything, not till you came
back from france.*

"you surprised me then," he said, "surprise me now, have never
stopped surprising me since." a well-considered diss and com-
pliment emerging from a cloud of alcohol & smoke.

but what exactly did he mean?

i ought to ask him when he's sober. but for now, i'm going
to rest, close up shop, go back to look for you, bright curl,
in nature:

i went empty to the river
and what did i see?

concentric circles
reaching for the breeze

called back patience
reminding trees

(cheerful toddlers
tumbling on the path

benevolent mothers
fish beyond the grass

reassuring cardinals
baby squirrel aghast)

wait till all effects ease

57

20 years to live. what happened in the last? i'm kind of antsy to be turning 50. i don't mind the big number (sort of like "looking" for my age), but if i am lucky, there won't be many more.

20 years ago, i would have been 5, and you already had andrew.

the joy of my first baby, yes! and i was busy, finishing my thesis (still a year before i was through) with jonathan, settled, living in new york. but still, i had my braces on. my 31st birthday had happened in new york, while i was

pregnant once again, with angie (in the blue t-shirt dress), daily swimming laps inside the pool.

a regular then of columbia's substandard gym. so, in fact, that was a long time ago.

after came a new era, with angie born,

and everybody coming to new jersey (time marks more with change of place). so my 32nd came nearer to us now, here in the garden (state), though then in the quiet, stream-lined house, where

she, your darling girl, was just a babe in arms,

and my life-long job was brand new.

you met olivier,

and then, that summer, things went swinging out of kilter.

you saw the moon,

and met again my brother luke. twelve years had passed since i had seen his face. and then i totally lost my bearings, almost had two love affairs (one with music, one with art), and

started writing poetry for real.

then, olivier (the first conversation, december '88). we sat down at that xmas party,

and your life began to go helter-skelter,

with that old codger phil (less ancient than i am now) stalking me as i turned 33. and that summer,

olivier's first love poem,

in june '89,

shot right through your heart,

so when he pulled out of his marriage through the next fall,
the tide turned, and

the shit began to hit the fan.

58

there's nothing worse than hurting somebody you love,

waiting to leave someone who needs you.

that, without a doubt, was the worst of times, misery from
the new year till august, when jonathan and i split apart. and
things stayed horrid well after that too, horrendous for a long
while.

and meanwhile, olivier

stuck with me, through and through, was willing to deal with
all the muck that stuck to me before, which we all climbed
out of eventually: me and him and even jonathan, once robyn
came back (around),

everybody landing safe and sound?

i guess not, but so i'd thought, though all felt terrible down
there, or should i say, back then.

time goes up and down or sideways?

and there's no use hiding or forgetting that. of course (of course?), we did the best we could, but the truth for me and jonathan was heart-wrenching.

like any love's ending, like any splitting apart,

and this trickled down,

making children

afraid to love too.

59

but here's a picture of more returning fears…

hey lee,

when i called your house, to touch base with your wife, it was so eeerrrrie to hear your voice, like you were still just there, when in fact you were supposed to be nowhere. i want to know

what happened to those ashes?

have they yet been spread on merry grounds?

and what will happen to your own?

20 years is nothing. one shouldn't expect more. 70 make up a rich and full life. 50, not so bad, i have always felt this in my bones. so lucky to be making it to 50. three splendid living children,

just me lost along the way

one good, then happy marriage (one decent divorce), nice career, teaching.

you even wrote a lot,

whatever i want, still do.

60

what's to be done with all that writing? finishing, polishing,
binding, that takes time, and i

still don't know what to do with it.

and if anything should happen now, it would be horrible to
slug through the mess. so i'm trying here to be responsible,
sort out the widow's mite, meager good, from all that bad.

keep track somehow and finish what you start.

when i gave birth to andrew, and was for the first time
filled with joy, i thought: i'll get to have him 40 years, thinking
i would live till 68...

*ok, ok, enough of those accounts... where was i when you last
went off to france?*

we had signed our wills in june, the day before we left, and
then, all of a sudden, there i was, in papi's room (which, once
restored, accepted gentle light), writing back to you from
france. and yes, even then,

half that new light through,

i couldn't think of you.

still nothing on your mind, except for dodging — food.

does that mean my mind was empty?

this is how you lose your place.

don't know what to do. my direction disappears, must be hit-ting on a thing that blocks it.

learn to search integrally, look into it.

61

in the meantime, here i am, yes, in france, in the very room where papi died. in a room with: YOU. and i was thinking all last night, how awful certain memories must have been, of him connected with this room. for his loved ones knew just what happened to his body. the white line, the gasp, olivier's careful dressing with clothing chosen by mamie, and then

the garbage bag.

so different from what happened to lee… who knows, who knows what's best for cast-off bodies?

so it's better if you just write to me,

ask you to come and help me, like before,

ask me to watch over all your children,

let them grow happier every day… the point is that we won't abandon

living, feeling, thinking what could be or could have been, no matter how i'm weak or often fall,

everyday advancing into darkness,

help me learn to die yet keep on living, till all can see a lasting

light.

62

before rome

the usual antechamber
of life a delay
the arrival of baggage
somebody else's

in countries that spread
themselves wide but
not enough for the full
nest of my american

selves constrained by
not wanting to fit
anywhere including
with whitman

(with whom i spoke
a few times waiting
to see who'd kiss me
sweat me a fresh tear)

i plan to make use
of each monument
no matter how many
seconds or fears

till the trumpets
or memories training
call me back
through the years

for you rome have
been living forever
abiding while the
world still cares

for a ruin born
senior to jesus
(even)
the original *grand-père*

or like she said in what i found reading:

la memoria ci tradisce o meglio siamo noi a tradirla:
ciò che pesa di piú giace nel fondo e, per non compiere
sforzi, dimentichiamo di rammentarlo.

alba de céspedes, IL RIMORSO

before i set again to scheming.

63

my jealousy, my sisters, the baby in the car. a crazy scene last
night in the stifling heat. or maybe that was just this morning.
first view,

an infant,

smiling, at the wheel.

and the mother?

she was nowhere in sight. then another car or truck smashed into it. and i, who was looking out a window, went outside to offer help. the mom appeared, yanked the baby out, swung her to and fro. so i went back into the storefront to criticize. you're not supposed to move

someone who's been hurt.

whence tina shows up and contradicts me.

and before?

a college scene, a boy wishing he weren't back in new bruns-wick (again). but i advance my theory. one is happy and sur-prised on first landing. it's the second time, reality sets in ... with my sisters still lurking in the background,

provoking you,

denying me somehow. so i say

none of you care about me.

that's why they barely came to the party?

but you still put your arm around joe and his wife,

trying all the while to be decent. when it comes to the others, it boils down to this: i'm JEALOUS (so i say that right out loud), while tina and ellen mutter to each other: no, that can't be real, maia thinks she's jealous, sure, *&* thinks she cares for

nothing but the family.

but she's been 15 years in pure wedded bliss and was well-
married also before that. so, it's really just a ladder that she
climbs up and down like a monkey. she's perfectly fine.

fine brown, and all that.

64

getting it back together, but unfaithful. crazy once again, the
scene last night. me, an employee working for a bratty girl,
i do her every whim, and i also have my son,

in fact you carry two,

precious, like my daughters. i'm packing up one's suitcase
and explaining: why i'm going to quit my job.

but before, your sister finds she too now has a girl,

one she's never recognized before.

you're the one who's helped her

do this.

and this girl,

once deformed, retarded, responds to this new love, and

grows into a beautiful child.

so now i'm free, and

on the prowl again,

responding once again to men's desires.
  this time, i sit passive and

  let one man, who's long admired you,

kiss me. he chews upon my cheek, which, all of a sudden, makes
my moral sense return, allowing me to

  throw him off.

for now i see that i'm complying with treachery, even if i'm
doing nothing at all. i mean, it wasn't me planting kisses or
biting on his neck. and i really want to

  make things right.

so i awake for the second time this morning. when i woke
before

  your eyes were yellow-green.

65

  in the parking lot

    there was something about a car
    i drove but then couldn't
    get to budge and sisters
    going along with it

    then a visit to an office
    of another time with hugh
    my nemesis saying what's
    a portion — just kill it

66

but somewhere also standing there was snow. it would make sense if i could mark a birthday for ondine. she was conceived in february 1980, and aborted on the

ides of march.

but they counted her conception 7 weeks: so, two in march, four in february, with cycle started one week previous? oh well, i'm going to call it

november 13.

makes it symmetrical with andrew's (born in january), just like matt's august 16 matches angies's june (odds & evens, two months apart), creating bookends for the holidays and summer.

anyway, ondine, november fits you well.

a month when everything is dying.

67

so why not stick to some integrity here.

we were talking about lee's death,

and tears began to flow, but i didn't want to feel the sadness, so instead i just kept flitting about.

hoping to avoid

strong emotions. freshest memory before his death was his voice, saying:

happy birthday!

and me (kind of a wise gal) cracking:

happy birthday to you too!

acting like i couldn't have cared less, or cared more about work, which has no importance whatsoever.

you've learned that along with everything.

i'm blue, but not much of a mourner. hardly cried for lee, but in truth i miss him, as much as others do. i'll always miss lee an awful lot.

he should have been in france, instead of you, at that defense.

for sure, he should have. and this fall, in his honor i'll teach *L'ILLUSION COMIQUE.*
    affection for lee, that is what i feel. lee (the lemur), and gladness. such happiness to see him always: come to have a drink, or get your turkey, drive with us to lambertville and snow.
    mostly smiling and just there. that was lee for me. mostly legs, mostly nose, but also breaking-blue, light-crinkling eyes.

and the trauma of the hospital?

that was real, for it cut my feelings off. i could swear i was not there. just a marionette, led through all the steps by doctor shepherd.

a body just abandoned, that was his death.

when lise dies, i thought (and that would happen soon), i'll want to help to put her body to rest. this, a part of any child's learning, and i was so afraid of that.

you didn't want to see it

coming. though it surely was. and, as usual, i anticipated way too much, imagined, just like lise did in her little poem, that they'd lay her body out on some sort of stone, then pop it in the oven. and that would be that.

same will happen to you before too long.

they'll bring the drawer in, then maybe out. and we will both have suffered so many times just this fear (of death).
　　but it doesn't matter how many times you suffer through it (or you don't). death comes to take you anyway. so i'm writing about death,

so you won't be surprised

whenever it comes knocking.

68

i mean we could crash in a car right now, like in that scene last night, where the car got violently overturned, with smashed skulls, mashed guts, and broken body parts all over the sidewalk. or we could just go down burning in a plane,

or get some sort of sudden sickness.

like jean said during dinner last night: *à nos âges, un cancer est vite arrivé,* a heart attack, or some such thing. but if none of these arrive to get me first, then i'll have to help lise and write about that

here, first, with your dead ondine.

so that after the barbecue,

the image of the person's still standing.

thus, hetna's white hair is still blowing in the wind. she's tall and beautiful like never in my life. and mischief is still barking.

true and not true.

his ashes are assembled in the small, wooden box. that heavy box delivered somewhat strangely by u.p.s., which i hid for weeks inside his doghouse, before we had the time to as- semble: together to bury it

beneath our spreading tree, while

lee, who seemed just to disappear (abandoned by us all in the hospital to shake) was whisked off alone (to sizzle in a box), he, my darling

lee, was not well tended to,

not buried near as well as mischief.

69

but those heavenly eyes turned back in his head, while his body was lying in the hospital... that i never saw for good, that keeps slipping out of memory. instead i see

a twinkle of real life

with his inveterate sense of humor. we went for a drink the
first time we met, to a place i'd never been, nor returned since.
one drink to consecrate our office-sharing, which extended
through some darkish years.
    that must have been august '87,

when you with babe-in-arms, angie,

still smoked cigarettes, and lee's wife could barely walk, she
was so pregnant. lee's giant baby about to come. yes, true memories live on, but stronger than these & more tangible by far,

proof — is what you find in dreams.

70

so good, so strong, so satisfying. lee was back again,

your friend again, last night,

and starting to make it somewhat regular. and the particu-
lars were: sheila, his wife, had now also passed, but was still
around (in the old flesh, announcing the official status of
the case), whereas he had been made new, resuscitated. and
he looked just great,

enthusiastic.

he was helping me and mine to move into a new place, and
had just cleaned the kitchen in record time while i was fiddling with the closet. and then, as i was looking through the
rooms of this big house, i saw that all around me,

everywhere — lee

had left signs. detailed posters about how to avoid ants, and
how to manage all kinds of practical conundrums. and jessie,
his boy, was so talkative. so each and

everyone — rejoiced,

including lee. smiling, and glad that he was back.

71

an underground play

MAJA	a middle-aged writer
OLIVER	her husband
MATTEUS	their 12-year old son
ANITA	first dream-narrator (a 14-year old girl)
GEORGE	second dream-narrator (a mexican-american gentleman of 50)
CARRIE	third dream-narrator (a whimsical woman of 30)
LEE'S LEGS	the lower body of a very tall subway rider
ROXANE	a 23-year old resident of rome
ONDINE	a long lost child

scene 1

*subway station in rome. maja (small, plumpish, swedish woman), oli-
ver (tall, handsome dutchman), and matteus (beautiful curly-haired
boy) walk down a long red-tiled corridor, then turn, solemnly descend
a dim, wide staircase, opening on to a grungy platform. all three stop
in their tracks, between two stairs, and listen to:*

(a loudspeaker)

i passeggeri sono pregati di non lasciare il loro bagaglio solo nella stazione e di riportare tutti comportamenti sospettosi alle protezioni. grazie.

MAJA

(resuming her descent, daydreaming a bit, but trying also to connect with the moment, fiddling with her bag and hat) look, oliver, did you see how these subway cars are covered with signs? like the ones we used to ride in new york... *(then calling to her son)* matteus! come here, remember to stay next to me or papa. otherwise we might get lost. did you remember to write down lynn's address?

MATTEUS

yes. i have it down. don't worry, mama. pass me the camera. you said that i could film today.

OLIVER

EUR. we need to take the number 3, then change at colosseo. that will take us to the termini — exactly where we want to go.

(the train rumbles up, a nearly empty number 3, they all step inside and sit down)

scene 2

(the inside of a nearly empty subway car. maja and oliver sit together on one bench, matteus, alone, on the bench across. oliver studies the map, the guide, smiles at maja, takes her hand)

MAJA

(*anxious, perceiving everything in motion, as always. the train going forward with her thoughts left behind. she digs in her purse, then folds her hands. how to enter in or stop time? turns to oliver, begins to chat*) i'm glad we've taken time to do this. i hope that we can use what we have. but i'm not sure what will come of it. six days in rome. all for ourselves. maybe i'll begin to see, to feel again. maybe matt can make a movie. the way he's sitting there, it really takes me back, back to riding subways with my nephews in new york. young boys, before they study others' faces, they always think to set their own. it's great to see lynn again. her kids, so cute. how tired she looked. you look tired too, and me, i'm exhausted. perhaps we shouldn't have come. i always set things crooked somehow.

OLIVER

don't worry, my love. of course, we should have come. of course we can't leave now, but we'll adjust, get used to how things are.

MAJA

the mosquitoes, the heat, the babies' cries…

OLIVER

the burden we are certainly imposing. but mostly we'll be out and about. it's true we're very tired, didn't sleep last night, but tonight things will be better. you'll see.

MAJA

(*looks long and lovingly at matteus sprawled out on the bench, peering this way and that through the camera. then, taking on the role of coryphaeus, she speaks directly to the public, dons a silver mask)* what a boy, what a fabulous boy! so beautiful, sweet and strong. all my children. who can i tell my love for them? how can i tell it well enough? make this reality stick. it's no longer just on-dine, the one ripped out, who's asking me to pull it all together, find out how to put what matters down.

(whispers)

(as if coming from everywhere) but it's you, you, horrible, this is all your fault.

MAJA

is it really all my children now, and others perhaps? our des-tiny depends, theirs and mine, on me mining to move this forward, timing how to put it down. *(too much responsibility, maja removes her mask. her shoulders slump beneath the burden, she sits a spell in solid silence, then shudders and purses her lips, sees herself reflected in the subway glass. heavy eyes, set and squaring chin, corners of the mouth weighing, she tries very hard to perk up a bit, readjust, fiddles with her mask, then sets it down)* of course, i do not need "pretty" anymore, just to settle into something graceful, learn to string all scenes through something grateful, settle gentle into night. *(long silence)* perhaps i'll make it once again through detours, cobble out a future from the past. i'll call on all the host of my relations, single out my ornery oth-ers, who through their secret accidents and incidents speak through dreams to point me on the path. *(she puts on her silver mask and calls out to the first dream-narrator)* anita!

scene 3

ANITA

(the subway car darkens, the glass turns into screens. in the first panel on the left, anita, a small, smooth dark-haired girl appears. she does a cartwheel, then stands high on her tiptoes, and whispers too, but with sweet, small hands cupped around her mouth) mama, grab a hold of this, my dream.

    i was about to go pee where the pool was, in the fancy tiled kingfisher room. and i felt so energetic, so blithe, and on my own, in my own fields of energy, finally. i had been composing songs in a parking lot, and i realized that my only problem was — i didn't ever write things down. pristine melodies, fine lyrics, passed through my head all the time, and i just listened to them, listened to them, never bothering to write them down. but now energy was swelling in my body, so i took some great big hops around the parking lot, and saw that i again could fly. then i thought, let's make the most of this wild day. i'll go to the green lands on the other side today and enjoy the smallness of my limbs, spend some time with this lithe feel-ing, running and flying through the park. i only stopped by the pool because... why not put a few laps in too? and there just before i ducked inside the dressing room, in the crisp bright air outside, playing by the pool, i saw: a perfect family of five, all matching with pink bathing caps. *(anita disappears)*

MAJA

(still masked, calls out to the second dream-narrator) george!

GEORGE

(george, a cancer patient returning from the dead, appears in the second subway car screen, hovering over a mic, breathy voice comes on the air, shoulders slouched, peering into the darkness, sneering like a stand-up comic. gruff, ironical with a slight cough, he stuffs his hands inside his jean pockets and grumbles) or how 'bout get a load of this. i heard it on the bus, gossip from a lady named roberta.

jack and jill, they bought a house, not on a hill but at 4 river drive (in the village). it had 16 rooms and was yellow. roberta was turning this over in her mind, and was thinking, oh my god what is jill going to do, what will she do with all that space? when john and she found out about the move, they were spending the night at jack and jill's old house, the first one they owned, in east orange. jill had called to say that jack was kind of pissed about the capital they'd spend, which was first supposed to be 53k and then turned out to be 73, because of transitory bad luck. so roberta, politely but with genuine interest, inquired "did you have trouble maybe getting a mortgage?" jack said "no, we got that, thanks to jill's plan. but i had to pay more for the house than i wanted." so roberta answered meekly "well it's amazing that you're finally moving to new york." taking it all in stride, jack said "yeah, it will be good, right in the midst of the theaters, for jill." all this… commitment to the arts?

well, roberta was duly impressed. and the next thing you know, she and john were going to see the new house, though they decided they should first stop to get a drink, approaching this artificial village. it was somewhere like we've all been before, & yet was more like a location in the city — a gray, modern one.

MAJA

a city lit up like in rimbaud's *VILLES?*

GEORGE

sure, like that. so eventually, they did stop inside a bar, and
john went off somewhere, while roberta, in honor of the good
old days — where she used to be closer (in space) to mexico
and to (the time of) being herself married to jack — ordered
herself kahlúa and cream. but what came looked like ginger
ale instead (or maybe champagne?) and tasted like cream soda
with bubbles. once she had a sip and recognized this slowly
(not to be what she wanted), she got the message to the wait-
ress and left.

she then went to perch herself, alongside john, in a tree
outside the new jack and jill house, and called through the
open window to say: hey! she'd come all this way to see them.
but an old gentleman came to the door, someone, who she took
to be roland, a kind and starry, clever-eyed fellow (related to
jack), but who was perhaps more uncle vanya than roland, or
perhaps someone else i do not know.

MAJA

or maybe he was related to hans, the stiff-necked grandfather
who lives — so briefly — in *THE MAGIC MOUNTAIN?*

GEORGE

whoever he was, he called out to our waiting couple, "can i
help you two? jack and jill are very busy right now." but roberta really wanted to see them. so she insisted, till jack came
down to let them in, whence she saw inside this magnificent

place, which was all blank yet painted faint yellow. and then she asked, while climbing solemnly the stairs, "jack, don't you think you'll miss east orange?" and jack said: "no, roberta, not at all." *(the second window-panel screen darkens and george disappears)*

MAJA

(masked again, calls out) carrie!

CARRIE

(the third dream narrator appears, a sandy, whispy-haired woman. she assumes the position of the thinker, but swings her crossed leg and begins in a husky voice) i was sleeping next to tim, but in a different house, and we had our little baby, eddie. the disposition of the rooms was different there from that of our real house. and i was thinking, yes, i'm sleeping very well, experiencing the in-between so heavily, but i also have to, really have to, pee. so i'll just crank up the courage to cross the living room and kitchen space, then tiptoe into the narrow white bathroom.

MAJA

just this side of baby eddie's room. *(which is square, gay, bright and spacious)*

CARRIE

i did this quietly in a rather adept way, but then lowered myself awkwardly to pee, as though i didn't have control.

MAJA

as happens necessarily when one is handicapped, as has happened necessarily to cassandra, and will happen one day with heather — two babies who lacked oxygen at birth.

CARRIE

once there, on the pot, i began admiring my woman's body, the smooth torso coming to a v.

MAJA

a bit like brie's, in the tub, in TRANSAMERICA.

CARRIE

and then finally i did start to pee. but oh my word, i'm afraid i missed. *(everywhere, thick splotchy spots of brownish pee, splattering about, flooding the whole place)* and i was thinking all the while, what is tim going to say? such a horrible mess. it's all my fault. but then, very bravely in reality, i stood up and truly dragged myself off to four other walls to pee.

scene 4

MAJA

(puts down her mask. the subway car lights up, more people are inside) it's time to speak about my waking (self again), about this writing and its life. you all remember, don't you, my good friend tom? he was loosely based on a composer i once met, whereas johannes, i found him in a bar. so, you see, i can in fact bake characters just like others do, concoctions from

amalgamations. and there's nothing wrong with that. the one i have in mind now is not yet clear. she's the daughter of pietro (an american sculptor i met at fred and heidi's) who himself became an avatar of vincent, the gallery guy who hired aleks. yes, i guess that's where she came from — roxane. and what fascinates me most is her frankness. ondine, can we please bring her to light?

and while we're waiting i'll spend time... reminiscing *(maja assumes her mask again)*, recalling what's occurred in the past. *(the word SUNDAY lights up in red upon the mask just above the left brow)* i've seen so many churches, glory to thy name, and rome is much more beautiful than expected. but it's all crowded up in my memory today and i'm not sure what to string here but pearls.

at the airport as we arrived, a clinky noise — the jingle of anticipation. proof that i could speak italian, wasn't kidding when i told matteus how it swings. and the shuttle's swimming team, a load of hefty, chatty girls somehow brought me back to giorgio, that red-haired volley-ball player from genoa, seven feet tall (who i took once to nogales in a volkswagen bug, before interpreting he'd got somebody pregnant). then, lynn and her three babies in the stairwell, a very holy sight, followed by a rough and sleepless night.

i went to bed with babies fussing, mosquitoes in the heat, then woke again, again, again, could not resort to anything but read. that's how i often know i'm traveling. so, sadly, since we've arrived, *(MONDAY, TUESDAY, WEDNESDAY light up on the mask)* some of the pictures did not seize me, i could not see ST. TERESA nor the PIETÀ. the finest works of art, they could not breathe for me. i mean the glove that keeps me numb was really pulled tight. that's much of the way it was in rome. but *(THURSDAY, FRIDAY, and SATURDAY light up in turn)* there were some magic moments with matteus. after exhaustion in the FORUM — our feet became our dogs —, wild flowers in the PALATINO. and even some man-made things got stuck inside my head. proliferating busts and bodies, a hermaphro- dite couch, heads of gods and emperors, suckling wolves. and i also somehow glimpsed a few paintings, (*a slide show begins, maja comments on each picture with an aside*) GALATHEA, that's the one we bought a poster of. *L'AMOUR SACRÉ, L'AMOUR PROFANE* — the naked one's the one who should be dressed. and now, coming back to me, a few glances even before that, (*TUESDAY lights up again*) crowded frescoes, raphael, look- ing down at us, while you (*she points hieratically to oliver*), oli- ver, pointed plato out to me, while i was pressed and fearing we might lose our boy. then there was caravaggio's *VOCATION* (*WEDNESDAY lights back up*) with matthew stunned amidst his taxes.

OLIVER

that's just how i feel.

MAJA

and tiziano's SALOME (*THURSDAY lights again, at which point maja removes her mask and keeps it off*). *DAPHNE AND APOLLO* were bernini's, and i remember borromini's broken lines. of michelangelo, i saw the whole, more than any part, except that eve was buff, and the sibyl who (*she nudges oliver*) you say looks like me. and i remember stepping down grand staircases: that of FARNESE palace near the TRASTEVERE, the widest, in the gallery BORGHESE, and one that tumbles from the TRINITÀ DEI MONTI, with its flock of nuns ascending.

(*lee's legs finally appear, while maja continues*)

the subway in rome is mostly lumbering, and that is how i feel, as i'm staring at the legs of a very tall man, who looks like lee, with shoes long & narrow, laces pulled around the feet, tight.

(a low rumbling noise gives way to silence, then to maja speaking again, now directly to the belt buckle)

MAJA

i say, i saw your shoes and legs first. then up to your waist. but i couldn't see your square torso, nor those blue eyes blasted back inside your head. those and your upper half must still have been lying in the hospital — after all that came had come to pass — for all i could see here were your legs, long, long, and couldn't discern what was missing on top. and the suddenness, the jolt, your disappearance made me think more along lines of hollowness, a similar great hole, scraped inside myself, the day they took — i let them take — ondine. such hollowness assures hallowness? some other place i'll see, ondine.

   sudden death is so heroic, the falling down though real, so glorious, because we simply can't believe. our peace remains forever in shock. not like the coming death of oldsters or our own, where we have lovingly considered consequences, long before we've picked the box. calculated all the details. studied all the nooks and crannies. the caving features, feet, touched by the cold, the gradual sinking and the stench, free radicals and cells arranging for a new attack, removal of the sap of life.

   all of this slow churning joyce and beckett sang before. but i can't see or buy their conclusions.

> not true there is no
> ending and no hero
> not true that we're
> not anybody's child

you, lee, in your armor, photo fenced beside my desk, i'm ask-ing you from here to help me (what a feast for eyes, your torso's fencing on my desk), gentle, kind, and pure, my good friend lee, consent to set again upon your awkward, stirring legs — long stems as near-inept as my two stubs for stepping through this stunted earth, this place we dragged to from paradise.

they prove to me, your legs (they often come and go), carrying a myriad of torsos. so i'll keep my eyes securely on your buttoned bottom half, not make the same mistake as orpheus, hold to my conviction you're still traveling, although i might not see you clearly with my same old eyes, until i too have crossed… i'll see you whole when time has reached the station.

(loudspeaker)

(now seeming to come from lee's legs, among the subway passengers, his belt buckle lit up by a spot)

IN ROME

sometimes you see
heads without bodies
sometimes bodies
without heads faces
without noses or lower
frontal planes without
protruding parts
but always you see
layers of centuries
stone and ornament

and no matter how
much this is moving
(because you know
all is beautiful) you must
walk in and round about
for it's moving in

a manner that is fixed
with still one layer
of beauty buckling
beneath another

making the whole
city armored in guilt
nailed up on the cross
taken from the cross
and so many piled up
instants of so many
storied myths saying
this is why we kill
what moves us most

scene 5

ROXANE

(COLOSSEO. *inside a different subway car, the door is open. roxane steps in. the doors close. dirty blond hair pulled back in a blue bandana, her eyes wander a bit then light upon maja, now standing in a crowd near the door, flanked by oliver and matteus. roxane's parted lips say nothing, but her eyes appear to speak as her voice comes over a mic set back stage)* you are... perhaps, i see, my mother? or is there something else between us?

look at me, i'm stripped of all my mystery, bare before you. here, my clear blue eyes and spotless face, straight white teeth. my young girl's face. no knots of look how pretty, nor of ugliness, my body also simply *is*, wrapped up in these clothes *(white shirt, blue skirt, white sandals)*, neither tall nor short, nor fat nor thin. everything i am's neutrality and clean, refusing like a nun all experience. never have had sex, never have known love. never tried, nor failed, never have known hope or

disappointment. refused, i have refused all experience. pre-
served only my pride, my spotless i'm from god. will not give
in till i am through.

you, with all your veils, your hat, your whitening hair, your
charming entourage, this man who fawns on you, this shining
son with curls, and other children i don't see, the older two,
walking in the world, the one that's in the wings, the hidden
girl you'd bring through me to life. you with all your clothes,
your passport in your bag, your sagging eyes and skin, and all
your gentleness, your pen, your fear, your sloth, your indeci-
sion. you with your regrets and all your appetites. you who
for all time have set your fingers clutching death — they say
the cord that bonds will set the fingers clutching death — take
your clothes off here that i might look at you. i'm the door,
the gate you must go through.

MAJA

(responding to this weird proposition — not exactly shocked, but still
a bit surprised — looks away a moment then clears her throat, speaks
to the public through her mask) i thought that i was minding my
own business, trying to adjust. had no notion that my yearning
was for multitudes of girls.

i have a perfect daughter walking on this earth, and one
i lost before this life began. what could this young woman be
wanting here from me? here there is no cord, something in my
groin? she's dull to me, pristine, and unattractive. and yet i'd
like to kiss her on the mouth. but no, i have to block impulsion.
this could be the gate that leads to death.

instead, i'll make it write for me a few more lines, prolong
a little longer my mystery with my veils, for if i can get through
my... story, i'll see what these compulsions are about.

i'll have to pray to make me patient, wait while all this
heat and restlessness calm down, turn this itching impulse

into activeness, let the one who guides me lead the way. and for music? while i'm waiting, how shall i mark time? time. again. i hear ONDINE.

(the opening passages of ravel's tone poem fill the car for a few moments. maja removes her mask and listens. then)

OLIVER

(chimes in) take the way of reason. step a bit aside, and ask her questions, so you yourself can see, better understand. who is this roxane? who has you cornered in the train, asking you to kiss her on the mouth?

ROXANE

(roxane appears intrigued, becomes more docile. begins to speak) if i'm so brazen, bold, acting like a nun, refusing all the things that decorate young girls (the pretty, dark-eyed wit, the shining helmet, curves, the smile, the satin skin that gird your angel, the blue-green questioning eyes, the long blond dancing waves that frame ondine), it's all the fault, i guess, of vincent, who brought me to this world just for himself.

i never knew who might have been my mother. an egg? i guess, just used by vincent, who always was in love with earl, but wanted me to be his daughter (not even to be shared with earl). i never minded this when i was little. vincent and me and lots of other girls.

my aunts who're living here in italy, and swarms of nannies who came to be my friends. my favorite of these was aleks, that polish girl you met. she lived with us in paris till i turned thirteen and painted me: 100 portraits. those years were the happiest i knew.

then lexy got her own studio, we moved to new york, and vincent fell in love with pietro. he put me in a boarding school, where i tried to just be normal all the way through, first at st. anne's, then at smith. but then *(roxane smiles at maja seductively as if trying to get her to come out, cut her loose from her family and especially herself)* i just accepted: i'm not interested in life. i've come to rome to die with my two aunts.

MAJA

(coughs and sputters, wondering why roxane has fixed on her like this, wondering why it's she who is provoking. usually it's maja who stares the other down, as if possessed, or just by accident. but this time she is sure that she's not guilty, although… she wants to kiss her on the mouth) death, you say? that's what you want, not me. i have children, matteus, still young, andreis and angelica, just grown, and ondine, of course, who never did begin — the child i would not let live. she's waiting near a cave that i discovered long ago. and there i promised somehow to redeem her. none of these accept the games i play with death, and i have chosen life with oliver.

so, smile away and try to draw me off the path, set your clear blue eyes on me, long as you might like. for me, you'll be the road not taken. since it happens i'm surrounded, i'll just follow through with living, let myself be carried by the tide.

ROXANE

tide of life! *(her mouth becomes contorted and she laughs)* what makes you think you know the tide? all you ever witness to is heaviness. heaviness of chores, heaviness of guilt. trying to construct a home a house a cave, even for ondine, a trap. all of this recording, this mad writing. nothing but construed illusions. meet me on this train, for i am presence, taste what has no aftermath or residue. then you'll know you swam — the tide of life.

MAJA

i'll not budge an inch. if it's true you're clean as death, you will come to me. otherwise you're just a trick of life, trick that i'll not choose, so i'm not guilty. even if you try to kill — you kill me — even if you separate me from my very self, i shall little more than take your picture, less than write a poem, come up just with this: a flimsy fiction, a play to show the urge i've had to breathe immortal air, then frame you as i wrinkle and fold back in the dust, sew you in the scrapbook of my life.

ROXANE

i know you want me gone, but see and touch me. i'm still here. regardless of your taste for miracles. remember me, i'm not an apparition. if i were, why would you want to kiss me on the mouth?

MAJA

perhaps it's just i see you too want things from me. you want to gather words, experience. you crave my hat, my veils. you're looking at my son, admiring my man, wondering, behind your proud refusal, what can this worn woman bring? images in-fused with stories, mostly french — *L'ANNONCE FAITE À MARIE, PARTAGE DE MIDI, LA TENTATION DE SAINT ANTOINE* — with touches too, i guess, of thomas mann. and under all these veils, my body is a cross, desire that was forged between two poets. like you, i've made my efforts to look normal in the world, but my soul's implanted firmly in these letters. that's why you're asking me to write you in, clear for you, a clean but sultry corner. finally, i guess (i learned perhaps from proust) your smile's pulled a string of memories. memories from my long-forgotten body of 19, memories of my first girlfriend, nora.

first to ever dote on me, build a nest for me. we loved each other well. i accepted, chastely, she desired: women. but when she wished so much, one night when we were drunk, to show just by a kiss how much she needed... i ran away in frenzy to the nearest church. the doors were locked. i turned my back on nora, on that aching kiss, moved out the next day from our apartment, back to hellish home, where love had always only been a dangerous trap. i, who had been touched by scores of creepy men who could not love me, i would not, could not kiss her on the mouth.

ROXANE

(*mutters*) scusi, signora. (*steps across maja's path as the subway stops, takes one last look at matteus and oliver, then disappears into a crowd of passengers that exits*)

scene 6

MAJA

(*still heading toward the termini, maja, oliver, and matteus sit down again side by side, maja turns to oliver, and asks*) how will i write this? don't know what to do, don't know what to say about the subject. look at christian art, no one ever worried what they had to paint. me, i have to make it all from scratch. (*then turns to the public, puts her mask back on*) and as for you, on-dine, i couldn't see you anywhere except in roxane's face, every other thing was but a sign: the tiny wildflower on the MONT PALATIN, the fluttering cloth inside the TRASTEVERE church, breathing life against the stone and lace. these were but the signs of heaven. and then there were those signs of hell: the dream about the twins, two bouncing, blimpy heads, tumbled down no doubt from rows of bodies.

LEE'S LEGS (appear again, voice-over)

remember to remember, create.

MAJA

(slumped, removes her mask) translate into words how far i feel
from all that's real? how far i feel from calling — ondine. no
wonder my dear lee is closer on this trip. i had a dream, intense, last night. we were together on his land — merry grang-
es. it was morning, i guess. and i was trying to distinguish
things from others. but his big lumbersome body kept coming
up toward me. it would emerge, come forth, very close to me.
he was smiling and perfectly well. i know we spent a patch
of time together, smiled, laughed. but now i can't remember…
anything he said. i only know that he was fine. like hetna, at
the family barbecue: straight and white and beautiful, dark
glasses. the truth, it always comes in dreams. george! come
back and speak: my dreams.

GEORGE

*(a spotlight falls on him, who narrates through a mic while looking
intently at maja)* how about that horrid scene we played last
night, concerning strikes that turned to war in quebec.

we were walking in the old city. had sat down for a while
on an old man's steps to say goodbye — "goodbye to you my
darling daughter." then we did some banking with tina. we
had a real gob, a fistful, of checks we could deposit. then, as we
resumed our stride, picked up some speed — our sense of pur-
pose and direction — we ran into a mob, as did a group of kids
who ran before us, saying "you'd better go around. the police,
they are not friendly here at all." and the next thing you know
we're at the station, where a cruel, young, officer points straight

at me, and motions, "her, you've got to get her out." so, at
the end of the scene:

> they put you on a truck
> with four men going
> to be executed
> all looking sad and sighing
>
> the wisest was an old
> chinese man with long
> bandana-tied hair and
> crinkly red eyes crying
>
> while another man
> mexican gave tomatoes
> to us all for this was
> to be our last meal

MAJA

(*resumes her mask*) oh i could tell you lots of endings, ondine,
not the kind you went through with no planning, but the kind
that is prepared throughout a life. you're always traveling
down this street, avoiding this or that, or waiting for a lover
or directions, and generally, you're holding lots of checks.

> bulging out of your fist
> there's always money
> all you have to do is sign

but there's always also somewhere else you have to go.
another turn or stop, till suddenly, you're not in charge of
where you're going anymore, just being carried along with it.

and the only thing you realize is we're all in the same boat, or maybe the same truck.

in the last scene, it must have been a phantom of father's, the blue willys... anita! let's hear how you began.

ANITA

(takes the mic) me, i emerged from the first russian aristocracy, no doubt, which actually was half japanese.

so nicolai, my father, didn't have a legal wife, nor even his own proper family. but he did have a child by accident and then decided he should get married, which turned into good news for me. there were serfs all around and everyone — including father — now had to learn what russian nobles have always done— produce easter eggs from serfs is what they do. and the process of producing them is painful. you have to put your head, and the whole top of you (your torso, you might say), deep inside a straw bundle, and then agree to be covered up in shell.

well, i never was exactly a serf, that's for sure. but i agreed to undergo this process, to help to set things right for nicolai. so we all went off, my two sisters and me, three maidens to get covered up with shells.

MAJA

what a lot of rot. let's hear from carrie.

CARRIE

(carrie takes the mic) me? you know, i only dream of real estate.

in the last place, there was a large room with a dirty whitish carpet, shades that didn't work, and sort of blue sixties' put-together furniture. and the deal was my mother-in-law had bought this house, for us, and for others in her family. i was not sure we could come back ever to our house (in america), which, in this scene, was not the place where we live right now, but some bigger version of the "hearst" apartment...

MAJA

where i lived when i was young, on riverside drive — a happy, airy place in manhattan, to which i often return.

CARRIE

but it turned out there were no exits in this place, which perhaps is why it was perched in france. and there were issues, lots of issues in the house. in particular there were two butts, or *mégots,* one of pot, one of tobacco, which at the same time showed the cruddiness of everything, but were also bits i wanted to keep and smoke. on the negative side, there was also jacqueline, talking to me about the price of dentistry, with me saying, "sure, it is the same in america," though one can get it cheaper in mexico (which my own mother used to do, who hasn't any problems with her teeth). and there was also, on the neutral side, a sister-in-law, who i don't know (this woman was tall and wan and thin and english), coming in to embrace our mother-in-law and asking if we'd thought to buy "star" cereal. then, mixed in there, somewhere with the positive, was my own sister, tina, who had brought from new york tons of clothes for me to try on, and i pretty much liked most of them. but my favorite dress i never did try on, because it was snatched by my other sister, ellen, who looked great in it. so i was jealous of her (i'm always jealous of her), but i liked the feeling of being cared for by tina. and andreis, he also liked that feeling. oh yes... and somewhere in this picture, mixed up (with the positive and the negative), was a storm. i took a look through the window at the horizon, which was simultaneously threatening and fantastic, steel-blue.

MAJA

this last dream, the worst, i'll tell myself. the sequence is a fast forward. it marks the end of my leave. here is just what i remember. *(takes the mic)*

many scenes with many members of my family. very dark, featuring my brothers, theo and luke. i woke up telling this to oliver, everything with regard to luke. i had been visiting him on many occasions and telling him i was making progress with my work, that my confidence was building, that what i am writing here might be worthwhile. he smiled at me and stared at me in an equivocal way, so i wasn't sure if it was pure or impure love. but i decided i would not evade it, just stay there and take the intensity of his look. then i cut to another scene, involving theo instead of luke. i was visiting a place, very vast, something like an underground rome, but it also was a bar or nightclub, with a ballroom dancing floor, and theo was one of the people i met there. as usual he did not pay attention to me, but he was somehow irrevocably *with* me: looking, thinking, talking about others in relation to himself — yet somehow very hooked in with me. and i found this unsettling, annoying. it was difficult for me not to be able to hold his thoughts. so, toward the end, i cut the scene again, returning for one more visit with luke instead. but this time i had to go up a long flight of stairs.

there were torches and people chanting all about, praying all around him in a large wooden barn. and here, there was also a young man who darted up the stairs, and turned out to be an avatar of theo. he swung the door open and told me to enter, through the passage on the left, as he was about to hurl a candle into the barn, because, he says, the solution (finally found) is that all of us are going to burn.

(maja turns to oliver) well, no wonder i awoke upset from all this, and rolled over to report it to you. *(an aside to the public)* poor oliver, he never gets to sleep. remember, you told me kindly "it's just an awful dream," but i say it's connected to reality.

OLIVER

how so?

MAJA

well i feel guilty toward my brothers in every way, and luke can be locked up in his self-righteousness. fanaticism does exist. or maybe it's simpler: i'm getting close to death. i'm going to burn, and it's starting now to happen in reality. i'm very hot. my hair is growing white and menopause itself's a kind of death.

OLIVER

that's hogwash, don't you see? you've always been like this. reacting just like that to all your fears, of death, and all the rest, as though extreme old age were right upon you, ever since you turned thirty-three. the fear you have, that makes you startle in your sleep, and poisons the first hours of the morning, it's the same you've always had, the one that was sown through your family, hurting you since you were just a child.

MAJA

you're right, i am afraid. i'm made of fear and hate, fear and hate for all my...

OLIVER

no *(oliver protests, shakes his gentle head)*, no, you aren't, that was just a dream.

MAJA

(whimpers more a bit and moans, then settles her head down on oliver's shoulder and sings) last night i was swimming in the river, dear. i wanted to lay with the grass, to be discovered, and desired by the whole earth. but i was playing games with someone in particular, most likely, it had to be a man. (i guess i really am a woman since my power plays are always with a man). i was planning to leap around the rocks, fly, and spin the way i always do, when suddenly this loneliness wasn't freedom anymore. i was cast at sea, lost among the deep rushing waters. then suddenly you came, emerged like neptune from the sea, saved me from the black stream waters, and it's only because of you that there's a dove hovering between my waking and dream worlds. now there's a passage between.

scene 7

ONDINE

(the subway car has darkened again, a swimming pool appears in screen one, ondine suspended in the air, standing in a simple white nightgown with long ash-blond hair falling to her knees appears through a scrim on the upper right side of the stage and declaims this poem)

> a clump of clouds a bee a square of blue
> an i-shaped shadow in the pool
> and three brothers playing *pétanque*

three women resting down the hill
with husbands climbing nearer to the plank
and children too with mirth and cries exploding

of this and truth and tales wide-hung
some women may still bear fruit while
others like mary rock their young

scene 8

MAJA

(the pool disappears, caravaggio's VOCATION again lights up in subway window [screen] two, a spotlight falls on maja who wears her silver mask and speaks to oliver, who's now become a statue by her side) yes, i too was startled by st. matthew, the tax collector, wondering, why me? i too felt the darkness and the call. but the darkness didn't really happen, start to happen, till my life turned toward november that fall.

i was sitting in the house on the avenue, crouched in what was my office at the time, perched there, just like here, at my computer, when a verse came to me. something about a branch crossing another branch and groundhogs left with no place to play. that was years and years ago. in november, snug inside my first new jersey home, a peaceful house, where things first became empty, then fell apart when darkness fell, after lise came there with ellen in january — everything turned cold then, almost to stone. or perhaps that whole drama had been set up just before, by my own brief encounter with oliver, our first conversation, in december. he was wearing tweed, and i was wearing pink (my corduroy dress)

i remember well his beautiful young head, cocked politely, quietly, and listening. he remembered too. "that's interesting," i said, no sooner had his soft voice begun to speak. back when we met, amidst him and him and maybe her, and others (some i do and don't remember). no wonder the big boys called me in.

for it was right around then things began to break between jonathan and me, though trouble had been brewing to begin with — lots of love, but trouble too. we swept it under the rug at our wedding, then stored it in our best sealed boxes. but the turmoil beneath began shining at me, looking through the glass, waiting for a crack to break through.

and the crack started like this: i had met someone, through father's brother, ron. he was tall and violent, strangled chickens, but also liked my little poems, a performance artist, named raoul. he came to our house with my uncle and my aunt, to a party for our boy's fourth birthday, and then went out for a long ride with ellen, whereas i stayed back to focus on my

children.

oh my god, andreis, how cute he was back then. if only i had known what he'd find ahead, such darkness and such cold...

IS THERE A WAY THAT I CAN MAKE AMENDS?

he used to chew upon his coat sleeves, 3 to 4? and played under the table when guests came near. but looked so happy when angelica came.

a tender boy, so glad to receive his sister,

then cried two years later when jonathan and i broke up. silent tears were rolling down his cheeks, i had made them fall. but then he was up, jumping on the bed. and stayed insecure and anxious, years after that. they were both insecure when sleeping, first in their own beds in the rented place, then also in the place i bought. and by day, i knew andreis wasn't comfortable,

but somehow didn't act. i wasn't cruel and i was always looking, loving, and tending. but it's true somehow i didn't always
act, paralyzed perhaps by my own guilt, and those were hard
years for them, formative years,

6 to 9 for him, 3 to 6 for her.

and then we upped and moved again, and when oliver and i
got married, i put andreis upstairs and slept below, not with
oliver, but with angelica. upstairs for boys, downstairs for
girls. everyone divided till matteus came along. help me now
to make amends...

and it was again heavy last night, wasn't it, oliver? the hard
talk we had concerning

matteus, when he was 9,

about him giving our babysitter's grandson a bloody nose and
her giving him, a spanking. how come

matteus never told you this before?

i suppose he was protecting... her?

you really should have asked more questions.

MY CHILDREN, I AM SORRY ABOUT THAT.

and, ondine, my ondine, did i tell you this? last night, lee
came calling once again, and i'd give anything to tell you what
he said. but right now i'm not remembering my dreams well.
only this snippet from a long time ago. i had asked how we'd
know when to put mischief to sleep, and lee said: with dogs,

it won't be as hard as you might think. he'll ask for it, when
he no longer eats."
one day will i no longer eat?

like on the day you walked to and from saint-cirq-lapopie?

the purple haze around concots
doves and bells
ondine

i remember i felt light at the halfway mark. happy too to
have the shade as i marched on. there was no roadkill and lots
of butterflies. i hardly saw a larger creature, a few birds maybe,
and some critters, and heard more than i saw, scampering or
scuttling through the brush. when i got up the hill leading
into the village, i got compliments from strangers for my hat.
from the church i saw some swallows doing what they do,
diving through the air above the lot. and sitting in the grass
amidst the roses was nice. the sweet-pea hedge was cool and
fragrant too. my face was soft and radiant inside the bathroom
mirror, though my thighs were burned from all that chafing. to
think i'd walk twelve miles in a long narrow skirt.
the way back was somewhat boring. long and hard, but
everything alive looked beautiful, just like you, ondine, and
all the places people lived were stately. i couldn't tell what
you might like best. those white flowers perhaps? they stood
out to greet a small white butterfly, and a yellow one too, very
pretty, and coveting a spray of bright orange poppies (sprung
just for you).

*(then, standing slowly, maja lays down her mask as the train pulls
in the station)*

scene 9

(the subway car darkens again and the third window screen lights up with a picture of cave paintings)

ONDINE

(ondine walks on stage, sits down on maja's lap and puts her arms around her neck) and then?

MAJA

i found the cave, ondine, where everyone took life, foot and hand prints in PECH MERLE. 24,000 years held within a day, horses, bulls with women, and the endless water drops. you weren't there, my girl (bambi on the lawn can't be danc- ing all about). and it wasn't like our cave, warm and narrow, soft and sweet, our own cocoon. but it marked me for you all the same. no one knows, they say, just what went on there. a temple — space for prayer and sacrifice. the color of the whole, a faint red clay, with bloody, spittled paint in spots. and lines, some finished, some trailing off, designed just right to hit the curves. not how we would decorate our walls, but desperate just the same to tell the story, to anyone who might just pass.

> more attuned with this
> underground are you
> than to what i finally
> read of giraudoux
> hogwash he made
> lines for stupid plays
> better they be funny
> or threatening
> like the small dog in koltès

72

now i'm thinking i could almost tell you stories...

three characters

asking for a frame, as usual, with me in there too, the narrator.

and me?

for you, there's nan louise,

a sly and surly grad student going on 26.

with russ dolman, a sculptor, whose home is in vermont, and my long-dead grandmother hetna, for i glimpsed her in the night. we were going to a concert in a car.

i'd been missing grandma

for so many years. she was

the anchor

of my world, kept me for my naps four through six.
sherry, cigarettes, and stacks of novels. disdained a bit by lise, but respected by pop, she was piano and t.v. to all of us. before her daughter's birth, she'd been

a musician

of note, mostly classical, but she also worked

in vaudeville,

played the orpheum circuit from 1912 to 1919, for gangsters like al capone, and with figures like mae west.

then, when lise came, she settled down

and taught.

73

she'd run away from home (an iowa banking family) in her twenties

to find her place with sal.

a slight, intelligent man, with a twinkle in his eye.

hetna was grand,

a striking, corpulent woman, with pale luminous skin, large reddish-brown, almond-shaped eyes, and dark auburn hair that she wore loosely braided down her back.

grandpa sal was a musician too.

he'd given hetna his card, when he swung through town, and heard her play some schumann at an auxiliary tea. his band was looking for a lady pianist. he

played all the strings

though he liked the banjo best.
    he was a polish jew from liverpool, son of a poor family who'd moved to chicago when he was thirteen. and there, he'd taught himself a lot, everything he knew,

but he couldn't read the notes

like hetna.

74

russ, by contrast, taught art and design at highbury and other nearby schools. he'd made himself a name in europe, china, and the states, and was settled deep in academia.

a genial man,

not too tall, a little plump. but always tastefully dressed, in dark simple clothing,

a soho look

that fully masked his body.
he had an open, meaty face, with curly gray hair & blue-gray eyes (nothing to hide there). his manner was all naked sincerity. his hand outstretched, he looked at you straight, with a steady, sensual gaze, whose intensity was offset (just a bit) by a small, but often breaking, crooked smile.

nan louise wasn't sure what to make of that smile.

sometimes it looked sheepish, like a vulnerable plea. at other times, it hit her like a smirk. but she liked him nonetheless. his talk was warm and unpretentious, and he wasn't shady,

his stance

was relaxed, that of an ordinary good man, who just happened to be, was raised to be,

an artist.

75

so it shouldn't have been a surprise to see his old red car,
pulling around the driveway of his stately vermont house,

when he came like a gentleman

up to the front door, to fetch: you (nan), and me, and hetna,
determined to transport us to the concert hall,

courteously catering to hetna,

of whom he'd never heard before. i thought at first he might
want... who knows what from nan,

imagining him quite narrowly,

or as somebody concerned about my writing. it never crossed
my mind he might care for other things, have passions besides
art and power (reading and sex).

you'd never pictured him a moment tinkering with cars.

but i decided i could ask him about this one, not out of curiosity,

you'd never stoop to that,

but to open up a topic that could lead back to my fraught...

tell him it reminded you of another old car,

one made long ago by a certain mr. mack (father's friend),
back where i grew up, that codger from brooklyn, who lived
for decades on our compound.

the first old bloke to grope you after geronimo the 3rd?

(who'd sat me on his lap when i was 4). yeah, that one, mr. mack, who brought down my first blood at age 11.

your father dubbed that guy a genius too.

mechanical, he said, because he'd built his engine from old appliance parts.

76

russ listened to my story with his usual frank look, said he wasn't as adept as my old neighbor, had just fallen in love with this particular old car, which he'd found sitting at his aunt's house in the sixties. it was a 1936 jaguar,

hardly a creation of his own desire.

with the help of a local garage, he'd finally made it work, and somehow kept it running ever since.
    it was an open car with nice proportions, but it had no dashing paint or chrome-work,

no smooth, sleek lines.

so it didn't look like a jaguar (its shape looked more like a tractor's to me). and i couldn't say much else about the car, knowing little about anything except writing, music, dance. but i was so beholden to russ for taking grandma to this con-cert that i began digging, in my purse...

for money?

no, prying to find

the right key.

77

and i deigned to wonder why hetna had come back, and

why we were going to this concert.

it had to be for our sake that russ had agreed, and somehow
in cahoots with hetna. but he took this mission so seriously,
was so much more attentive to hetna than to you, nan, or to
me, that i felt baffled. and this puzzlement increased when

grandma began to morph.

she was hetna, alright, come back to life. but as we led her
across the driveway to the old red car, she

wavered,

appearing first as the hunched, old woman i'd known throughout my teens, taking three pushes to rise from russ's easy chair,
and then unable to stop lurching forward, as she tottered
head-long across the floor. but then she straightened up, and
broke into a stride, to become finally a blondish woman, lean
and tough, with a sixtyish sort of face, sporting sharp hair and
handsome features, with something of hillary's beauty, mixed
with another, drier woman's face, one i'm sure i've never seen.
and then, as she entered the car, she

began to crane her neck,

as if seeking her reflection in the mirror.

as if in taking on that image, she became

another.

78

i hadn't a clue how this old bird had sprung from hetna, or what she had to do with me and russ. and yet i acquiesced,

determined to play a part.

and when she settled in, i was much relieved. for once we got going, she became hetna again, still hunched, and formless, though

spilling ancient mysteries and grace.

and she wasn't, as i'd feared she'd be, placed next to russ up front. rather, seating her securely behind him, and explaining he was worried she might get cold, he handed me

a woolen blanket,

and asked me to sit beside her,

to shield her shoulders from the wind.

i'd wanted to be up front,

wanting to be close

to the driver, but also knew i had better keep my distance. so i stayed put, patiently seated where i was, and did my best to look indifferent through the rear-view mirror, crossing ten miles of vermont hills, the green, green grass, white framed houses, and scattered red barns,

with nan's chestnut locks,

now blowing in, now away, from her small pink mouth, against a pillowed, pale-blue sky.

79

the concert hall was on the outskirts of highbury. the atrium appeared

both open and closed,

like the marvelous MEYERSON HALL in dallas by i. m. pei (though on a scale more intimate, less grand), and with a terrace ultramodern and pleasant,

lined with horizontal fountains

like the OPÉRA DE LYON. the building's walls, the walk, everything in sight, was made of clean, pale gray cement, but lined with long blue-painted boxes of marigolds, with

here and there a splash of red geraniums

raised high on poles in hanging pots.

80

a good crowd was gathering for this sunday matinee. the elderly had come in finery, the young were wearing jeans and light tops.

and all were opening doors for hetna,

and as we entered the hall, russ offered his right arm to her for balance, while she steadied the other with a smooth wooden cane.

so we just followed meekly behind.

yes, with you, nan, carrying our bags and coats, and me feeling both subdued and anxious. for all this ushering and care
for hetna reminded me of bright nights in my childhood, of
evenings when the high-class ladies in our town, subscrib-
ers to the musical society, would come to her house, perched
upon our family's "compound," come to hear our grandma play.

you would shine the punch bowl and the tea-cups

through the afternoon, then dress in my prettiest blue blouse.

proudly let the first guests pat you on the head,

then run out in the dark,

to feel the gathering,

the surge controlled by my two brothers, whose bouncing
flashlights ushered in all the guests' cars,

beams shooting

through our parking lot.

81

as we made it down the aisle, the orchestra began

the din of tuning up.

russ's seats (as usual) were the finest in the house,

center of the third row.

i felt happy to be there, the two of us together, with russ and grandma between. but no sooner did we sit, than russ popped back up, had to go back out and make a call.

so bewildered once again by the commotion,

and depressed to feel the artist pull away once more, i began to wonder... why'd he bring us in the first place?

why not grab our coats and leave?

but i was trying (in those days) to be patient. so i told myself this might just be an exercise, a strategy specifically designed to

kindle more desire through a thick wall of respect

and make it all the stronger — flame.
    but when he returned, my hopes fell flat. for less than kindling, he was carrying three programs, and pointing to a picture on the front,

eloise, playing the cello.

82

she's got what you're seeking, whispered russ. he'd been wanting me to hear her since the day we met. a friend from berlin, today she'd play us elgar in e minor. she had what we'd come for.

a knife went through your throat.

but i just smiled.

so this was it again.

i'd often had to face

green-eyed monsters,

sometimes when i'd least expect.
     such gripping fears had consumed me since i was a child,
left me so depressed i couldn't grow. my role had been the runt's,

the last shall be the least.

my siblings were all destined to be greater than myself. then
there were my privileged peers.

around your neck, a heavy stone.

     and there was envy over judy, joan and jill: the adopted
girl whose parents loved her, the tall blond sassy girl with
boots, the blue-eyed girl with ribbons in her hair, while my
brothers teased me and abused me, and my sisters fanned
the flames.

everybody stepped on you as though not small enough.

told me i had no place in our house. found, they said i was,
a small desert snake,

under a big rock.

whereas,

somehow, they'd lost their precious sister.

a snow-white girl with cherry lips & long dark hair, and
were stuck instead with me (surviving),

fine brown.

83

plain, i felt, so plain, so long identified with ground, that
i could hardly lift my head, and so began a valiant search,
a struggle to stand, and draw some worth.

first focusing on your lumpy body,

trying to stretch it out, make it thin. jump and twirl about,

to give your hidden beauty birth.

around 14, i almost made it. one day i sprang like fire on the
stage. my eyes grew depth with make-up next to small red dots,
my legs could bend and burst.

> but then everybody tried to seize you
> till you crashed
> and fell back down

> gravity imposed its lids once more
> so you tried to flee
> your desert sideways

> skirt across the ocean
> skipping over ice to sow
> a seed or two in *douce france*

and there indeed i fetched myself some distance and respect. got my hands on cream puffs, unrelated men, developed
how to scheme with taste. consumed all i desired, then spat
it right back out, practiced swallowing, then puking with my
torso, throat, and face,

till this pattern became a sacred habit,

automatic reflex of escape.

84

and then sitting in the dark, years later, disappointed by
the yearning that was gnawing at my ribs, amidst the bustle
in vermont,

you simply changed…

i no longer yearned for the "artist." what i wanted would be
coming on the next train. all i had to do was turn and catch it.

that's when eloise, shining, silky,

in her dress, her pale and comely face, her long, cascading
streams of silver-gold hair,

floated down the stage,

greeted the conductor with the slightest nod,

blew a kiss to you, and me, and hetna,

then wrapped her knees around her heavy instrument (anchor
to the ground), her bow perched like a wing on air.

as she played, our pain weakened

and grandma slowly straightened in her chair, every stroke wiped out a wrinkle on her brow, and left me lighter, fuller, knowing,

needing nothing finally to articulate.

listen, i could listen, no longer felt the need to speak.

instead you could just see,

fill my eyes with hetna, who was slowing turning back again toward her own youth, yet moving through the figure she'd morphed to once before, the face i'd glimpsed in russ's driveway,

a face russ might have shaped,

which i now saw carried something of his own.

what was there to do but take that in?

for there was nothing left but flesh & stones between us — hetna, me, him, and nan, with eloise playing lightly, playing deeply,

changing forms to timelessness.

85

so i was thinking we could stay, close our eyes

in bliss,

when in the silent break between two movements, the world
shifted yet again.

now russ was still beside me, but grandma, she was gone,
while eloise, on the stage assumed the face i'd seen before, the
handsome, aging woman, with the short-cropped hair, pretty
eyes and forehead, square clenched jaw, merging with the
woman in the driveway. and now her strong tan arms were
simply sawing strings and space, while her ankles, slightly
thick, were spilling over the edges of her round black pumps,
very firmly planted on the wooden stage.

and the vision you had first?

that shining face and dress with streams of heavenly hair,
they'd somehow disappeared into the rafters. and russ, he was
just sitting there complacently, calm fingers tapping mutely
on his lap,

just listening,

as though nothing were missing,

as though presence itself were there.

86

it was hard to deal with, such a circus. too great a trial for my patience, and

you didn't want to to lose hetna,

though i'd never asked her to come back. now i knew i needed her to stay, stay

with the gliding spirit

that eloise had been. so i grabbed my shawl and left the concert. search for them, i would, though i did not know

where to begin.

87

out of town, i ran, pounded down the streets and concrete sidewalks, past the wood-framed houses with their wide, green lawns, past the old red barns,

flying,

till i reached a quiet wood.
     there i could see nothing but the tall, dark trees, inviting me to lose myself beneath their tender boughs, where i wan-dered till i sank from tiredness,

weeping for all those you'd left behind,

mourned the loves i'd lost or cast away,

whether eloise and sal, or jack and jill,

the world that used to be my childhood,

mother, father, sisters, brothers,

everyone i'd clung to, each one i'd despised,

everything desired, then tossed.

till my mind was finally empty and i stretched out on the earth.

that's when eloise came back

> floating through the air
> not the seasoned cellist
> sawing on taut strings
> but the angel with the wing
> that plucked the air

88

and she laid down beside me, pressed her tender body up against my weary skin, while her silver voice whispered in my ear:

see, i've come back, please let me in.

i kissed her shining head, clasped her in my arms, drew her to my breast, prepared to hold her there forever. but then she gently rolled and slipped inward,

disappeared once more into your own small frame,

said she'd stay a while in my body,

where we both could rest and breathe.

sleep fell on us both, you tucked in my side. and hetna too, with all her fleshy folds, swaddling us tight inside her dreams.

89

when dusk fell i saw headlights in the distance. i stood and shook off leaves, careful not to trouble spirits

rooting in your chest.

and what do you know, there was russ again, rumbling down the road in his red car, searching for us through this patch of wood, coming for a bow, since it was he who'd run this show, backwards, pointing to the path

lit through the rear-view mirror.

he turned the engine off, sat there straight and still, as the blood-red sun ducked down in silence. i ventured closer bit by bit,

timid as a deer,

trying not to spill the rising secrets.

90

BUY (ANOTHER TICKET)

the night before
i was in the airport in tehran
where i just wanted to get
to another airport in europe

but i couldn't get out of any
of those bare forsaken spaces
each time i'd make a move
my bag would be lost or stolen

so i'd have to return for
another pit stop a passport
or sleep in some miserable hotel
kissing the plane — alas

let's hear another.

91

annie was invited to deirdre's. a bright sunday in july. light, white, the morning air. warm and breezy.

hardly a cloud in the sky.

she let her puppy out, 6 am.

birds on the back porch, singing.

brandy's short loud barks were coming from the front. while annie was preparing breakfast for her son, charlie, coffee for her husband, fred, a cardinal flew by the kitchen window.

that was a good sign.

she popped two waffles in the toaster, poured charlie's juice, and decided to invite eileen over.

mothers, sisters, come along!

eileen was three years older, recently divorced. two weeks before she'd moved to a nearby condo. an apartment in the middle of them all. and annie wanted to spend time with her. why not take her on the drive? ride together in the car to deirdre's house and

kill two birds with one stone.

92

deirdre was annie's ex-mother-in-law. they'd gotten along famously the past few years, since stan and susan (max's older twins) had moved away. max was deirdre's son, a banker. two years before he had remarried, sadie. and they all got together, on holidays, or whenever stan or susan were in town. family was solid ground.

annie was the youngest

in a sprawling west-coast clan. but she never could stand all their hullabaloo and hazing. often knocked down by all their sun and crashing waves, *never in control,*

now pummeled, now left high and dry, she anchored herself far away to stake out some direction and stability.

things hadn't been easy,

but she now felt at peace, like a gently watered vine in her own garden,

learning bit by bit to grow.

so she got anxious when eileen upped and followed her back east, wanting to try her hand too at writing. she'd found a job in a publishing house (the same one in manhattan where deirdre'd interned as a teen), then plunked all her stuff ten miles down the road from annie, in new jersey.

93

annie loved to make people happy, she longed to make deirdre and eileen happy

and feel buoyant at the same time.

deirdre's partner had recently passed away. so she too had moved closer, into an assisted living community, down by the shore. annie had wanted to call on her for months, but never could find the time. all through the spring, she'd been trying to complete (bring to a point, polish and unwind) a little story. but she had papers to correct, no time to herself, could hardly find a minute to write or rest or breathe.

charlie was never the problem, nor fred. fred was always helpful, gentle on the inside, kind and smart without, and a committed writer too. he asked almost nothing of her. he and charlie, all they ever needed were her eyes, smile, and bursts of attention from time to time to stroke their palms or brace their heavy heads,

gather up their fears at night.

so, free at last (for the summer), she decided

this could be the day.

a perfect sunday.

she'd devote it to a drive to elsewhere,

spend time away with deirdre and eileen,

and take along her little guy.

but charlie shook his curls, pouted full lips, "no way i'm gonna leave brandy behind" (puppy named for liquor streaks running down his fur). so she decided they could

bring the dog too,

and phoned eileen, telling her they'd soon come to fetch her, around

10ish by the east gate.

94

sunny harbor was about an hour further, nestled (according to the slick brochure) in a neat, quiet spot beside the sea.
but when annie turned in the drive, she was surprised to see

the opposite of calm.

the place was bustling with all kinds of stands and stores,
a beach, a boardwalk, and some buildings backed up to the
ocean. a sign inside the parking lot pointed to a dock, where
residents could leave their boats. "it's odd, don't you think,"
mumbled annie, "that these duffers would be interested in
boating?"

old age isn't what you think.

eileen snapped, "most people get their golden years together,
turn over a new leaf," then clenched her jaw in silence, and
surveyed the lot, pointing annie to the closest empty space.

annie wasn't convinced,

she never was, by whatever eileen said, but let the hard parts
of their difference go. searching instead for more porous, common ground, she noted

these apartments looked peculiar,

nothing like retirement communities out west. several small
buildings conjoined by a large façade with thick white walls,
covered in what eileen called *crappy crepi.* annie thought
she once had seen a place like this. maybe in atlantic city?
but eileen just shrugged, as if to imply,

like any mall or theater in the northeast.

95

the sun was high when they walked in through the wide front steps, and crossed

a stream of people pouring out.

seniors, escorted by their relatives, of course. but there weren't only oldsters inhabiting this place,

a number were young

invalids.

some missing limbs, others walking on crutches.

annie saw mostly one-legged people at first. brandy started to growl and charlie looked uncomfortable and nervous. so she suggested the two of them could wait outside the building. she and eileen would ask deirdre out to lunch, then they'd all have a stroll

along the boardwalk.

96

the sisters took the elevator to deirdre's (6th floor), slipping their way through the crowd within. annie was small & pale, with fine red hair. even features, pretty green eyes. simply dressed in jeans, a long white shirt, a dark blue raincoat, red sneakers.

eileen was taller,

and more conspicuous, with cowboy boots, a flowing black skirt and a colorful guatemalan blouse. she was a striking brunette, with a low sexy voice, sporting lots of attitude and make-up.

annie rang the bell,

deirdre got the door, greeted them at once with a bright, cheery voice. she too was an imposing woman, with a handsome ruddy face, sparkling eyes, and short, neatly clipped white hair. she'd been so looking forward to annie's visit, but was put out at first to see eileen had come along.

deirdre barely knew her,

had met her only once, 20 years before, at max and annie's wedding, and had found her way too flighty and dramatic. but deirdre knew her manners, when to behave, so she masked her disappointment with a handshake and a smile, and asked for news of charlie and fred.
   annie made the usual apologies for fred, he was a journalist besieged with deadlines, "we've all been overwhelmed with work this spring," and began telling deirdre about the new puppy.

charlie and brandy waiting downstairs,

"they're right outside the building," she exclaimed, "so i guess we ought to leave right away." "too bad," deirdre said, "i've just put coffee on" —"well then, no," eileen broke in, "we don't need to rush. charlie will be fine — i'm dying for a cup — and could we please have a quick tour of your place? the layout looks... intriguing."

97

the inside walls looked the same as the building's façade, sporting the same icky stucco. but that was the least part of their "interest." the living/dining-room, where deirdre had first invited them to sit, was shaped to begin with in the most standard way, a rectangle emerging from the outside hall. but the back of the room's shape was bewildering. annie couldn't make heads nor tails of it.

the walls tapered gradually, then rounded to a point,

enclosing within something like a moat,

a deep semi-circular canal.

so the apartment as a whole gave the impression of being half-boat, half-house (rather than a boat house or house boat). for instead of any other normal room or hallway attached to this main one, there was another little boat-room anchored in the moat, with a small row boat that squared off on one end, producing in effect a large double bed, equipped with a mattress, a comforter, and cushions. "this," said deirdre, "is my bedroom, the whole is designed to keep us afloat,"

not like other places that cradle to the grave.

here they put the emphasis on action,

water sports, fishing, fulfilling more than dreams,

setting out to see what life's about.

98

annie felt puzzled, even queasy about this, but eileen took it right in stride. and deirdre was pleased by her enthusiasm, so they all sat down and started visiting, spat out jolly bits of conversation, catching up over this scrap of family news and that, till they finally went outside to

pick up charlie.

there he glowed, golden curls shining in the sun, trying to teach new tricks to brandy. and deirdre was so pleased to see him. such a bright, funny kid, really sweet and clever with them all.

she'd been awfully upset when annie'd married fred, but she'd always looked on charlie kindly. so she asked him about school, remarked how much he'd grown, a foot or two at least since christmas! "soon you'll be taller than your mom," she quipped. charlie was

going on eight.

99

the foursome decided to walk around the grounds, let brandy off the leash, work up their appetite for lunch. there were palms and oleanders, all kinds of plants that seemed quite out of place. annie was baffled by how shoddy the whole complex looked. the exotic plants suggested luxury, so

why couldn't they pay for better upkeep?

and the connection between the residence and the grounds wasn't clear. far from opening onto a harbor, as the apartment's odd design led one to expect, *the back walls were high and dingy, almost prison-like,*

and the "gardens," though not far removed from the beach, were filled with vacant spots, with rubbish strewn amidst random patches of dry, dead weeds, whereas annie had been picturing lush, green grass. was this a retirement retreat? or a resort somehow thriving

with dead spurs.

but deirdre and eileen were hitting it off beyond belief, and annie found that amusing. they'd got talking over lunch about playwriting, a passion both shared. on and on they went about this play and that, and the many conferences and workshops they'd attended.

eileen said she would come back to sunny harbor for one of deirdre's shows (written years before). deirdre said she'd introduce eileen to one of her best friends (a producer). though annie was repelled, she decided she was glad.

deirdre and eileen were getting on so well,

why not let them pitch and ramble all they liked.

100

meanwhile, charlie downed his sandwich in a flash. so annie let him go to play with brandy on the beach, feeling she should stay behind,

finish this lunch with the ladies, put her two cents in,

since after all, the afternoon was off (and running). but right around dessert, *she couldn't take it anymore.*

she was bored sick, began to wish the day was over. if only she could strike out on her own,

find an escape,

a temporary break.
 so, after she had paid and made her way out of the shack behind deirdre and eileen, who were planning once again to walk down by the dock, she said she had to go back upstairs.

she'd left her hat and bag…

inside,

could she also fetch something for deirdre or eileen?

101

the sun was still high just after 2 o'clock, as annie returned toward the residence from behind. despite the odd architec‑ ture and sickening nursing smell, she felt curiously drawn to these buildings. first she crossed a large, run‑down pool

she hadn't seen before

then stopped to look around the grounds once more.

here too were disabled people,

several missing two legs rather than one. some were only trunks with arms and stumps in wheelchairs. others, badly crippled, were being pulled around in wagons on their backs.

and the assistants were far from well themselves,

hobbling about on canes and crutches.

from time to time, a resident would suddenly take a plunge or be dunked into the water by a helper. annie felt repulsed, but was also intrigued, musing to herself that

getting old is really tough,

when a wagon with a cripple knocked into her knees, and pushed her fully dressed into the pool.

102

now i've fallen deep, she thought. but the cool blue water was inviting, not like the grungy grounds or odd buildings. so she opted not to jump back out, but settle in instead, pull off her soaking jeans and sneakers, plunk them on the side,

swim around a bit,

rejoicing in a change of scene. diving down in her underwear and shirt, annie felt protected and revived inside the pool.

silence all around this floating theater.

she enjoyed her round but slender, small, pale limbs, the red flames of her hair, the flatness of her belly as she slithered around the blue-tiled bottom

where no other swimmers were in sight.

103

when she tired, she got out, and explained her accident to

gina, a nice young girl,

who was cleaning up some drinks around the pool,

pretty with a clubbed foot.

gina was kind and sympathetic, handed annie a warm towel,
then dragged her jeans *&* sneakers to the dryer. grateful and
refreshed, annie wrapped herself inside the fluffy whiteness,
and resumed her mission to collect her hat. whence, heading
for the steps, she crossed an old gentleman she thought she
knew, partially hidden behind huge sunglasses.
  yup, there he blew…

rob, deirdre's dead partner,

standing by the bar, drinking with a friend, babbling away,
as though still bubbling in the mix.

and he didn't seem surprised to see annie,

just greeted her warmly, kissed her on the cheek, and asked
"how're charlie and fred?,"

which led annie to wonder where she really was.

she shook her head and tried to concentrate, but then got
distracted by an image,

her own reflection in the mirror.

behind the bar her face was shining, looking beautiful, her hair tangled high in a dark red mass. here & there, a curly strand fell on her brow. and her cheeks dimpled, as they had in her youth.

so, she didn't really feel like searching outward anymore. she smiled and took her leave of rob.

104

encouraged she'd survive the long afternoon, she made her way inside the strange building, nodded at the folks lumbering about, headed with a light step toward the elevator.

the crowds were all gone.

the residents had left, retreating for siestas,

except for two lingering men,

holding back the elevator doors, as though waiting courteously for others to catch up. annie thought at first that

one was legless.

he had buzzed gray hair, a weather-beaten look, a strong square jaw, narrow blue eyes, and he was shirtless. the other man was young, dark, and slightly built. warm brown eyes, a beautiful arched brow, and gleaming broad teeth.

the doors closed.

they started to ascend, and annie lowered her eyes.

staring at the floor with some relief, she saw the older man's hidden leg and foot come into view. he wasn't missing anything, was all there, and like the young man, muscular and handsome. but this made her feel uneasy in a different way, ashamed that she could see him, and self-conscious.

the closed metal box approached the 6th floor, the two men coughed. the boy pulled a switch and the graying man hissed, "all we need to save is her face," while the boy sneered,

now you'll get your due.

glaring at her, smiling over teeth, were grins that twisted wild, threatening lips.

annie's little chest, her heart, began to pound. the elevator slowly mounted past deirdre's 6th floor, stopping only at the top: 13. she now saw she was trapped. it's going to feel like hell, she thought. they'll beat me, and i'll

never make it through.

105

but then, desire quelled (just like that) what annie had just felt toward both

bad men —

the draw toward this place, her pride in her pale face, her pretty eyes and mouth. the joy of her white limbs, her wish to probe the depths, all she felt

turned instantly to dust.

and yet somehow she retained reason, managed not to panic, her thoughts remained clear. she knew she wanted out, to run down, then out, the building stairs. then home, back home with charlie to her garden.

and she saw her only hope was to confuse these men somehow,

lure the devils with her dark side.

so, she gazed up at them both, straight inside their eyes, smiled like she wanted to submit to them. play, she'd learned to play, get inside their game.

the pair relaxed and laughed,

stripped off shirts and pants, prepared to take it easy, have their fun with her,

till annie flipped the switch,

opened up the doors, and slipped right past their gripping legs and grasping hands, ran as fast as her two feet could carry

trembling little legs, thumping down the stairs.

she pushed the heavy door, headed for the car, but then remembered

she still needed to get charlie.

106

there he was, still shining in the distance, walking on the boardwalk with his pup. so, she slowed herself and turned, walked back toward the silvery pool, where rob and other residents were gathering. out of breath, she was, and rob was engaged, still chatting away with friends, as though he'd never stopped.

now that she was safe, she thought that she should wait
to say goodbye.

time — this time, buy time,

dive (instead of fall) into the pool.
      and there, once immersed, she soon forgot about things
past, lost track of harsh attacks just like of boredom. began to
just let go, swim around again, stretch out a line or two,

wiggle through the plot,

kick away with lunch, all that just had happened in the box.
      and yet when she came up for air, it struck her again: how
odd these people were. all kinds of decrepit creatures, some
of their parts gone, others fully there. people chatting like all
was to be expected. the maimed young, they were here, the
dead were even here,

swimming in the pool

alongside annie, whose head popped up again close to rob's.

107

now he made it clear he had been searching, "i've come back
for you, my dear." he was so fond of her,

his deer?

and glad, he was so glad she'd come to visit: "pretty, you're so
bright inside this basin."

his eyes gleamed.

he knew she would come, had long ago told deirdre she'd return. and yet his pull was less forceful than that pressure in
the box. close had been the call and strong the downward
thrust inside the building.

here the draw was less, no grip, no cutting off,

no heat, no clutching legs or fists, not even sweating. so annie
thought less about the danger. since rob was here,

perhaps there'd be no death?

and she'd seen she could flee threats. felt proud and glad of
that, so her heart swelled from rob's sustained attentions.
    but then she spied eileen, who'd jumped beside her in the
pool, and saw

her sister had come prepared to fish.

she was swimming round and round, and she was casting.
hacking minds, connections of all kinds. then she started

hovering near,

swimming alongside annie right in tandem, forcing her to retract once again. so annie decided to duck, then bob — plunge
her feet straight down to the bottom of the pool and then
spring up for air. eileen, she knew, would never leave the top,

her body stretched out long upon the surface.

that way she could skim through conversations,

lay her whole self out

in sheets of prose.

108

so annie just kept bobbing, rarely stopped to chat, resting only to catch her breath from time to time. but she longed to know all rob had been through: had he really died or just crossed over?

had he really left his flesh?

was this his solid core, or the truest body of illusions? she asked him too about the boat-apartments: could they really carry seniors out to sea?

rob was intrigued

with all this questioning. the freshness of her face had dawned on him in life. so, he

did his best to focus and respond.

but soon he got distracted by eileen, began to swim behind her long, lusty body, pursued her like a fish, while annie kept on bobbing up and down.

she felt like bait

until, with one great splash, rob caught eileen at last, and saw she was less fine, less shimmering than annie, whence he let her go,

swimming round and round.

after which, annie felt safe and whole inside, like she'd be able to unwind her windy tune.

all she had to do was keep on bobbing,

while eileen's flashy plays might come to nought.

and then, while she was drying,

just outside the pool, ready to say "bye" and "thanks" to deir-dre, who'd just waved to her, to rob, and to eileen, who'd fi-nally come to join them with charlie and the pup, at that very moment,

eileen asked rob,

as though he hadn't died,

who he'd leave his money to?

and once she uttered that,

this sister shrank,

dissolved under a splash of disapproval,

like the wicked witch, from the bucket inside oz.

"how dare she be so brash," scoffed deirdre, "so crass before my dear departed!" somehow annie knew then that her reach was higher than eileen's, and her roots extended deeper. for though she might catch herself fending off petty thoughts,

never would she spit such venom.

and since rob was still there, since there was no death,

why bother to prepare for leavings.

109

so annie drove back home and forgot about eileen, left her standing there, like the water in the pool where she'd been preening.

she played a new cd,

joked with charlie and his dog, felt fine about her "time" off.

but when the next light came,

pulling her scorched eyes toward another denser day,

her spirits sank.

she was heavier than she'd thought, and rolling side to side

instead of springing.

and though she yearned to rise and see that cardinal once more, hear the barking dog — this time forsaking all thoughts of shooting birds with stones, so as to catch instead the gently falling free things — alas,

she could not move.

stiffly wavering, she was,

between a thought and wish,

and her limbs were

somehow rigid, yet flailing.

110

i feel stuck — ahoy —
what could this mean?

outside my window
the thin green day
browner than it ought

to be
is waiting for a
silent singing voice

to bring me back
what's bonnie

let's hear another...

111

jim and i had twins, two adorable kids, not identical, a
boy and girl. and with them we received

fine presents,

all sorts of things (for children), and we were proud,

proud and gratified parents,

with family and friends all about. and agnes, our governess,
was also helping around the house, cleaning this and that.

the boy,

chubby and magnificent, got

plenty of attention,

a lot more than

the girl,

who was also beautiful though

smaller, hard to notice.

a true enchantress with sparkling eyes, a button nose, and light brown hair, drawing you right into her face.
    i was cuddling her one day, a shining afternoon in april, when i realized, oh my god, i'd forgotten

her name?

at the time, i thought i knew what we had called her brother, so decided not to panic, and assumed: it's got to come back, i've just forgotten because i'm getting older.
    so calmly, steadfastly, and with firm belief, i continued to care for my girl, as though each little thing were in its place, just pausing once in a while, trying to recall her name.

was it cassandra?

that crossed my mind. but no, i thought, jim and i couldn't have called her that because we could never have let slip a name we knew so well, and

cassandra brings bad news.

but still i looked it up, did some research, and found that cassandra could have been appropriate:

cassandra. greek mythology. a daughter of the tro-
jan king priam, [...] was given the gift of prophecy by
apollo. when she cheated him, however, he turned this
into a curse by causing her prophecies, though true,
to be disbelieved.

so now i thought, sure, cassandra and i,

your name is june,

(thanks to juno or to writing this in june?), we found ourselves
cuddling in a bed, in the midst of a social situation (where
i often find myself though i prefer to be alone). and then i
realized it was

time

to change cassie's diaper, yes. so i did this with no hesitation,
without any fuss, though it was sure to be a terrible mess,
and i was awkward throughout the operation.

shit got on things,

but eventually, not dallying, and with all the diligence i could
muster (as well as plenty of water and wipes), i was able to

clean everything off.

my baby, cassie, was pleasing, presentable again. and the hands
on the clock had moved, a number of ticks. by now we'd spent
more than an hour together, huddled, withdrawn from the
party way too long. so it was time to show her off once more.

you gathered your baby girl,

tight-wrapped in my arms, and resolved to go forth, face
the world with her.

112

but first, i decided to confess to jim, find out from him our
girl's actual name, which i now remembered i had forgotten.
i asked him to whisper it to me, only to discover

he'd forgotten it too.

so i began searching through the gifts we'd received, hoping
to find clues, perhaps a card or a label marked

to x from

y and z, maybe something from aunt susie or uncle stan... but i
couldn't find one anywhere, so i had to make the search public,
revealing my lapsus even to

georgia and marceline?

my sisters, who confronted me of course.
	marceline was smiling and understanding, georgia, a bit
more stern. but they were both concerned, had questions, and
didn't hesitate to help by pressing: "what's the boy's name?"
asked georgia. and marceline chimed in, "it must be related
to the girl's."
	my ears burned with shame, as i shrank smaller & smaller,
having to admit before my inquisitors that i

didn't know the boy's name either.

and neither did my husband, jim.

their names had totally escaped you,

like drawings on a magnetic plate.

113

and yet what was worse than this forgetting and the humili-
ation that ensued, as

this secret was revealed,

was the horrible feeling that

your sisters were glad and prepared to hear it.

they had known it all along. indeed, georgia informed me,
in her usual forthright way, that they'd been waiting for this
moment to say:

the twins themselves did not exist.

"june, you made them up," georgia quipped, "they're figments.
and now you have to let them go." while marceline, conceding
that jim and i were great, sighed in a syrupy voice: "you and
jim are wonderful for each other, but you don't have, never
have had any children, can't possibly know what parenting's
about."

114

this seemed ludicrous at first. georgia and marceline always
blew things up. and they had always been spiteful,

envious of all

i had "accomplished," as well as of my marriage with jim.
    he and i'd been living with our babies for weeks, caring for
them, cuddling them, and showing them to friends. we were

so happy that they'd finally come, though perhaps a bit late (jim was 46 and i, 42).

you'd saved the best for last.

but as i started grasping for the evidence, those white paper straws, proof with which to tell my sisters, let them know i was tired of their shenanigans,

so they could leave off their judgments,

much to my horror, i couldn't lay my hand on any of the babies' things. their toys and clothes, their cradles and chairs, their bottles and feeding paraphernalia,

no sign of them was anywhere in sight.

everything connected to our twins had vanished. but i still remembered somehow that

cassie was there.

perhaps she was with agnes, in the living room, since i'd gone upstairs before to search the house for gifts, and jim had been there too, playing with our boy (and worrying less than me about the name thing).
so i left georgia and marceline in the kitchen (where we three had sat down to talk) and hurried back to the party in the living room, to scoop my daughter in my arms once more. jim was there. agnes was there. everyone was there, but

your heart was pounding,

for the twins themselves had disappeared.

115

i tried to retain my wits, to keep my composure and my balance. here, after all, was a room full of old friends who could witness to our family's weeks together.

your twins' absence now seemed only

a dream,

a slight misunderstanding,

or sleight of hand,

a slip of the tongue,

a joke. but then the nanny who'd been helping me with household chores came near.

agnes,

yes, agnes, the swiss governess, walked up to me, smiled, and offered me a drink. and when i said to her, trying to strike just the right note, "agnes, you've been caring for my children now for weeks, and you're so good to us, dear, tell me, please…"

where might the little ones be?

"june," she said, "i wish i could tell you and would love to care for your kids, should you and jim ever have any, but…"

you were devastated,

sank to the floor,

all in a heap,

began to seriously doubt myself,

admitting confusion and defeat.

116

where had our children gone? that evening, jim and i went
out to dinner, to consider our dilemma. how had we forgotten what their names were? neither of us could come up with

a clue,

there was no direct action we could take. our words were sad
but civil, with schubert's

DEATH AND THE MAIDEN

playing in the background.

the light drained from your eyes

and our tenderness was gone, but at least we still had each
other to rely on and the hope that our children would return.
this sustained me through endless hours of grief, and still
holds me today.

but when my love is off at work

> i often find myself alone
> pouring over an
> endless *book of names*
> trying to recapture
> my infants

and it's only this exercise that keeps me sane and helps me to ward off my sisters, who still call me every two weeks (both together — one ear each — glued to their double-phones).

they mean well, i know it, and often give me good ideas, even while taunting me about my struggles and explaining over and over how jim had been no help against my madness. it's now well known to be genetic, they say, and we're all prone to this — *folie à deux*.

> then someone gave
> jim a kimono
> reminding me
> i had one too
>
> so i packed my
> pride inside out
> and wore it to
> the frigging zoo

117

prosimètre (pas de six)

i could remember that a deer was curious —

why do you keep cowering inside?

so much so that she came to greet me by my window. 6 am, a large white frame, my office window pane, which is also

where you rock and sit.

i have no other room.

this writing is my life,

my surest place for living bit by bit.

118

a pale blue sky, with dabs of pink & green, spilling on the new horizon.

the lilac hedge was there, witnessing,

standing in the foreground, at attention.

your deer was chomping on flowers about to burst,

much like i chew gum. purple petals stretching out from leafy tender stems. and underneath her breath i heard her muttering,

when will you come out, mother?

how can we bring out, sisters,

the gossamer of our father?

won't you see, breathe, touch,

feel the magic that he's spun.

119

valery on horseback through the woods is trotting
her clear green eyes are darting through the brush

valery has a great coat a riding stick and boots
mud all over those boots and a loose white shirt

tucked into her old gray jeans with holes
on each worn leg where her pale thin

knees gently peak out as she nudges her
black horse to ride faster on and on

valery with her gold hair tied tightly at her neck
her wide pink mouth her olive skin and wisps

valery is looking for her bambi on the lawn

120

i can't go out today, though he promised me

our father?

that if i pass the test, he'll let me fly away (inside a wide balloon) and feel his gossamer forever.

now he wants you to stay put,

let others come to me, that's why he sent you first

to announce the coming deer,

this series of temptations,

or characters.

121

valery's the first. you've seen her in the world. talkative
she is, and smiling. in front of you in lines around the plane.
it's easy enough to see

she has a life,

she's earned it through her tempered, striking beauty. but what
she wants is really to cross over, not to be the object of af-
fections anymore. not to be a star, but to jump right through
the screen, get the camera in her hand and shoot the movie,

crack the whip.

122

next clare appears, a dancer in her mid-forties. a patient, sensitive teacher, a kind and nurturing soul,

who lives with jürgen,

a german architect, in a great white house in charlotte, north carolina.

clare is plain yet appealing,

medium height with short dark hair, and warm brown eyes.

she has legs like cyd charisse,

narrow hips and heavy breasts.

she tried but wasn't able to have children.

found ways of mothering (her instincts) by training and supporting young girls.

123

but now clare wants to shape, to form something else,

a work that she might call her own.

she longs to create, to offer to the world, not just exercises in the studio, endless repetitive routines for all those girls.

now she wants to draw up something beautiful,

wind up moving figures that might stick through time & space,

touch people,

even strangers in the audience,

    where they see, hear, speak,

and breathe.

124

    a dance for a small troupe that could somehow cross the space

    between this stage and "life."

she's wondering what she has to work with, turning steps &
situations over in her mind and thinking about valery,

    while singing…

        i bet val could rise
        she's got talent in
        droves and beauty a star
        though she's always
        ducking the limelight

        i cherished her
        taught her as though
        she were my own
        once abigail donned
        that gaunt death mask

        the pretty darling
        was just thirteen so
        val and me (her father
        often gone) we stuck
        together from that time on

till i introduced her to nick.

125

who's nick? that young man there, gazing through the frame, and smiling. he's standing

next to valery.

handsome,

debonair.

with light hazel eyes, dark skin, thick black curly hair (mom's a scot, father's nigerian). he's lanky, tall, & graceful, like julia, his twin, who's dancing now for ALVIN AILEY. but clare hard﹣ly knows her, never taught her once, since she was sent to boarding school. it's nick that clare knows well. she often says "she knew him when," before he got so

smooth, sophisticated.

nick must have been fourteen when they moved across the street. played basketball all day, always shooting hoops with boys around his age and, from time to time, with jürgen.

jürgen, where is he?

striding down the hall, waving "good﹣bye darling" through the doorway, tall with sandy hair, squinty eyes, ruddy cheeks. 48, but still looks great, always liked to stay in shape…

126

nick met valery after the nutcracker, a huge holiday bash,

the year they turned 18.

and now they have decided: to get married. clare's delighted,
not just because she made the match, nor because

he's such a good catch,

he's got a bright future (a residency nearby) and soon will
be an orthopedic surgeon. he's also kind and brilliant, quite
committed, clare is sure.

it's valery, it seems, who always drags her feet.

always putting off the wedding date, the shopping for the
dress, and invitations (even) for their scores of guests.

why, clare has barely seen her for weeks.

whereas nick,

he'd just stopped by that morning.

127

he knocked on her front door, just before he left for work,
wearing a dark suit, soft gray shirt, pale green tie.

looking warm and friendly, like always,

but somehow also puzzled or perplexed, as if he weren't quite
sure why he'd come.

> hello clare it's
> good to see you
>
> julia? she's fine
> just moved in with

gus but been away
on tour all spring

ma's surgery?
was rough but the

cancer wasn't much
she's fine now too

doesn't need a thing
how are you clare?

how's that aching
back and jürgen?

128

then nick's broad grin settles on clare's chest.

those heavy ample breasts

that heave behind the brace he'd laced her in last spring, to
give her round shoulders something like a rest. his almond
eyes had twinkled while

his supple fingers pressed,

traveled up and down her spine, her hands, her arms, her neck
and shoulders. he'd been happy to find the corset, administer
the tests. and here he was again,

tending to clare only,

his smile and his eyes inquiring. and though she wonders what
he's after, why he flirts so much, she imagines he's still true
to val, so brushes off

his glance,

asks him where val's been, why so hard to reach? "she's off again," he says, "gone to southern pines, has things out there she wants to do…"

is always somewhere else,

or so it seems.

looking for someone else,

or remembering, perhaps, someone from her past? or

rehearsing something still to come.

129

here, anabel slips in. but wait, i have to… break

this line, this story.

> are you there
> i keep on asking
> under the autumn
> sun stepping on
> the dead and falling
> leaves i'm lost
> cannot convoke
> the thoughts that
> breed from dust
> nor grasp the form
> of ghosts i grieve

go on, go on, i see you're trying, mother,

crying to bring back ondine.

130

anabel's on the porch. her small pale thighs are spread a tad apart. they hardly make a dip in the hemp hammock.

her little feet fan out,

with polished pink toes,

lit up on the tips,

about to dazzle us like nabokov's

butterflies.

her stretchy dark blue skirt's hiked around her hips. her chiffon patterned blouse is falling open, the lace of her silk bra just barely peeking out.

her sweet madonna's face is peacefully composed

resting on a mass of curly, chestnut hair, displaying unabashed to the mottled blue sky

finely molded, even features.

nothing to catch the eye on here, except for tender upturned corners of

unpainted crimson lips,

and two heavy crescent

fringes of black lashes,

bordering translucent

moon-shaped lids.

and lined up underneath on the gray, tattered floorboards, her

pink strappy heels

kicked into the corner in a heap.

131

on the other side of the porch are two white wicker chairs, where victor & sam, anabel's lover and her brother, sit quietly talking. they're gesturing a bit.

victor's small and french,

early thirties, going bald, with bird-like features, deep-set eyes. he's impeccably dressed this morning (as he always is): a dark green long-sleeved shirt (rolled cuffs, an open neck), and ivory-colored linen pants. he's slowly drinking from a chipped red mug, trying to down the awful coffee sam has made.

sam is large and rugged,

about 23. he's got thick, close-cropped hair and is clean shaven.

a soldier at fort bragg,

today he's wearing jeans and a red-checked cotton shirt. but he's not drinking coffee, he's cracking his first beer, for

sam is not a character,

he acts more like a prop. he sits and drinks, and rocks, and sits and drinks.

132

it's eleven o'clock in the morning on this early april day, the same day on which valery (gone to southern pines) is riding. and after nick stops by,

clare sets out to work.

she carefully picks her music: bach, camille, and hersch,

sketches out three patterns in her studio,

but she's having trouble thinking, linking all the steps, doesn't like to force her work, so sets herself instead to puttering. magnificent, it is,

this large white house,

a dream

she had designed with jürgen.

six fine rooms around a courtyard (three open, three closed) with here a cozy corner, and there a vast expanse. some rooms have tile floors, others oak or cherry wood, and pristine walls with lovely modern paintings clare had learned to pick, along with flowers, sculptures, potted plants adorning gleaming doors and windows. all of this set neat

around a garden with a pond,

which harbors three white ducks, one black swan, and a sturdy *art nouveau* green metal table, where on summer mornings clare often likes to sit. now, for the first time in the season, *she changes the water*

in the birdbaths, and cleans her whirlpool tub, thinks perhaps
she'll use it late that afternoon. ease her aching back. why stay
inside on

such a lovely day.

the kind of day that often blooms in north carolina.

133

why even down near southern pines, at anabel's, a ratty, run-
down place, thirty miles from fort bragg, a junkyard with
a shack that needs painting, with two rusty cars and sam's
orange, souped-up truck on oversized wheels,

*the richness of the soil, the thick green grass, the spanish moss
and longleaf pines,*

they make you wonder

why wouldn't everybody want to live here?

here in north carolina, where wildflowers shoot riotous among
the downy weeds.
    just beyond sam's truck,

a purple flowered vine

drapes softly down a forty-foot magnolia tree, holding braided
(through frayed rope) a beat-up family swing,

an old black tire,

where anabel, sam, and georgy used to play.

georgy, where is he?

that child will have no part inside this story.

he's gone for good,

off in jail.

no chance of getting out,

nor emerging from the dark

where we might see him.

134

strange as it feels to be here, with her father's corpse laid out, inside the small front room,

anabel is glad to be back home.

from time to time she lifts her chin and shoulders, awakens from her dreams, picks herself off the hammock, plants her tender feet down on the splintery boards, then wanders inside to perch upon her mother's lumpy chair. and there she sits,

watching over her father

in the dimly lit room. while staring at his dummy body, she gathers all her wits, but doesn't have the nerve to kiss or touch it.

robert

was its name. she remembers now how upright he'd always seemed before.

walking tall and vigorous

before she had left home, though his face was often drained of color, always overworked. mostly sullen and silent. but every now and then she remembers long ago when

robert's face had lit up too, and filled with laughter,

laughter from that throat, and everywhere within a particular warmth and glow that he always seemed to catch from

virginia,

belle's mother, his wife.

135

when anabel was four, they'd all three dance and prance around the living room (brothers stayed outside). but that was long before...

virginia lost her mind and robert turned to non-stop drinking,

no longer to drown out his stinking job (defense contracting, the plant), the "dumb-ass" war, but more to forget about his wife's infirmity,

her mind's wasting away inside that army nursing home

where he'd had to take her, though all agreed (even the doctors) she was much too young.

when she turned fifty-two, she

who'd always cared for everybody else (a nurse, she long had been inside that same old home),

stopped recognizing names and faces,

even her own kin,

and began to wander out in search of strangers every night.

"home" no longer kept her in.

136

as anabel grows tired of thinking, victor sends her back to sleeping.

first she dreams she's quiet
then careens obsessed
choking tears of kindness
down with draughts of rage

a knight's recording
table sees her in distress
happens to spin by
shows her how to dress

how mingling with
wolves can roundly
press each broken bit
of fancy long saved

137

next anabel wakes up again, lights a cigarette, pulls a small black book from her huge pink purse. inspects her precious nails, and pretty fingers. she thumbs through dog-eared pages, circles names and numbers, then hands the book to vic, who moseys toward the kitchen phone.

he dials the first numbers. no answer. he reflects, then flips backwards, till he reaches s, and quickly locates: jürgen and clare schmidt. gets clare on the phone (who was just about to nail her first dance…)

"allo clare oui je
suis ici victor gris

l'ami d'anabel dupree
l'amie de votre amie"

a friend of hers? of
valery's and jürgen's?

anabel's back home
her father just passed

and she hasn't forgotten
all kindnesses

though she'd long
been out of touch

been living in france
with victor for

the last two years
had asked him to call

let friends know about
robert's funeral

"her brother sam and i
we're here with anabel

the service will be held
at sand hills in 3 days

we're hoping you'll
attend with jürgen and val

i don't know why
we can't reach val"

138

anabel's face finally lights in clare's mind —

a small, slovenly girl,

who'd always tagged along,

singing silly songs

to valery. no determination, no control. too slothful to become
a dancer. not well-groomed, squirrelly, & always chewing gum.

a sneer was often plastered on her way too made-up face.

a bad influence she'd always been on valery. once, she caught
them laughing, half-naked, smoking pot. still, virginia had lost
her mind, and now her father too was gone...

so young and so alone.

so clare was glad that victor had called, thought, for sure, she could get valery on the phone, speak to her herself, about this funeral. later, other things... but first she dialed jürgen to help work out her next moves, before responding.

139

order all her thoughts, make a sound plan, scatter spring and chaos to the winds.

> dear do you remember
> anabel dupree? a fort
>
> bragg girl who studied
> dance with me
>
> a spacy raggedy girl
> not serious i recall
>
> but always hovering
> around my studio
>
> while staying here in
> charlotte with her aunt
>
> well today i got
> the strangest call
>
> her father has passed
> and now she's back
>
> to bury him her friend
> victor called and it was

strange i thought
that he would ask us

to the funeral to
come and bring val

why i didn't even
know you knew her

jürgen tell me about
that nor did i know

anabel was still a
friend of val but victor's

tone was so insistent
his voice so intense

that i said sure we could
help him track val down

he says that *you* and i
were kind to belle and

though she moved away
she's still fond of us

while i could hardly even
dredge up who she was

he says that she's lost
touch with all around here

except her brother sam
a soldier at fort bragg

it's good that he's there
(their mother's in a home)

they're so alone since
now the father's gone

her father whom
she hadn't seen for years

it was moving how
devoted victor was

how could i refuse
i said i would find val

and thought to ask
them over this evening

to join us for some
supper in the garden?

victor sounds quite
interesting from paris

and maybe we should
also ask nick and val?

tell me what you think
jürgen? it's funny

how victor kept insisting
you knew anabel

he said that she still
cares about you jürgen

140

jürgen hems and haws, but still confirms the plan, in this way skirts the question that clare had gently posed.

how could he tell clare he'd known anabel like that?

played with her like that. he hoped, he thought and figured

she'd never talk of that.

now that she was grown and living, well… in paris.

such a little girl,

flirting on the porch,

foundling on the porch,

fondling on the porch. so many years ago, a habit he had formed when he was drinking hard that year. he'd lost the contract for the building in berlin, missed the boat at forty. now, no way to get back home. still, he was making a fine living here down south with clare.

anabel, she was a…

pretty slip of a girl, parading like a slut.

a precocious little thing.

a fingered thigh, a willing, open mouth,

a secret covered spot.

a beating heart, a vortex of desire.

141

so why don't we sink deeper within this rushing scene, swim along in clare's river dream.

finally, you and me,

my prodigy,

and also val, your queen.

me upon a park bench waiting. you with your pale green eyes, and

slinky golden hair,

beckoning all to come on,

let her kiss you.

first i see her standing there

like, rising from the sea.

but not like botticelli's venus, covering herself with arms & hands, hair blown long by winds that look like angels, ready to be cloaked.

no, here, she's more domestic and familiar, like titian's simple beauty,

wringing out her hair,

as if preparing for just one more picture, one we don't yet know. or like ingres', where *a golden looking glass, lifted toward her face,*

substitutes itself for that cast-off, empty shell, drifting out to sea in titian.

birth has given way to reflection.

142

thus we are surrounded by a crowd of chubby babes, who don't need to drink.

cherubs at our feet,

who finally give us courage to look out of the frame, and dare the world to

come on, come on and kiss me.

you purse your pale lips against a stormy sky,

a romantic theater backdrop,

as though poised and thirsting for a cloud to break, yet looking askance at me as though to question...

what is all this reticence about?

143

i keep my acrid distance for a while, turn my back and twist my mouth.

try to fend me off,

feelings tied in knots, sitting down alone, returned to judg-
ment. what's love got to do with truth or beauty?

witch in your own trial, fire in the womb.

for me, those cherubs look like demons. but sleep has lasted
long, long tonight, and i'm also in a fog.

but the heavy graying air has put your moral sense to rest,

so i loosen all my strings.

just let go,

let her place a hand upon your breast. it's swelling from the
bottom but springs light to the touch, small globe resting in
her fingers. and i let you touch her breast as well,

trying not to cringe and spit.

and eventually my reticence weakens, begins to fade away. until
through my own volition, my own free will, she seeks your
other breast, and i concede,

we're caught.

i see that deep within somehow she needs you

and thunder hasn't struck.

so i'm going to stick with this... allow myself to

plunge into deep waters with me,

follow down that path.

   but nothing further happens, nothing more than this. and it seems you're safe abandoned by the world at large, like sap-pho living on her island. and here i'll sit content, because we know there's proof,

   reflections show we still long for each other.

144

   and then i fear your aunts will come & shower us, as we're weary and want to eat.

   but they never show up.

they never cared for us.

   instead, i see lise,

with (for money) her old-fashioned forgetfulness and a touch of the plain crazies. she wants to buy us soup. but the first place we find's... a burger joint that only offers wraps.

   so you go to lunch with her, and lose me for a while.

yes, i take her by the hand to the next place and the next, where at least we can buy (manhattan) clam chowder. there we fill our bellies, get just what we need, until

   finally leaving lise behind,

i somehow lose myself.

145

then, i drive our old car home with belle's brother, and next to him, also, my childhood's best friend.

steven's back to life?

the one who died of aids. we're young again, of course (at most, thirteen). and we're trying to find our way back home. i'm driving steady, steering fine, but the blue car's brakes don't work, though i set the

pedal to the metal,

no resistance to the floor. i try again, again, until we glide right by steven's house. where, since i can't stop, i

switch places with sam

(who always comes through). he turns round and round until we finally break

in a kind of wrecked-up hillside forest,

a dip in the road where the blue car stops, and we get out to see what we can see.

magnificent, it burns, the forest with the trees.

but it happens by sheer magic that we also

find a truck behind a building.

it's sam's, i guess. so we can put the ruins of our blue wagon inside.

once we load up, we can go.

146

then we reconsider, think it might be best to just abandon
this pile of junk, leave the boys

and head inside,

step lightly through the back door of the building.

it's a gas station-post office,

according to the sign, though it also turns out doubles as

a print shop.

"sure, you can make copies and buy stamps," the salesgirl says,
"but there's no way you can leave that car."

i go back out

to tell the guys, but see that they have left... then, start to make
my way alone along the forest road.

night is falling swiftly all about.

there's a faint, light purple hue with dark green pine boughs
inside these woods. bobcats jump at me, with glowing yellow
eyes, electric springing claws, and i'm afraid.

147

and yet we've found our way alone so i am

sleeping,

not back home inside my painted brick room, but somewhere else within the family "compound." i think we're up at grandma hetna's house with little matt, and we're watching quite a lot of tv.

something unsettling comes up on the screen.

we don't want to watch. so i fuss and fiddle,

press the buttons, quick,

till at last the screen shuts off.

and there's hardly any fearful aura left.

we're solid and secure, enough to walk out in the dark.

we make our way

across hetna's yard to the main house, where tina, luke and ellen, theo, joe and i lie crouched in scattered rooms,

gathering in pockets

in the corners.

148

and it's here i find father, dark and handsome, curly, young and strong. somehow like himself, yet like obama. he's told me he won't go now, neither plunge back into drink, nor return to war, and pats me and my child on the head.

it's great to have him

here with us,

and this time it's for good.

the pat upon the head, it's as real as real can be.

where rhymes converge with rhythms,

nothing has ever been forsaken.

149

more like burrowing a hole
than breaking through

this adventure into fiction
twice a day i dream

the string might break
fly me up unfettered

through the air instead
its endless scratch and digging

grinding just to mind
something that's there

150

go on, mother, tie another knot. seal your naked trust in me, ondine.

valery

is seeking her bambi on the lawn,

while anabel beseeches

a prince (or king of france)

till they scoop us up

to play at dawn.

151

purple traces in the far-off sky, when val puts down one arched olive foot on the polished hardwood floor, next to the high bed (her mother's cherry bed) with flower-sculpted posts,

where she has lain long, sleeping.

across the spacious room, the moldings' tender crests and creamy thick walls bless an ancient cedar chest, strewn with riding clothes, where tall black boots rest quiet,

biding more lost time,

till combing out her golden waves, gazing through the gilt-framed water at her glowing flesh,

val anadyomène,

bored with all her riches and beauty, decides it's now high time to

get dressed.

152

her mother's bequest, that cedar chest. she'd died with a cough and a sputter (a lump and a song) in her breast, when valery was just 13.

abigail

had been a sweet, soft southern belle, loving to her last breath

dale, valery's father,

a tall tobacco farmer. but once abby died, dale retreated from that (old plantation) world, quit growing tobacco to breed stallions,

bought himself some studs,

where he and val could find reprieve, recover wind from death.

a cool, calm mansion in southern pines.

valery had shown she could live there, playing with dolls at home or going off on her own, riding.

153

and down the road from southern pines, that's where

val first set eyes on her pixie in distress.

at the end of an aimless path, anabel.

standing on a shabby porch

in a baggy muslin dress,

flicking words off fingertips,

winnowing with her lips

silver whispers,

skipping round in circles,

whirling.

154

the girl was barely 6, her chestnut locks were tousled, her knees grass-stained, her bare feet were muddy, her house poor and plain,

but valery was lonely,

dreamed of playing. so, she hopped down from her horse, walked briskly toward the porch,

curved her parted lips,

smiled and started waving, arms stretched high, beguiling,

till anabel hopped down the steps,

began to put on airs for this mistress who seemed

almost a queen.

and to the probing question that valery put first,

anybody home?

anabel replied, "daddy's gone to work, mama's not around." she was home alone, but

that she didn't say…

sam and george were gone (down by the pond)

fishing.

155

so valery smiled again, and patted down her horse, "a birth-day gift," she said, "you can pet him too,"

adding she was now 13,

"i'm living down the road," she ventured, "on my daddy's farm. i can have friends over any time."

tomorrow, could she play?

anabel would ask. so then valery returned, many times, with her nanny's car, to take her new best friend up the road to southern pines, where they could make-believe with rabbits, ducks, and dolls,

tell stories

like those

mysteries she'd been singing.

156

    this, the prize you're seeking? this wisp of a girl with silky hair, who'd turned to a ghost in a far-off dream,

    a white phantom figure,

who'd danced in circles on the lawn,

    around and through the body of a fawn.

a tender, spotted yearling with knees close drawn and great, dark-eyed

    lashes — long, long.

or perhaps, just another... reason why we're always stalling,

    fleeing.

157

    it's certain that val longed to regather in her arms,

    the pale little legs,

the small curved lips,

    the smooth rubbery hips

of winsome anabel, whose tiny scarred chest bared for her caress

    a spot

that val had found

riding.

for now, here again,

before and later too?

tall and golden, strong, valiant on her horse, meandering all alone,

on the trail of a green morning

in the carolina sun,

valery came hunting on her splendid black steed.

first galloping fast, then ambling slow, then more even-clipped or trotting, till finally recalling the exact june day she'd first seen from afar

a baby in the brush,

the spotted little deer, with no mother around. how she'd longed to lift her, to

offer womb and breast,

to comfort at long last that

fledgling creature on the grass.

158

and belle was still there too, waiting, on the patch at the end of the path. almost hidden by the weeds, stretched below the flowering tree,

fetching anabel

standing on the porch, disheveled, barefoot.

mumbling magic words…

a dervish, nymph, *&* fawn, twirling. her fine brown silky hair curled around her neck, forlorn, brothers never home, mother, daddy gone.

valery alone had spotted her,

abandoned, till she rode back to the farm and told her nurse, "i found a new friend." could they drive a ways to fetch her? down the back road to fort bragg,

bring her back to southern pines

for playing? janine said fine,

dale would like that too,

this would would help disperse their sorrows.

159

carry them away from grief, disease and death. such a painful death, abby's thirsty parting. it still woke dale at night, and val was brave by day, but

still crying.

so every day through three long months (april, may, and june), the lass with her newfound friend would while away the afternoons.

val would play the princess, bride,

the lady, mom, or queen.

and anabel the child,

fairy, nymph, or slave,

the flower girl

or maid-in-waiting.

160

but sometimes through their play, the devil knocked too, and shot through anabel

a jolt, a shock,

a burning twitch, a noxious throbbing itch, an urge

the urchin could not quiet.

nor could she imagine where it came from.

val was her big sister,

her savior, her adoring queen, whereas

evil came from bogeymen instead.

161

so whenever val pleaded, anabel cast eyelids toward her own two feet,

tiny sculpted feet,

small round toes and heels, tender to the touch, with here & there a splotchy stain of green, or fresh brown dirt.

gazing first at her ankles,

then upward, where floating through the trees, amongst pink clouds in the sky, she felt the cooling breeze,

and gave herself completely,

thinking — should she ever die, due to val's strange touch,

her spirit would fly up

into those hollows made for everybody's keeping.

her body, she could give in spurts like these,

first to val, why not? and then to princes, knights, or kings, to whomever might just come along beseeching,

till she'd forget she'd ever been

a lost child,

rocking empty cradles in the wind.

162

anabel, the fearless, bravely played the game, took all tips
between her lips,

but also spat and trembled

clinging through the years to valery,

the only one who'd seen her, dancing on the porch.

the first who'd heard how she could slip into the world,

had finally come to fetch her through the daunting woods,

and get her through each brush with loneliness.

all other loved ones... gone.

163

anabel's song

father father sinking into earth

gentle fingers made
to brush away the dirt
pluck up seedlings born
through loamy girth

never purer candle
whitening heaven's shrine
calling on all wind drops
firing up the mind

never purer hand to pat
the soil than that
which daily pierces
through the grime

ondine alone remembers all of this...

164

the ducks were swimming round the blue-green pond, when
clare set out

the white linen cloth

with the silver for her evening party.

how to seat the guests?

anabel and nick, victor and val, in between herself *&* jürgen.

now clare is wearing

a black silk tunic, with slits along the sides, and underneath

a dark red swimming suit.

she had managed a fine moment in the whirlpool, around four.

she had to watch her back,

take care to rest her shoulders, if she wanted them to work, last
through all five classes later in the week, keep her energy up,

finally pin down something that might stick.

the music she'd decided on was

brahms: for cello

instead of paco (for guitar) or, for piano, bach or hersch.

165

something in the air? perhaps she'd find out what.

nick flirting with her or she toying with nick?

when both had made their pacts with val and jürgen.

and all of them connected

through the past,

somehow tied to anabel,

whom she herself had barely noticed, wiped clean from her
slate,

till the future, which had telephoned

through victor's tenor voice, ringing out the toll announcing
everybody's death,

slipped the lost girl back in the equation.

clare feels deeply happy in the silence about this.

she welcomes the suspense,

prepares to find out why, by simply pulling six parts together.

five fleeting phantoms interacting with herself.

this becomes the substance of her dance.

166

her pas de six begins with

three white ducks and three black swans,

swimming around the pond inside her garden.

jürgen has a white shirt on.

he enters contrite. adjusts the silver on the table. tells clare
she's looking lovely, rested, offers her a drink. then sits down
to read the paper, trying to avoid her eyes, whose warm, dark
lights keep settling on him. and even before

the doorbell rings,

he jumps up to solemnly escort pretty anabel and her sleek partner in. victor's also wearing white. he gleams against

anabel's short black dress,

her bare legs, pink polished toes, and the same strappy heels cast off on the porch hours before. but now her chestnut hair is neatly gathered, elegantly swept back into a japanese comb. at the door, she warmly

kisses jürgen on both cheeks.

tells him, "it's so nice to see you," then, more timidly, gives

a quick, light hug to clare,

tells her, "gosh, you're looking wonderful, haven't changed a bit."

clare is glad and pleased

to be greeted in this way. and now she's quite impressed, though she hadn't been before.

she stares at anabel,

sizes up her figure, sees the beauty in her face, tonight almost devoid of make-up,

sees this urchin's finally taken root,

so, she feels, she needs her

in her dance.

167

jürgen stands there awkwardly, offers to get drinks,

walks across the garden

to the terrace bar, comes back with two tumblers,

a kir for anabel,

a small splash of cassis, a half-glass of chablis.

a mint julep for victor,

whose color-coded outfit is now reversed (a white linen shirt on top of dark green pants), and whose drink blends sugar, cracked ice, bourbon, in a frosted glass,

with a sprig of home-grown mint,

thanks to green-thumbed clare.

victor says he likes it,

more so than *pastis*, the garden drink most popular in... (where he's from).

but jürgen only asks him about paris,

the records he's produced, and begins to air his views on europe,

till victor turns the tables,

points to THE OBSERVER next to jürgen's glass, and

begins to talk of american politics, with clare.

"what's interesting is this..." and "what do you think of that?"

lines to fill the emptiness of evening.

168

so anabel and jürgen turn away from talk. the moment's finally come for them to dance. they rise and walk together as though preparing to take off,

circling the pond three times.

till jürgen deftly stops, and seizes anabel. first, it seems he'll lift her in a graceful arabesque, but then

he simply hoists her

to his shoulders,

pins her thighs

around his ruddy neck, where atop his sandy head,

she stretches out both arms, in desperate gestures.

she points to jürgen's heart, then clasps and rubs her own.

then hides her face,

speaking as though behind binoculars: the fingers of both hands, cupped around her eyes,

she tells all

to any ears that hear, while peering

through this makeshift mask.

169

surely it was something, jürgen's

loving,

that was part of it (part of what she seemed to be saying),

his loving was quite strong,

not exclusive, of course. and she never could be sure whether

his passion was meant for her,

or if who he wished to conquer was rather valery or clare, or maybe even

her own future lovers.

whatever it was, there had been fire in his eyes and between their bodies,

a magnetic heat

that kept drawing his hands toward her,

grasping what was hers,

her eyes, her lips and hair, her neck, her thighs and wrists.

following her everywhere

around the yard, inside the house,

trapping her surprised (at times)

in corners.

170

so she allowed him more & more, to touch her everywhere,
couldn't say why not

press his body close to hers.

and after a while frolicking like this, two weeks, maybe three,

they had come to a mature agreement.

they'd decided they could stop there, just stay buried

in the silence for a while,

after having walked down a winding road together,

living the same adventure for a time.

and by exchanging drops of blood (like sam and georgy used
to do)

they had made a pact,

promising not to tell,

wrong as it might be,

a secret that felt most

...unselfish.

171

for knowing it was wrong, putting vanity aside, accepting parts of life that all were meant to have, the fate of experiencing the world (as though through others),

this seemed like the least bad thing to do.

and strangely enough, no sooner did anabel

let jürgen take hold through her,

than suddenly she lost

her own desire.

by this i mean,

his bodily parts

no longer drew her in. instead she was repelled, for they

began to seem quite crude.

and yet she didn't know what to do, for she was loyal, would

never change horses

in the middle of a stream.

172

happily, after a time, jürgen tired of the lapping *&* got hungry,

so he lowered the child,

pulled a squash out of the mud

with his strong left arm,

sat there in his underwear and ate it.

anabel laughed,

thinking it was funny at first.

but then preening in clare's garden,

and stretching out his foot,

he showed her his old toes.

this her soul could not abide.

173

so she stretched her arms out wide, accepting to fall back into
the blue-green pond, knowing at that moment

she was careening toward death,

plummeting into the depths.

jürgen knew it too,

and cried out distressed,

    for he loved her still,

and was sorry she was leaving.

174

    but as she was falling to her death, plunging backward into dark waters, mouth gasping its last breaths,

    a wind came along and she was

blown into the atmosphere, high above the earth.

    sucked into the heavens, she was flying.

and this was right,

    just what she'd always known,

so jürgen became glad she'd had the courage to let go,

    give up the solid ground and sacrifice.

but they were also wondering: would she ever get a rest? because the

    draw up in the air

was more than winsome, the vast expanses, the feeling of the rush and

    brush with eternity

remained... frightening.

175

so jürgen catching anabel brought her down once more. they walk back to the table, to sit a spell, sip their summer drinks, and address themselves to victor and clare, till

a knock comes at the gate, and

valery enters furtively,

wearing loose black jeans,

a black t-shirt, with

golden leather sandals,

matching a large bag. her blond hair tumbling around her waist.

her green eyes light on anabel,

her deer, while

nick strides in behind,

still donning his

long white coat.

176

valery greets victor, jürgen, and clare, a peck on all six cheeks.

then embraces anabel,

walks her to the pond, lays a hand upon her shoulder, and
sings:

> me galloping
> over the land
> you striving to
> find a place
>
> *supposing once more*
> *we were to gather*
>
> desire up in arms
> now that you
> have recognized
> my face
>
> *no we don't*
> *belong together*
>
> you settle here
> inside this frame
> while i go ever
> further on the chase

177

valery holds anabel, who's now begun to weep, accepting
she must go through this

mourning.

she pulls an antique looking-glass out of her gold bag,

a two-way mirror set inside a gilded frame

adorned with shells.

a gift she'd bought for anabel's twelfth birthday,

but then forgotten to send home from school.

valery is sorry,

already she must go.

she can't attend the mass,

the funeral at sand hills.

she's got to fly away

that very night, she has to leave.

her movie shoot begins again at dawn.

so while anabel has found

her prince or king of france,

valery still seeks

her bambi on the lawn.

178

ondine, i dreamed last night i had to finish you. but once more this ended by

not being —

and morphed into

a perpetual thesis.

thirteen pages to complete in just so many days, then repeat, repeat... yet it was conceivable i could finish it, proceeding — one page per day,

if only you could feel,

if only i could think,

if only we could start

on time. but on this particular day, nearing 5 o'clock, i was once again

dithering hours away.

trying to set up our situation. clearing lise & tina, ellen, far out of the way,

procuring for yourself

coffee, gum, and cigarettes, to make room for countless other

consolations.

179

lise wasn't hard to find, and then dispatch, though she kept pestering me (of course). she was younger than today, with no memory loss, just

prods here and there

to push me forward.

everyone's got to try,

or so lise always thought, it's great to even have the opportu-nity. but her older daughters, oh,

your sisters,

it's always the same old scene. they are several steps ahead of me. joined at the hip and literally right upstairs, where

ellen has admirers,

swarming all around, falling at her feet, and

is parading almost naked,

looking very, very nice.

so you're trying to rise higher, and yet find some relief

in the comfort of the loft where tina resides.

180

yet when i softly explain i'm completing you,

ondine,

the weight of my sisters really trips me up, often making me stumble & repeat myself. "anodyne," ellen asks, "is that what you said?" "no, iodine," says tina, "that's what she meant." i just shake my head, and say either no, or om, for what i'd clearly said was "*on —*"

they're always messing up my name,

making me shrink inside. so i have no other recourse but to flee,

take your distance.

but while i'm trying to get away, safely come back home, i find i'm caught between

two different sets of stairs,

can't leap from one platform to another. so i resolve to forget about hopping from side to side, and settle on descending through the in-between.

181

there i ignore my sisters, go about my business. and as i descend to find my way,

get back to your own world,

tina keeps on talking, in a loud and constant voice, giving me directions, but i no longer mind.

once on the ground floor,

i roam around a bit and run into

a tall, appealing fellow.

who's blond, with longish hair. he sounds like

an aussie or a brit,

and has a big red dog,

bouncy like an irish setter.

he seems interesting enough and,

talking just with you,

asks me lovely questions and proposes that we smoke. i sense that things will lighten,

i might have a chance.

182

then ellen returns. here she comes again,

traipsing down the stairs.

she's looking for me, calling me, and persuades me to follow her back up.

and there she shows you how to jump

between one staircase and the next. so up we go, zigzagging.
and as we round the last bend,

back to tina's room,

i see that ellen and i,

you've both been stripped to underwear,

though ellen had been wearing her flimsy gown before, while
i was fully dressed.

her long lean body

impresses me so much. it's clear that

yours will never measure up.

but on top of this belittlement,

the long and short of it,

she says to me (half kindly) as though she too had to suck it up,

you've always been a cute and pretty baby.

and she's glad, though my heart's broken, i've come back. that's
when i knew i'd never finish raising you,

ondine,

my time will all be wasted

growing up.

183

and yet, through scenes to come, your light appeared again, although i thought i'd lost my

bearings,

hours before, forgotten even where i'd buried truth. something quite essential kept happening in the night, as i saw new

visions of your character.

dragged around france, witnessing the way

men made mincemeat out of her,

just because she was sixteen. had no clue how or where she was,

stranded all alone,

paraded like a kid from place to place. small and slightly

round with bangs and most appealing

in a checkered hat, clowns and dancers came to entertain me,

while the main man who wanted you,

an impresario of sorts,

always looked on sly

as others came to ask me for a dance.

your father, he'd consider your reactions,

carefully measure each chance.

184

so again you broke — had to break in two — and began to
wander off. left the whole untimely scene, through the back of
a hotel, to see if i could get away through water. first i drifted

close to DISNEYWORLD

(in a somber boat), dismissing endless plastic pirates. then,
extending, floated into currents more like

lazy rivers

with expanses all about. by this time

we were older,

had to settle, and i could see my own part poking through in
all these escapades, could even think ahead, see inside

the woman you'd become,

who's mostly kept hidden all she had been through.

how'd you manage that?

by keeping a safe haven, an apartment in new york, unbe-
knownst to all, even my old self. a place where i could still
pretend i'd not yet married, never settled down, never given
(nor denied) birth to children,

kept all options open for your life.

it felt dishonest that i still had the lease,

and somewhere in your drawers, the old key.

but i'd never gone so far as to collect rent from

characters of all kinds,

squatters, who'd been living there for years,

more or less respecting all my stuff.

185

why, had it not been for the mail that started pouring through my dreams, delivered with sand, from

a box you'd left in france,

random items all untouched:

dresses, shoes, and blankets,

bed rolls,

pictures from your youth,

a few where i was

beautiful and shining,

others where my face was

blotted out,

i'd have never seen the link, grasped the tie between

   your tender open being

and that dryer, older woman, who'd ignore you,

   hiding ondine,

till the dam broke and she had no other choice,

   coming to see at midlife she was barren.

honing efforts not to waste the precious present, i was

   finally trying to make a life

yourself.

186

   the bard said it — all. real estate, weaving stuff from dreams.

   so next, we're

in a beach house with joseph *&* cathleen, and also my daughter

   amandine.

she had

   a little cut

or some such thing.

   and to heal it,

i wanted to borrow a small piece of cloth, to use as medical
tape. a bit of

the inseam of a baby's sleeve.

so i asked joseph and he asked cathleen, but they never got back to me. this forced me to search all over this rented house, and what i finally came up with was a rag.

you cut off a little strip,

and took it to

fix your daughter's finger.

then we moved into the present, the scene changed.

we're in another family setting,

very different. i'm supposed to be visiting someone and also taking with me part of my own kin,

children i suppose,

but i'm no longer sure who these kids might be, nor whom we're going to see, though i think it might be annie & charlie. but the question for this reunion is:

does anybody want or have to go?

tina proposes

some of us split off

and ride around the city streets together. but there's something of a problem, a hang-up here. for father too thinks

this is a solution,

since lee and earl, my colleagues, get along so well.

they've befriended my whole family when i wasn't around, had no idea that they had even met. father keeps on saying how terrific earl is. and me, i'm saying yes, he's nice, and he's effective. but it's lee, i think, who's really special, and no one seems to notice him at all.

meanwhile, there's a noisy powwow going on to decide how this reunion can finally take place.

trying to cut through the layers of this mess,

defuse all of the fuss and complications,

you suddenly spit out,

look, you all don't have to go back to annie's house. right now she's waiting just for me. it's i who have to go, and since i must, i'll be

glad to take along the children.

then someone forcefully shoots this down

perhaps it was lise?

saying,

no, maia, not you,

as if all this could finally come to that.

complacent, i linger behind, and go to fetch an extra blanket. i think it's from my neighbors', the winfields', car, since i'm slowly moving back toward the beach house again, and thinking everyone and thing will come together. i'm even taking out the garbage, straightening too, as if i could *get rid of things that don't belong.*

then i realize that the stuff i'm

carrying

in my arms is not what i meant to take outside. it's precious drinks instead:

water (for the babies),

diet ginger ales.

so i take myself in hand, gather all my courage and faltering discipline, lug these heavy boxes back up the narrow stairs, the straight white wooden steps up to the steril house, where

a child that's not yours is waiting.

i've told her parents that she's walking. it's very clear. i saw her take a step or two with my own eyes. she's crawling fast and climbing everywhere, but it isn't sure that anyone believes me. and as i'm preoccupied with this, i'm still not up the stairs.

that's when you see tina circling in the lot,

she's going to take me shopping and i'm really glad. we go to a clean market, where she picks up things, quickly, for the whole party,

big slabs of meat, baklava, and dark pink buckets of peppermint ice cream.

that is what i best recall.

then, as this reel is ending, we head back to the car, which is way far off, shining in the vast parking lot. tina's in a hurry, as is her daughter, tam, who joined us in the store. they're tearing back to organize the party, but me,

you're just too comfortable, too well fixed-up to run.

i'm seated on a weird inverted scooter, something like a pogo stick with a cushy seat. and it's very pleasant, going up and down, feeling rhythmic pounding, contact with the pavement though i'm gliding on my seat.

this contraption bounces

faster than i could ever walk. in fact,

it feels a bit like flying.

i don't want to get down now, run, and lose my breath.

so naturally, you lose your sister

and my niece.
what's more, i can't find the car, go past the lot a bit, end up where there's nothing, not even any streets. so i backtrack and i tell myself they're looking for me too, when suddenly i think i hear their voices and even see the headlights of their suv.

and somewhere in the middle of this low-lit scene,

which feels like soothing water as i draw it from the well,

there's something like your mother's body,

rolling, heaving, not like a beached whale, but thirsting, quiet, and softly palpitating.

a throbbing, inarticulate, mass of weak and wrinkled flesh,

which used to block, contain, all this resistance,

as well as all your power and our secrets.

now it is just lying, breathing there, with nothing left to say.
and there's a link that can't be broken between her and me,

but it's been transferred to the realm of the unnamable,

in which i feel i'm sinking too.

187

the emptiness you feel is an illusion. i'm walking down the
street with christian. and i've been told to tell him that my

first book of poems

will be published soon, but i'm really not sure what his reaction will be. i'm hoping to get warm (congratulations). christian and i were supposed to meet at a subway

in a remote part of paris.

it's a place i've visited before in my dreams,

but never in your waking life.

the landscape is sort of *montmartrois* in the sense that there
are hills and stairways. but the steps are broader here, and
what this neighborhood's associated with is restaurants more
than art. tons of bistrots, many featuring pork. plenty of spots

are far from attractive. there are streets covered over by giant buildings, and also dingy highway overpasses. there are
underground galleries, cheap industrial parks, but for some
reason i always want to walk around up here.

this is your own part of paris.

it's the second time i've met christian here (the first was a
misunderstanding). he told me he'd be sitting in a café around
dabrancourt, but i'm several blocks away and around the corner, so i have to huff and puff to even hope i will catch up.
somehow, eventually i do.

christian's sitting there, kind as always.

we have a drink together, a coffee or some such thing. and
then we begin to take a walk. he is perfectly courteous, willing to please, so i decide to grin and bare it — just tell him
about the book.
    he listens to me keenly, as he always does. when i tell him:
christian,

devine,

he looks at me inquisitively and utters:

quoi?

a bit shyly, i again say *devine,* this time placing the accent
squarely on the second syllable. but all that follows (my command) is

silence.

so, then i say, christian, my poems will be published very soon. and all he says is this, *d'accord.*

d'accord?

that means o.k. o.k., which means so what.

your dream

is smashed to bits by this reaction.
    but i am stubborn and resilient and i want to save face. so i say, christian, i was told that you would really want to know, so i screwed my courage up and told you.

silence from christian, nothing but silence and distraction.

he's feeling more and more like he'd like to get away. con-siderate, i help with the transition, ask him, "christian, when did you publish your first book?" and he answers, "well it wasn't around here and i was younger then than you." after that our conversation ended.

there was nowhere else to go.

so i woke up to greet this january morning, but hesitate to join the real world, because there i'm blocked by great patches of emptiness (in which i cannot write). whereas if i can stick with just what happens in the night, i believe i'll never have to stop.

these stories of the night

aren't quite coherent. but at least they are ongoing and non-stop. and *you don't have to worry if they're real*

or made up, because my world's been taken in by fiction, which means perhaps that

we'll be (two).

188

so let's go back inside that time where i can function. move around quite freely, roll around in bed, merge with you,

ondine,

inside my head. i know there's still a story lurking near brown hills. maybe found in utah, or nevada?

one of those dry scapes, out west.

yes, the setting is for sure the great american west:

beauteous, grandiose,

with rocky hills all about... oh now, on closer look, yes, of course. i see it has to be

arizona.

surprise, surprise. those sparse,

thorny plants

are so darn sexy. prickly pears, and tall saguaros, with their many arms lifted to the sky, *shrubs that you can't touch,*

bushes you can see through, plants that really hurt, because they

stick inside your skin

and sear their

silhouettes right upon your eyes.

there's no place else on earth that's fashioned just like this. that's why, though i have left, i still must be from there — sonora. mexico and arizona. i am, you are

a daughter of the desert,

where women just like men are dry and tough.

189

so i happened to be riding around this landscape of my youth (mountains around)

as you often do,

bouncing up and down, jolting on the bed

butts on the deck! (sounds the navy cry)

of someone-like-my-father's pick-up. but in this particular instance i'm more or less grown...

enough to host and care for children.

when we round the corner of an especially austere hill,

you see there's something man-made,

something like a newfangled oasis.

it's a huge pond-like structure

with a complex building perched on top,

sprouting tube-like branches all around it,

like the glass halls carrying escalators at BEAUBOURG.
    and there are several underground passages. i comment
to my sisters that this is new in town, that none of it belongs.
but they're unwilling to commit. so i split myself from them
(as i often do), decide that i should check this place out alone.
everything's fabricated

in this reservoir of sorts, the water's quite shallow.

sometimes you see the bottom, with its white plastic,
smeary creases through artificial stones & pebbles, piled
high, the size of cookies. i swam a stretch, the whole way
underneath. it's easier to glide than moving in and out.

you don't like the feeling of intermittent air,

nor the grasping, kicking, beating on the surface. even i was
shocked to see the circle close so fast. this oasis was hardly
larger than a king-sized pool, a curve that stretched at most
a quarter of a mile. as i reached the starting point i saw my

family had come back.

catalina was splashing with my nieces, wearing pretty tank suits, red. the shiny wet cloth upon their glowing bronze skin,

all of this against the rocks,

the warm clay earth, the sexy plants and sky,

was reassuring.

but i was on a cultural mission. my self-appointed job was to determine what this bizarre concocted place was for. so i got out, dried off, and went inside.

there were people gathered round the entrance.

some were handing fliers out, saying things were happening on saturday nights, as much as you can find in any city in the east. there were locker rooms and sleazy bars,

and everybody looked the way they do in crowds back east,

the people haunting beaches on long island, the swim clubs scattered over westchester, or anywhere you go in DISNEY, florida.

women, children thinking

that they're on the cutting edge.

husbands dispossessed and drinking beer.

and all were glad they'd found this place among the desert rocks.

but you,

well, i was plum well-nigh disgusted,

preferred to give your body to the thorns, the sexy trees,

would rather dry, a prune, beneath the baking desert sun,

than stay inside this weird simulacroasis,

which offered only semblances of washes,

arteries deep clogged with fake blues.

190

no such thing as pure — fiction. we were, deirdre and i, in a hospital hotel. we were there together, and we were waiting. we had both heard the news about our beloved jan. our

heads were bowed and hearts were devastated,

both of us. there is no other word, both frightened and sad, and wanting to care for jan. but somehow there was nothing left to do. nothing but to take care of each other. the grief was palpable and we laid down together. the lion and the lamb.

deirdre was the lion,

though she was innocent of course, whereas i,

you were the sullied lamb.

it seemed sure that something terrible would happen to jan,

and you could not intervene,

prevent or help. nor could either of us pretend to console him. it was a man's world, all of a sudden, and we, the weak women, were there just to watch.

just like in the old days,

when the violence begins and no birth pangs are in sight,

women were consigned to wailing.

so this is what we did. we did all we could do, and passed the time together. i showed my respect to her greater age and power as we wept

copiously we wept,

tears filled up the bed where we laid down to rest. soon we were floating all around the room. and after a while we were tired, not because the end had played itself out, but just because we were (tired).

all your tears had been spent,

and i was looking for something to ease and occupy us both,

so you asked deirdre, would she like to knit?

she said she would,

though she didn't have needles and yarn.

no, she didn't, not on hand. but i still did, for

you'd left unfinished scarves for your children,

in a closet, tucked away, from one of many occasions over
the years where i'd wanted to learn to knit. i decided i could

try to go back there and get them,

slip into the old house where this closet was.

the knitting would help us with the waiting.

so i set out in the very early morn. the streets were dark
and empty, despite a purple dust of dawn. the plan was i'd
slip into my old house alone, grab the knitting from the shelf,
and run. then meet up with dee again at the grand hotel. some
place neutral, not anybody's territory.

the retrieval of the knitting was easy.

there it was, neatly tucked inside a bag, the beginnings of andrew's and angelina's scarves, both striped pastels, only a few
rows. but then, leaving, i crossed joe, who should have been
back with catalina near our desert home. and i can't say his
presence was reassuring (he was neither helping or harming
my foray in any way).

what was joe doing in your old new jersey house?

i have no idea,

tending to his own children?

i suppose. but this crossing with my brother hardly took any
time. in a flash i was in the hospital hotel again, and looking

around for deirdre, my fellow wailer. i waited a while in the
bar, then decided to

escape once more,

relieve myself in the ladies' room, when in the long, jagged
line, suddenly,

you see lise, your own mother, once again.

she's declined significantly from the last time we met.

utterly dumb now, and blind,

like lucky and pozzo in WAITING FOR GODOT, she always has
to go to the bathroom (just like me), but doesn't know at all
how to do this. she's bumping into the thick painted stall
doors over and over again, and my mission changes. i'm here to

HELP HER OUT,

figure out how to deal with her old decrepit self, this body
out of which i rose, and then,

help me out too.

yes, what's left of you, and me, and all my children.
    i'm thankful for that body, though disgusted by it too. it's
my lever onto hate, self-loathing. still, through it i also grasp
all i know of love. so without further ado, i now

take your mother under your wing,

and bring her along with me.

deirdre looks awe-inspiring as we approach, tall, majestic, always in command, not afraid to roar her feelings. but she looks at me differently than she used to. she's inquisitive, needy, benevolent, and she sings melodiously,

> i spied you in the distance
> but then you disappeared
>
> i thought you had abandoned
> seeds

191

love (and sex), they came back to me last night. i wish i could remember how they were, but it ended with me rolling, happy in lee's arms. this part was not sex, it was love.

rolling in the arms of your dead friend?

perhaps it was this morning, in the second sleep, when i was bound and determined not to raise my rotting carcass from our senior wedding bed, and attack e-mail problems by the billion. no, said i, i won't let the charm of morning go to waste this time, and laid my hoary head back on the pillow (hoary might be something of a hyperbole).

you're still pretty for your age,

if i... concentrate. nabokov says it in THE VANE SISTERS just right. but however good i look i am apparently not hot. few chili peppers on my student ratings, which were mainly what was there thirty years ago, when i fell over in my chair, skirt above my head, examining young men at columbia.

from the last row of the room, i pointed, then leaned over, to make a smart remark. (i wanted to correct a small mistake in french.) my chair, the desk, all overturned, my legs and col-ored skirt flew up in the air. the boys all clapped and cheered, so happy with my feat. i earned a full ovation from that class.

you were easy on the eyes in those days.

now the easy's all that's left. oh well, it's just this life, and just when i'm awake.

you still have magic powers in your dreams.

so, yes,

lee came calling last night.

we were working on a project in the department, earl, and me, and olivier. we were standing around, trying to solve a tricky problem, when suddenly earl says to me, why don't you ask lee? and i'm a little hesitant to do this... because

you know he's there,

i've always known that, no way...

no one could turn him into dust.

but i'm surprised to find his presence acknowledged by olivier and earl, since alone it seems that i am the believer. for them the story turned out differently,

perhaps some changing places at the hospital?

or he flew off in a plane, got caught up in a raid, and

somehow he escaped...

death? but i'm not in the mood to ask questions. so glad to find lee here, back again with us, reminding us that work's about affection, doesn't matter who is right or wrong.

yes, there he was, lee.

he was thinner, younger, shorter, slightly more compact, and had a slightly smaller nose. he was still curly blond with a few dark streaks, but his skin was neither pale nor ruddy.

and his blue eyes,

though twinkling,

had that navy, newborn hue.

was that your perfect body, lee?

but you said there was also sex?

that was me. all alone.

sex was nothing more than

this: i was flashing truck drivers, on some sort of flying bike. all i had to do was sit and feel the wind, forming

an obscene image in the rear-view mirror,

near the eye of one strange man.

192

cool runnings… nothing shrill betraying anyone last night, not so far as i recall. i was

just rolling

side to side, when certain visions came. one involved dancing. the hills around were rocky and green. so i must have been

in ireland

or some such place. there were bunches of my friends and relatives spread about, & me, behaving differently with each.

there was an old man

to whom i gave a chaste, prolonged kiss, a press of my two lips upon the forehead, which inspired him, enabled him to stand.

and there was also gina, the lame beauty from the pool,

who i happened to cross in the subway just last week, and

who, getting married, asked you to her wedding.

everybody at this gathering had parking tickets, and the alcohol was strong, particularly stiff. and gina was in fact pregnant, not feeling very well. so the celebration turned out bleak. and finally, there was awareness, burning through the clouds, that it was time for me to get in shape.

you wanted to get fit

so i could run, bounce, and fly. and to do this i designed a program, (no small amount of) stretches and ballet. i set myself to exercising,

not far from the old man,

the place where i had kissed him and brought him back to life. lying around that spot, i found a kind of saw-horse, a makeshift barre, and stuck my leg up there, sneaker and all,

craned your neck to see the mirror.

and through that glass, i saw

something short and round

about my thigh, and that my foot was turned in (downward), neither up nor out. but i decided not to be bamboozled this time, to remember certain things take effort. meanwhile, i'd focus on what's best.

shift your gaze upward,

where there was nothing great to see, nothing astounding near. but a few lines worth keeping,

the outline of the torso,

front and back. and for face hues, something pale,

like clarity breaking through.

encouraged by this gleam, i took off for a jog through the parklands, the grass.

there was a picnic on a hill, where some of my relatives had stopped to eat. but i just circled widely, waved & smiled, and when i made it back to

the green fields again,

alone with nature,

that's when you got high.

yes, i was running along, doing what's required, when the soles of my feet acquired a certain bounce.

your strides became long, longer, longest,

till they began to angle high, every time i touched down, pushing a bit further off from the earth.

soon you were flying,

though low, like certain birds, still retaining strains of contact with the earth. so now i know, if i just carry on with training, on and on, there's no such thing as not

reaching where i am.

and it's not true, like i've thought at times, that life requires only scratch and digging.

what's needed is

a lift,

an élan.

no matter how small.

193

careers and love (again). there were elements of time and place for sure. buds on the trees outside my window,

looking better from olivier's high view point

than from my own.

and there was a colleague of mine, a pretty famous guy, telling me, if you're the woman who i think you are, i have the solution. it's translation. but translation, he cautions, is not a *pis aller,*

you'll have to devote yourself entirely.

ah… devotion, once again.

and that commitment problem…

drew me willy-nilly back to an apartment in new york, a studio with white stucco walls.

you'd been invited once again to a party,

though i didn't know anybody there. to my left, on a sofa, were a few men, and a young one who said: so, i've heard you're into

SIGNÉPONGE.

i just let that drop. for even though i took that course with der-rida himself, in fact i wasn't paying attention, and even though he'd invited me to the party to get my copy signed, and there i

challenged the master with your little friend lacan,

i never even read that text, and so wouldn't know what we'd
be talking about.

whence, feeling out of place, i looked around the room
once more and found a different scattered body of three or
maybe four women (the rest were men).

one rough and wrinkly lady,

but with acne as though young,

asked if you still went to meetings.

i hemmed and hawed, muttering, what meetings do you mean?

she started to say "a … a,"

but then settled on "the saturday one".

that's when (in the center of the room), shimmying up &
down, in chic gypsy clothes, i saw vera, one of my old friends.
she'd made something of herself by becoming

a danseuse.

and she really had not aged a bit.

this made me feel dejected, lonely, and unloved. disowned,
i felt i was, by everybody there. and i was equally uninterested
in them, until at one point i was thrown back on a bed by one
of the young men,

and your desire was suddenly awakened.

but this guy just pressed his body three times against mine,
then stood and wandered off, revealing, behind, another man,
much older, who was wanting me to be … his … and i was getting quite intrigued.

but also you really didn't want to.

fortunately, somehow this whole scene changed. i got out and climbed onto the roof, noting every detail of the flat as i left. at first, it had presented as a studio, a nice, sculpted room with windows, but without any extra carved-out space. but then i saw it also had

an extra hidden chamber,

which in fact looked something like a hole.

a whole hole?

literally, yes, like someone had blown out a huge cavity in the back wall, and then put back up a thin partition. this little room was just about 6 x 10.

there was no bed, no furniture, no nothing,

but it was definitely serving as a bedroom.

and the bathroom?

it was fine, but very non-descript, so i didn't even bother to go in there. but on my way out i also saw

a kitchen with a low-slung ceiling.

a square space, with grayish-white stucco walls, and adorned with

easter-colored lights

strung up all around. the place was rough, textured, dark and light at the same time, and cheerful although dingy. yes, this might have broken loose from our ranch kitchen

in mexico, maybe coming from your youth?

before attaching to a rooftop-studio in new york (traveling discreetly through the night).

you got on the roof,

where i was happy to walk, get out to walk, for there was air, and where i also was convinced i had been

beckoned by olivier,

the one who cares for me, who's always there, all these many years, since first we met.

but somehow once i got there on this rooftop, he was ambivalent.

maybe wanting to leave?

to be with someone else? or just to be free, for heaven's sake, to be somewhere else. i was worrying about that, got distracted by such thoughts, and did not want to be abandoned, so began looking around once more,

searching for olivier and feeling uncertain,

wondering whether i was the traitor or the one being betrayed, which led me to get caught between my sisters again.

tina and ellen, always the same trap.

and here is how it happened this time. i was checking on lise, or meaning to do that, but instead of the regular answering machine, i got

ellen's voice, telling someone else,

in a low, dramatic tone, that

tina's daughter had ended up in jail.

i got ensnared in that disaster, anxious and upset, but was also feeling vindicated, like nothing ever goes right in my family. and yet

this cold, unfeeling reportage

on how my niece was now... i also did not know

how to digest.

i was about to explain this to someone or myself, when

tina shows up.

she's come to see me on this terrace that looms over new york. as she is approaching, i have no time to think, and just blurt the bad news out,

blubber it out,

while starting to cry:

your child is in jail, in jail,

(i say), i'm sorry (i said).

i should have been more clear, i ought not to have cried,
but i wanted to tell tina right away, and also for her to know

the story was real and sad,

not the constant theater, heartless news report, that was
always coming through the family (telephone) lines.

meanwhile, you're wondering about your own tears,

and fear they're less from sadness than anxiety. i need to talk
about this and manage to do that somehow

with olivier,

who, hours before, had seemed to abandon me, gone off to
his own tea party... as my friend, he'd strangely stood there
to help me with my brains, but as my love, he'd wandered
off discreetly, so

you weren't sure if you had him anymore

till the end of our talk. then i saw him clearly, waiting.

he was standing, near and far,

he was glowing.

194

dieter's lament, in san francisco, i believe, though i rarely go there.

and ellen was again a stumbling block and draw.

our flight was several hours late, a flight from kennedy, carrying out west: olivier, myself, and matt,

you were going

to california. just for a few days, a long weekend. and this was somewhat on business (a bit, of course), but also to pay a visit to my sister,

to connect with her finally,

and make things work.
    but when we arrived exhausted at the airport hotel, there wasn't any thing or place to eat, nowhere to park either. and while olivier attended to that and found a spot to put our bleeping rented car, i did my best to

get ellen on the horn.

since our plane was three hours late,

she answers in a tired, barely audible voice,

like this delay could have been my fault. so i desperately tried to figure out when i should call again. sometime the next day, not to bother her? but i also became "pissed off." i had dragged myself, my husband, all this way just to see her. the least she could do would be to act glad when i call. finally, she agrees, *you'll talk the next day,*

so i decide it's time i

focus on your children.

but at this exact point, my other sister appears. i should have known

tina would also come along,

i never have one sister without the other. but it turns out that tina both is and isn't involved in our weekend plan.

she's here on her own family business,

something to do with her children's careers, and she's

staying in another, better hotel.

basically, she complicates things a notch or two,

making you feel inadequate and hovering around,

but now won't play an active part in telling me

what to do?

there's nowhere here (for us) to eat, and there's nowhere near to go. the hotel is modern enough. but it's dingy, kind of gross. i want to leave, get out of there as soon as possible, but

olivier, he wants to do the wash.

we argue about that a little while. why do we need to do the wash? but eventually i let him do it, and wander out into a vacant lot with matt.

as you meander, you spy —

a long strip mall, behind the vacant lot. it has a dunkin donuts, a cheap walmartish store (or perhaps it's an old-fashioned wool-worth's), and an old-fashioned grocery store that's locked. but what i'm trying to get to & at the same time avoid is, for sure, the

DUNKIN DONUTS,

which once before had gripped me in my dreams:

> there were frosted
> doughnuts
> many of them
>
> half eaten
> with sprinkles
> strewn across the floor
>
> a child that was mine
> had eaten them
> and left me the remains
>
> from the bedpost
> to the door
> and i well i was
>
> left to gather them
> pluck and sweep
> them bit by bit
>
> till there weren't
> anymore my lot
> it seems is cut
>
> off from consuming
> all that's left is
> keeping score

but matt and i never actually made it to the doughnuts. instead, we were last seen trying to find some decent things to wear,

wanting to buy presents in the cheap all-purpose store.

i thought i spotted first

a red-checked frilly dress,

i've always wanted one of those,

for a baby girl.

but then on closer inspection, this item disappeared and was replaced by

a black chiffon play-suit,

which was weird, for a girl of 6 to 8. a very risky purchase all around. and it's there where i cross paths with my sisters once again.

tina comes back first,

encountered at this store. i ask for her opinions on fashions such as these, for i can see that she herself is

shopping like mad.

she's getting cheap but tasteful cottons out of a high-strewn pile of mixed-up colored things, a mass that looks to me like junk. and, as she's helping me,

ellen too returns,

as a voice on the phone, emotional, intense, though she's not much interested in me.

and you?

well, me, i'm just no one, nowhere at all. dissed, and not conforming to anybody's plan. but i still manage to feel

what's missing.

195

europe, i was dining with the spanish department in a beach hotel, on the western coast of france. and i was carrying

a small child,

of two or three, but who was upstairs in my room, sleeping.
a group of pizazzy faculty members sat down around me and began to laugh and joke. most of them were men. some i recognized, others i did not. one right beside me had a sweep of dark, curly hair, just beginning here and there to gray. he was a flirt and a talker i've never seen before. another was a gentle giant i know well. there were several women too, spread around the circle, one or two jewish gringas (like myself), trying to be cool, and a few american latinas in the bunch. no one from central america nor mexico. but we ladies were there mainly to wear dresses. the real professors were the men.

you wanted to be a real professor too,

as i always do, a working person interested in reading, with ideas.

but you were also a mom,

and didn't hesitate to emphasize that.

this was the peculiar nature of your life.

accordingly, i quietly asked who among these colleagues had brought children. but that topic really didn't fly. so i switched to: how do you handle undergraduates? whereupon i discovered that these spanish department types were much better at flyers and parties than we'd ever been in french, and i was planning to copy their approach.

so there's no question you were cunning and conniving,

doing business, shooting the breeze in this hotel. but still, i remained conscious that

small bodies were waiting upstairs,

bodies who had been attached,

and one in particular was still attached to mine.

this moved the giant, who had a mangled child of his own. he quietly put his large brown hand on top of mine, which was starting to get wrinkled, along with being small, white, and dry. because of his warm fingers, i felt more powerful and beloved.

this made you look outside yourself,

outdoors, toward an expanse of beach,

where you were impressed by the bareness.

there were europeans, americans, of every ilk and time, but they predominantly came in clusters, tending to form crooked lines, and

there were old-fashioned black telephones,

just sitting in the sand. somehow these objects or instruments marked the official entry way to france, whereas the beach that extended beyond (those old black phones) remained a kind of duty-free zone, where people could

congregate, make plans.

and since congregation happens around restrooms, i of course had to pee and got in line.
there were mostly aging women waiting in front of me, though also, occasionally, a hapless man, while teenagers were zipping by on dirt-bikes.

finally, you got into one of the men's rooms.

it was amazing — vast, and light,

and featuring nothing but a well-defined hole in the center,

where we were all supposed to go, though mostly

to relieve oneself.

196

short series, first with iranians and shoe stores. and me, carrying my things around in a plastic bag while searching for

nakedness and psychotherapy,

in a building whose number was 135, back in manhattan, where i was trying to grow up.

then there were rebozos,

which i don't wear, but my sisters do, looking stately and arguing which is best. there was a purple one and a white one, with various kinds of trim. so once more, just to verify rebozos don't fit me,

you grabbed a red one,

since red's my color. i wrapped it around myself, but this really didn't work.

it cut you right in half

and overwhelmed me. so instead of the graceful sprite, or

elfin spirit,

sometimes captured in my dreams, i became an ordinary ugly american, a dumpling of sorts, with no particular charm that was my own.

and then came a whole layer of triviality,

of ego pain, covering something worse,

your mother's admission that she didn't want you,

we were all father's plan. she'd just lent her body for the project. she had no use for bloodlines or attachment,

and difficulty in shaking off her womb.

but before even that, there was something far worse still,

cold and tremulous.

197

infidelity — certainly there was a moment when i betrayed you, not just you,

ondine,

but also

olivier,

and not just with anyone, with his twin. yet i was still trying to figure out how i could stay true to him all the same, because i knew i loved him most, and that everything

depended on him.

i'm not sure you want to hear the details, familiar scenes and situations, houses we were renting, trying to live in for a matter of weeks. and family all about — versions of our mothers, sisters, brothers,

and also this strange twin,

who wanted to hold my hand.

that's all you let him do, hold your hand?

but this seemed to be crucial to both him and me, for

it lifted and lightened your spirits.

this to the point where we were

barely any longer inhabiting this earth.

we were light as feathers, sheer, made-up particles of color
and light, and pure. we were pure as air.
    then, realizing

you could never go further,

he (olivier's twin) and i, we sat down and we rocked, grieving,
while our mothers and others watched us. and all were aware
that as long as we did just that,

this rocking had to be o.k.

even though it had to stop. for now, it was a kind of healing,
a sealing of the deal.

your connection with all others would forever remain chaste.

no more clutchings, barely touchings, no brushings of the
hands. no,

you would keep yourself henceforth ever close to olivier,

buried in his beard, for life.

198

triptych, again, in spain, though this was not really me.

you had iron-gray hair

cut short in a bob, and a body, tall & thin, somewhat board-like.
    i had ended up inside this stony neighborhood, with moss-
covered rocks, in a city (like madrid), and an underground
apartment that i liked, though the air had little light. it was
a studio, with a large bed in the middle. there was a desk,

a closet in which to hang one's clothes. and there was a door
to the outside, leading to a busy street. i felt surrounded,

in the center of it all,

though i also had my own dominion.

how do you know it was spain?

the location was defined by the nature of the street. it wasn't
the street of a small town or village. it was a street within
a neighborhood, a network of them, and between my little
doorway and the next big street, which connected to a wider,
broader avenue, there was a cozy little place to eat. a bodega
or bar, where i could pay money and get something, without
having to involve myself in cooking.

tucked behind my table, i could also observe the goings-on,
and this made me feel like i was part of them too. and then
when i was full, i could wander home, close the door, but still
not be alone, because i heard

a strain of something beautiful played on the guitar.

i could discuss things here with people, both inside and out:
talk with them, see myself up-close with my short iron hair,
with my terse, stiffening mouth, and somehow still bear all
i was reflecting. though, now, as i lie down again, roll over
in bed, i regret the glimmer of what i used to be. there's no
going back to the smallish, plumpish girl. beautiful back then,
when i was grieving and in a barcelona jail.

but at least i still hear

music pouring out of rocks

that grow and fall in spain, and know i'm part of their world.

***

next stop (and opposite), a barber shop, or rather, i should say, a salon, attaching it and us to a hotel and a very

fancy spa.

offering: every service imaginable, even washing you at night. so i was wondering:

how does one leave such a place without getting soiled?

and does everyone who pays for this nightly change her bed? but i decided not to get caught up with these thoughts, for i was here on a mission with my daughter,

amandine?

oui, and i was once again me and not me at all, by which i mean, i was forming and becoming

a different character.

i was rooted in someone else's skin, couldn't possibly get out, and there was little connection here with my actual self.

the woman you were now had straight brown-orangish hair,

and her face was handsome, masculine, but way too thin, with bags and dark circles all around her eyes. these weren't the kinds of bags that i now have, which often make my eyes look swollen and shut. they were the round dark bags of a southern european type. and my hair wasn't wavy like my own. it was tame, shoulder-length with blunt bangs, not curly, puffy, frizzy, but limp and drooping.

and your daughter had no connection to your own,

neither to angelina, nor to you, ondine. she was seven or eight, and blond, with a super pie-shaped face, and straight, almost white, flaxen hair. and what she wanted was a new haircut.

you wanted to please her, so you really did the rounds.

the last place i remember was a baroque, chinese-like spa, in the midst of a suburban strip mall that somehow also managed to be covered. but we couldn't get a haircut very quickly there.

we got attention all right, and from the head of the salon. she came strutting out in heels and standing (outside of the shop), fiddled with amandine's fair hair, and showed her how to pin it up while we were waiting. "i'd be glad to arrange an appointment," she said, "have your little girl come back for just the cut she wants, but it's impossible at present to slip her in."

i was frustrated by this delay, so decided to leave *&* keep searching. on and on, we went till two doors down, where a kindly lady took us in.

and there you still are now,

sitting on a bench behind my pie-faced girl, still looking toward the signs sparkling in the spa, waiting till someone finally comes to cut her hair.

before the picture fades, let's catch a glimpse

of us all together in the wide square mirror.

what i see is

other people, though it looks like we're also

removed,

separated from our own flesh.

***

which somehow brings us back to our dead friend,

lee.

he's agreed to rejoin the three of us once more,

you, olivier, and earl?

for a brief discussion of our books.

all four together, lying on the floor,

in some hotel in spain, which didn't seem too real, except we all looked much the same as we actually were. i was certainly myself, as i was back in those days, small and packed in jeans. earl was not yet oppressed, nor compacted, and olivier was just as he tends to be, tall & strong (already with his beard). together, the two of us were our perpetual selves, utterly in love, only younger, not yet tired, bent and worn. and the four of us were

talking about your books.

i found it quite amusing that lee would point a shot (at me) saying, "a book should have at least 400 pages," when i generally got closer to that number than he. now, nobody writes books as long as olivier's. but those he dedicates to me, and even on my own, i'm much closer to his count than are either earl or lee... but in the end, i don't get mad, because

there's a twinkle in lee's eye,

and what he wants to discuss is less the worth or count of written pages, but what should be inside. he likes: alcott, louisa may. and that's what i like too. so i know he's on my side,

he will grant what you wish,

which is to write (inside) some books about women and

to be a little woman too.

199

school, sitting near a classroom, at barnard. circling somewhere,

and following

around a student like angie (who is mine, but also not mine),

somebody you love and look after.

i was trying to get through the catalog, see which french classes i might have to teach, or at least be prepared to watch over. there were a number of them, such as E1, F2, which appeared of subelementary level, and yet had difficult subjects, such as

verse in baudelaire.

426

so it occurred to me there'd been some changes since my day. and then, i must have been sitting by the xerox machine in the hall, pulling out all the papers i thought i ought to have, when the bell rang for the next class and i went in.

weirdly, this was political science,

which made me think angie would be there, though i'd lost her in the crowd. since i felt it would be best not to chase after her or look for her amongst the rows, i made a bee-line for an empty seat.

the professor

was a wiry little man by the name of saint-yves, and he was here for every other lecture. he started out by passing out papers, and said we'd spend the first half-hour doing: group correct. what mattered here was smoothing out transitions from the last approved module to the next one.

saint-yves put on a red cap

with a long yarn train,

and began furiously erasing the board

while students tried to digest his comments, remarks he had freshly written (not wrote).

there was a woman in the room,

who made it clear that some of the students here had fellowships, honors awarded to do research abroad. they would now be leading the discussion. the issue was *how to respond to a crisis,*

and the point was to see it from every angle. this was something like an exercise that angie had mastered at her previous
school, an international crisis resolution. but this one was
more social, less high tech.

you were bothered by the privileged students

near the front. no doubt these were the ones with fellowships.

one girl

played the expert on religion and

piped up with a point on

john the baptist. she was talking about a dinner in which john,
she said, had been particularly well served, especially, she insisted, by *saint denis* (who later left his head atop montmartre).
she also mentioned further that this was the same

jean-baptiste

who some scholars, years before, had dared to call a miscreant. hearing this bit of french, my ears pricked up. i thought i
ought to join in, see what i could do to straighten things out.

a miscreant,

said i, means one who dis-believes,

has something like the doubt that troubled thomas.

after jesus, that's o.k. it's a problem we all have. but if this happened before, before jesus even came, well then john must have suffered something awful. his trial was not a privilege, but a terrible charade.

this girl, the expert, looked at me perturbed, like i didn't have a clue. "this was john," she kept insisting, "the baptist, who everybody knows, and everything he knew came on a platter." luckily,

saint-yves called next on someone else up front,

who had something smart to say on eastern europe.

he wanted also to hear from hillary,

who happened to have stopped by,

and also from the irish.

maybe that was me — the elf seated toward the back.

200

leases and deeds, my sisters (again), and real estate. this time, rambling around in

tina's new house,

which is smaller, leaner, cheaper than the old one, something sort of squished, trailer-sized, yet also in the world, free-standing. it would make a good set for

FIN DE PARTIE,

except that it has more than twenty rooms. the dining-room is separated from the rest of the house. tina's working in there while

ellen's singing in the shower.

so i begin gossiping with tina about problems with ellen's new boyfriend, his drinking, and her moving in and out. "josh isn't a fall-down drunk, is he?" i ask, trying to open the session delicately. "no, that's the problem," tina replies, "if he were, we'd know what to do with him."

i'm so jealous of ellen (and so glad to have tina finally to myself) that i'm happy she's preoccupied with her boyfriend and relieved she might not be too much around. but somehow, though she's gone,

she's still with us.

for it was she, before, who'd asked me with a grin if i was ready yet to move on the whetmore place. was it o.k. with me that she and tina rent it out? had i received the message from their office, telling me they'd found a tenant?

i had, but it had totally confused me, because as far as i knew i'd never owned a whetmore place.

the only place you ever had out west

was a small old house, on the corner of tree and plant. i lived there on one side, and had been forced to eat breakfasts with "grandpa" mack, but then eventually was able to move over to fix up the other side, which was modern, rather beautiful, with a kind of lofty feeling and red bricks.

i'm pretty sure i owned that place once, and maybe i still do, even though i don't have the first notion where the deed is, and the address itself is nowhere to be found, nor can i remember how the outside walls looked, as those had been

demolished

since my childhood. and i never had a dime to myself in that town. but still, i think i owned that place in name at one point. so it made sense if my sisters would ask if they could rent it (and it might be that they'd rented it before).
but whetmore...

whetmore?

a house of mine on that street, on the east side of town? i still can't begin to see anything there, except perhaps a vague memory that steven once lived nearby, (not saint stephen who was stoned but) steven,

your childhood friend who died from aids.

but there's something about ellen's grin, when i start to betray that i don't remember (how i might still be connected with) whetmore, which makes me want to keep it nonetheless.

keep your foot in the door,

if only not to give in to her, give to others what's mine so easily. i do this by acting confused, befuddled. "it's been so long," i say, "since i've lived anywhere out here. can you remind me why you and tina associate me with that place?"

perhaps after all, you do own it, and need to begin to worry more about what's yours.

perhaps. but before all this haggling about the house, leases, and deeds, i'd been with tina on a picnic. and tina proposed that i should accompany her back home so we could visit.

being with tina is always so much fun.

she's an extraordinary woman: beautiful, rich & bossy, fully grounded, yet charismatic.

her bonds are very strong,

all my children tell me this, whose favorite aunt she is,

we'll all be deeply grieved if ever she should die.

and now there's suddenly something messed up with her teeth (which is a real shame, since she can't stand bad teeth). but what i remember being even more surprised about than this decay was hearing that

tina now knew a certain song.

something like WE'RE GOING TO A PARTY.
　　i couldn't get over this, it was so cute, tina knowing and singing that song. so, i said, "tina, i didn't know you ever listened to music like that — whenever i'm in the car with you, we just talk." "what d' you think i do," she asked, "when i'm on the road alone?" "when i was young," i muttered, "too little to tell your troubles to, you used to listen to canned music." (the kind you are supposed to do your taxes to.)

things change, she said.

and then went on to sing:

back then i was gorgeous
driving around in a gold car
father was a pimp
my lover a tycoon

now i'm a single granny
who's cut down and budgeted
everything i own even
the enamel on my teeth

whereupon i piped in, "no matter, tina, you're still you, and have fantastic powers all around you. so when your lover, parents, brothers, sister, all abandon you — you'll still have me."

you, and me, and all her children,

yes, and because (or even though) she dressed me like a dolly with her dollars and her sewing hands, took me off to paris and through mexican hotels, paraded me down fifth avenue, and threw the two of us back into the world by preventing you from ever

coming home to roost,

we'll always have her also, ondine.

2.01

whereby we learn we cannot escape the lure of beauty contests, nor of swank hotels with

countless mothers and daughters,

of all races, shapes, and sizes, and also

a number of dancing men.

i say dancing, because they were. even the elevator opera-
tor who took me up to my floor did a kind of mambo ballet
thing. he was rather heavy, and wearing white tights, with a
silver leotard and red suspenders, something very odd. and
he really had no feeling for where things were in this hotel.
so after i exited from the elevator, i took the stairs.

we'd been foisted,

you and me,

on a separate floor

where there was nothing but games, and a door into our room,

tucked discreetly in the corner.

fortunately, olivier was waiting there, otherwise we would
have felt both anxious and isolated, since down below by
the pool, the contest was still going on and featuring again
the star of our show, tina with her daughter tam.

tam, like tina, was straight and tall, and sporty,

exotic and beautiful, and was dancing her heart out all in
green,

yet still coming in only in third place.

so tina was being forceful, coaching her on how to get ahead,
suggesting, perhaps the problem was the three pounds she's
gained, rather than some other less definable lack of grace...
but no matter, she and tam could still "work on it." and there
still were several contests to go.

whereas you got lost from the start in the scoring,

as i often do, for it seemed to consist of points, games, and matches, like in tennis, where everything slips neatly into something else. but i couldn't begin to figure how the system worked, since the fit was more zigzag and incremental than with russian dolls.

    still, once i realized that at some level everyone has to struggle both to count and to contend and

even the beauty process can be broken down,

i felt reassured and even tried (though no one encouraged me) to do one of the recommended moves.

    it begins with flattening yourself along the side of a pool. it's a pose for the swimsuit competition, but is very much the opposite of standing. you have to align yourself while trying to look good, as though suspended. you have to attach yourself and hover where there is nothing to cling to, which means that you're essentially festive and ready for fun.

you've got to have the quality

of a blown-up balloon, something light that can still manage to stay stuck to the wall,

stay firm and yet protrude in certain places.

and this can only happen when you're rubbed and rubbed just right,

till your sheer bulge attains magnetic attraction.

    well, after i tried this, and succeeded, i could finally relax, knowing i remained capable of doing what i still had to prove.

202

which reminds me… one last push.

olivier and i were in mexico, traveling, when my package of skin-care products finally arrived, delivered to the back seat of our taxi. i knew i would have to perform soon, so i began to

smear the stimucell

all over my face, in hopes that this would freshen my com-plexion,

bring back some of your lost youth.

i felt there might be promise yet for us to get where we wanted to go.

and, wonderfully enough, your product presented itself,

much to my surprise,

in the shape of a small, votive candle,

an aid to devotion

like the one you're lighting here,

to remind myself what use there is in writing.
    i was so excited that i opened up the package right away (which had been wrapped in cellophane), held it close to my heart, and there began to ooze,

from its waxy core, a warm rich oil,

which made me feel like silk. i rubbed it on my cheeks and it was glorious.

i was so happy with my find — it was worth the price, no matter the cost — and carefully rubbed the excess on my hands (like i was taught). but then the whole substance began to melt, so i saw i'd have to use the whole of it in just one shot, and also control the situation in the car, avoid the spilling & the mess,

apply every drop,

before olivier (in front) could realize what was happening (in the back). for the material mess would annoy him, awfully much, and he was already annoyed by something else, which was that we were now careening toward the border, the moment where we'd have to get our passports out, and we'd both forgotten where they were.

olivier is a force for order, always putting things away,

but now he couldn't remember where he'd put them.

so you with your calm logic retrieved them.

i stuck my hand inside a bag sitting open just beside his seat, and out the passports came.

we crossed the border seamlessly.

and i guess my hands weren't greasy. my finding felt for all like an offering, so i thought we'd been saved.

but then ellen appeared,

and the pain of having to contend, compete with her once more and all she brought along was intense, for i wanted to deliver you only, *and yet i was still not the star,*

though i'd written, just for you, a new set of songs.

you had created a whole cycle,

and felt elated about this, since i hadn't known i was able to write music. i had just heard these songs so clearly,

you coudn't help putting them down.

but when ellen (who is far more public) saw that they concerned her & others also and that i had managed to get these notes on the page, she decided she should try to sing them. and i let her.

she simply took our songs and was going to sing them.

the performance i was about to attend turned out to be hers. and i have to admit she did her best with them.

the first one was okay, though perhaps a bit flat.

but then things got worse, and as the cycle unfolded,

the fault turned out to be your own.

so i felt even worse than before — awful, guilty, that people were interrupting ellen's singing and leaving the room, going on to other matters, concerns that were their own.

you were standing by the door as everybody left, one by one.

i was devastated. not one single person even mentioned you — ondine — or these songs composed in a way never heard before.

no criticism, no compliments, just silence.

i was convinced that

everybody out there

would be unwilling to lend you an ear, they

would be forever unable to recognize your sound.

i was sad, for sure,

you were crying,

till ellen explained,

something had gone wrong.

she said in a gentle way, perhaps i should listen better to the songs myself. then i might understand that the problem wasn't with her singing, nor even "out there" as i'd thought, but rather

something buried deep within,

something i had overlooked.

that was it.

i'd *heard* the pretty songs i had written down. the lyrics corresponded to something mysterious and new, but no one in particular could sing them.

these missing songs would have to be delivered differently,

439

as melodies at once your own and not your own. and this revelation was at once depressing and encouraging,

it cracked a beam of hope.

i saw that with some patience, progress could be made. i could continue to search out the melodies, but then forget about having to perform them.

write only for those seeking to hear within.

avoid penning scores bound by

time and space,

producing tracks that come to naught.

sing silently instead

through our tuned voices.

COLOPHON

DREAMSCAPES I
— BETRAYALS (101 & 202 NIGHTS)
was handset in InDesign CC.

The text font is *BC Figural*.
Book design & typesetting: Alessandro Segalini
Cover design: CMP

Cover image credit: *Flora* (or *Persephone*, or *allegory of Spring*).
Wall painting, Villa di Arianna, Stabiæ.
Museo Archeologico Nazionale, Napoli.

Opening spread image credit: Antonin Artaud. *Les illusions de l'âme*, 1946.
Musée National d'Art Moderne — Centre de Création Industrielle,
Centre Georges Pompidou, Paris.

DREAMSCAPES I
— BETRAYALS (101 & 202 NIGHTS)
is published by Contra Mundum Press.

Contra Mundum Press   New York · London · Melbourne

CONTRA MUNDUM PRESS

Dedicated to the value & the indispensable importance of the individual voice, to works that test the boundaries of thought & experience.

The primary aim of Contra Mundum is to publish translations of writers who in their use of form and style are *à rebours*, or who deviate significantly from more programmatic & spurious forms of experimentation. Such writing attests to the volatile nature of modernism. Our preference is for works that have not yet been translated into English, are out of print, or are poorly translated, for writers whose thinking & æsthetics are in opposition to timely or mainstream currents of thought, value systems, or moralities. We also reprint obscure and out-of-print works we consider significant but which have been forgotten, neglected, or overshadowed.

There are many works of fundamental significance to *Weltliteratur* (& *Weltkultur*) that still remain in relative oblivion, works that alter and disrupt standard circuits of thought — these warrant being encountered by the world at large. It is our aim to render them more visible.

For the complete list of forthcoming publications, please visit our website. To be added to our mailing list, send your name and email address to: info@contramundum.net

Contra Mundum Press
P.O. Box 1326
New York, NY 10276
USA

OTHER CONTRA MUNDUM PRESS TITLES

SOME FORTHCOMING TITLES

AGRODOLCE SERIES ÆD

2020   Dejan Lukić, *The Oyster*
2022   Ugo Tognazzi, *The Injester*

HYPERION
On the Future of Æsthetics   2006–PRESENT

To read samples and order current & back issues of *Hyperion*,
visit contramundumpress.com / hyperion
Edited by Rainer J. Hanshe & Erika Mihálycsa (2014 ~)

CONTRA MUNDUM PRESS

is published by Rainer J. Hanshe
Typography & Design: Alessandro Segalini
Publicity & Marketing: Alexandra Gold
Ebook Design: Carlie R. Houser

THE FUTURE OF KULCHUR

THE PROJECT

From major museums like the MoMA to art house cinemas such as Film Forum, cultural organizations do not sustain themselves from sales alone, but from subscriptions, donations, benefactors, and grants.

Since benefactors of Peggy Guggenheim's stature are rare to come by, and receiving large grants from major funding bodies is an infrequent and unreliable source of capital, we seek to further our venture through a form of modest support that is within everyone's reach.

Although esteemed, Contra Mundum is an independent boutique press with modest profit margins. In not having university, state, or institutional backing, other forms of sustenance are required to move us into the future.

Additionally, in the past decade, the reduction of the purchasing budgets across the nation of both public and private libraries has had a severe impact upon publishers, leading to significant decreases in sales, thereby necessitating the creation of alternative means of subsistence.

Because many of our books are translations, our desire for proper remuneration is a persistent point of concern. Even when translators receive grants for book projects, the amount is often insufficient to compensate for their efforts, and royalties, which trickle in slowly over years, are not a reliable source of compensation.

WHAT WILL BE DONE

With your participation we seek to offer writers and translators greater compensation for their work, and in a more expeditious manner.

Additionally, funds will be used to pay for translation rights, basic operating expenses of the press, and to represent our writers and translators at book fairs.

If the means exist, we will also create a translation residency, providing opportunities to both junior and more established translators, thereby furthering our cultural efforts.

Through a greater collective and the cultural commons of the world, we can band together to create this constellation and together function as a patron for the writers and artists published by CMP. We hope you will join us in this partnership.

Your patronage is an expression of your confidence and belief in visionary literary work that would otherwise be exiled from the Anglophone world. With bookstores and presses around the world struggling to survive, and many even closing, joining the Future of Kulchur allows you to be a part of an active force that forms a continuous & stable foundation which safeguards the longevity of Contra Mundum Press.

Endowed by your support, we can expand our poetics of hospitality by continuing to publish works from many different languages and reflect, welcome, and embrace the riches of other cultures throughout the world. To become a member of any of our Future of Kulchur tiers is to express your support of such cultural work, and to aid us in continuing it. A unified assemblage of individuals can make a modern Mæcenas and deepen access to radical works.

THE OYSTER ($2/month)

- Three issues (PDFs) of your choice of our art journal, *Hyperion*.
- 15% discount on all purchases (for orders made directly through our site) during the subscription term (one year).
- Impact: $2 a month contributes to the cost to convert a title to an ebook and make it accessible to wider audiences.

Paris Spleen ($5/month)

- Receive $35 worth of books or your choice from our back catalog.
- Three issues (PDFs) of your choice of our art journal, *Hyperion*.
- 18% discount on all purchases (for orders made directly through our site) during the subscription term (one year).
- Impact: $5 a month contributes to the cost purchasing new fonts for expanding the range of our typesetting palette.

Gilgamesh ($10/month)

- Receive $70 worth books of your choice from our back catalog.
- 4 PDF issues of our magazine *Hyperion*.
- A quarterly newsletter with exclusive content such as interviews with authors or translators, excerpts from upcoming titles, publication news, and more.
- 20% discount on all merchandise (for orders made directly through our site) during the subscription term (one year).
- Select images of our books as they are being typeset.
- Impact: $10 a month contributes to the production and publication of *Hyperion*, encouraging critical engagement with art theory & æsthetics and ensuring we can pay our contributors.

The Greek Music Drama ($25/month)

- Receive $215 worth of books.
- 5 PDF issues of *Hyperion* ($25 value).
- A quarterly newsletter with exclusive content such as interviews with authors or translators, excerpts from upcoming titles, publication news, and more.
- 25% discount (for orders made directly through our site) on all merchandise during the subscription term (one year).
- Impact: $25 a month contributes to the cost of designing and formatting a book.

Citizen Above Suspicion ($50/month)

- Receive $525 worth of books.
- 6 PDF issues of *Hyperion* ($30 value).
- 1 tote.
- A quarterly newsletter with exclusive content such as interviews with authors or translators, excerpts from upcoming titles, publication news, and more.
- 30% discount on all merchandise (for orders made directly through our site) during the subscription term (one year).
- Select one forthcoming book from our catalog and receive it in advance of release to the general public.
- Impact: $50 a month contributes to editorial & proofreading fees.

Casanova ($100/month)

- Receive $1040 worth of books.
- 7 PDF issues of *Hyperion* ($30 value).
- 1 tote.
- A quarterly newsletter with exclusive content such as interviews with authors or translators, excerpts from upcoming titles, publication news, and more.
- 35% discount on all merchandise (for orders made directly through our site) during the subscription term (one year).
- A signed typeset spread from two forthcoming books.
- Select two forthcoming books from our catalog and receive them in advance of release to the general public.
- Impact: $100 a month contributes to the cost of translating a book, therefore supporting a translator in their craft & bringing a new work & perspective to Anglophone audiences.

Cybernetogamic Vampire ($200/month)

- Receive $2020 worth of books.
- 10 PDF issues of *Hyperion* ($50 value).
- 1 tote.
- A quarterly newsletter with exclusive content such as interviews with authors or translators, excerpts from upcoming titles, publication news, and more.
- 40% discount on all merchandise (for orders made directly through our site) during the subscription term (one year).
- A signed typeset spread from four of our forthcoming books.
- The listing of your name in the colophon to a forthcoming book of your choice.
- Select four forthcoming books from our catalog and receive them in advance of release to the general public.
- Impact: $200 a month contributes to general operating expenses of the press, paying for translation rights, and attending book fairs to represent our writers and translators and reach more readers around the world.

To join the Future of Kulchur, visit here:

contramundumpress.com/support-us

www.ingramcontent.com/pod-product-compliance
Lightning Source LLC
Chambersburg PA
CBHW030911050726
47498CB00003BA/690